Praise for *What Happened to Sophie Wilder*

"*What Happened to Sophie Wilder* is about many things—the New York publishing world, the growing pains of post-collegiate life, the rigors of Roman Catholicism—but at its center it's a moving meditation on why and for whom we write."
— *New York Times Book Review* (editor's choice)

"A crisis of faith is key to the disappearance of a young woman in Christopher Beha's *What Happened to Sophie Wilder*, which deftly renders the competing impulses—creative, intellectual, emotional—of young writers in New York."
— *Vogue*

"In this smart short novel . . . a young writer deals with the reappearance and disappearance of the woman he sometimes loved."
— *O, The Oprah Magazine*

"*What Happened to Sophie Wilder* is a remarkable first novel, which should especially be read by those who have given up on contemporary literature. Along with giving them something good to read, it will renew their faith in what literature is capable of achieving."
— D. G. Myers, *Commentary*

"This novel is excitingly alert . . . to the ways we understand life in terms of stories, in particular the stories we tell about other people. . . . The story Beha tells about Charlie and Sophie is a convincing contemporary love story, not in spite of its sometimes dizzying self-awareness but, in large part, because of it."
— *San Francisco Chronicle*

"Beha's beautiful, whip-smart first novel . . . is sober, unsentimental and delivered with intelligence and passion."
— *Washington Post*

ARTS &
ENTERTAINMENTS

Christopher Beha

An Imprint of HarperCollinsPublishers

ARTS & ENTERTAINMENTS. Copyright © 2014 by Christopher Beha. All rights reserved. Printed in the United States of America. No part of this book may be used or reproduced in any manner whatsoever without written permission except in the case of brief quotations embodied in critical articles and reviews. For information address HarperCollins Publishers, 195 Broadway, New York, NY 10007.

HarperCollins books may be purchased for educational, business, or sales promotional use. For information please e-mail the Special Markets Department at SPsales@harpercollins.com.

FIRST EDITION

Designed by Mary Austin Speaker

Library of Congress Cataloging-in-Publication Data has been applied for.

ISBN 978-0-06-232246-3

14 15 16 17 18 OV/RRD   10 9 8 7 6 5 4 3 2 1

To Ally, who changed everything

She is one of fifty thousand, so far as the mere ambition goes; but I am very sure that in the way of resolution and capacity she is a rarity. And in one gift—perfect heartlessness—I will warrant she is unsurpassed. She has not as much heart as will go on the point of a needle. That is an immense virtue. Yes, she is one of the celebrities of the future.

HENRY JAMES, *THE AMERICAN*

What characterizes the so-called advanced societies is that they today consume images and no longer, like those of the past, beliefs.

ROLAND BARTHES, *CAMERA LUCIDA*

ACKNOWLEDGMENTS

I would like to thank the Ucross Foundation for a residency during which a draft of this book was completed.

I would also like to thank: Sarah Burnes, Logan Garrison, and everyone at the Gernert Company; Lee Boudreaux, Libby Edelson, Ashley Garland, Dan Halpern, Michael McKenzie, Ben Tomek, Ryan Willard, Craig Young, and Steve Attardo at Ecco; all of my colleagues at *Harper's* magazine; my family, especially Jim and Nancy Beha, Jim and Alyson Beha, Alice and Len Teti, and Sanny Beha; Lynn, Bob, and Palmer Ducommun and Lindsey and Charlie Schilling, mostly for the groom's cake; Peter and Christine Moyers; and John Carr, Brian DeLeeuw, and Jim Fuerst for invaluable early reads.

If I had not met Alexandra Andrews Beha halfway through the composition of this novel, it would be a far lesser book, as my life would be a far lesser life.

ARTS & ENTERTAINMENTS

PART ONE

ONE

"YOU KNOW WHO I saw on TV last night?" John Wilkins asked the small group of old friends surrounding him. "Dr. Drake."

They'd been drinking in the St. Albert's library for less than half an hour, but Eddie was surprised it had taken even that long for the name to come up.

"The show's in syndication," he said. "It's on every day."

"Not *Dr. Drake*," Wilkins clarified, as though the distinction should have been obvious. "Martha. She was on Entertainment Daily talking about her new boyfriend, Rex Gilbert."

Wilkins still had his reddish blond hair and the pale, lightly freckled skin that made him look perpetually young. In the years since Eddie had seen him last, he seemed to have aged only by a slight thickening. He wasn't fat so much as dense.

"She's a big star now," Eddie allowed.

"Are you kidding?" Wilkins said. "She's all over the place. All the talk shows. *Reverberator*'s sexiest list. Must drive your wife nuts."

He said this last part like a joke, though it was true and wasn't funny.

"Jesus, Wilky," Justin Price said. "Cut the guy a break."

Wilkins waved Justin off.

"You still keep up with her?"

"We haven't really talked since she moved out west."

"You know who *I* saw on TV the other day?" Justin broke in again. "Handsome Eddie Hartley."

He was trying to help, Eddie knew, but in some ways this was worse. The edge of good-natured mockery his old nickname had always carried felt more pointed now. The last thing he wanted was for his acting career to be set beside Martha's.

"Is that right? Which of my masterpieces was it?"

"One of those old *Law & Order* episodes."

"Was I the good guy or the bad guy?"

"You were some kind of pervert. Putting plastic bags over little girls' heads or something like that."

"One of my finest roles."

"Have you gotten any big parts recently?" Tim Reilly asked. Eddie hadn't seen Reilly since their last reunion, so he couldn't blame him for the question.

"I gave all that up a few years ago. I just teach now."

"Not a bad fucking gig," Wilkins said. "Out at four. Summers off. I'd take it. I've been getting killed these days."

Eddie wanted to say that an opening could be found, if it attracted him all that much.

"The job does have its perks."

"Plus you get scholarships for the kids, right?"

"I don't have any kids just yet. But in theory, yes."

"Lucky bastard." Wilkins laughed, and his cheeks turned

red, his freckles seeming to bleed out into the rest of his face. "We've got two, and we're already sweating how to get the older one into preschool. Do you know how much that shit costs these days? Even if I make partner in a couple of years, I couldn't pay two St. Albert's tuitions and keep the place on the North Shore. It didn't used to be so expensive to be rich in this town. Now it's just the hedge fund guys like Price here who can swing it. Mere professionals need not apply."

Eddie separated himself from the group and walked to the far wall of the library, where a makeshift bar stood beneath a large circular window that looked out on the park. A banner stretched across the window: "St. Albert's School Welcomes You Back." Beneath it, the young woman working the bar smiled at Eddie with uncertain recognition, a once-common reaction that had become less so in recent years.

"You look familiar," she said as she filled his glass with ice.

Perhaps she was just flirting. That was still common enough.

"I know what it is," she added before he could respond. "You buy your morning coffee at the Flying Duck Market around the corner. We're the caterers for this thing."

"That must be it," Eddie said. "I'm the drama teacher here."

"That's so funny," she told him. "I'm an actress."

Eddie wasn't surprised to hear it. She was pretty—though not, he reflected, quite pretty enough.

"I work at the Flying Duck to pay the bills," she continued.

Eddie tried to think of something encouraging to say.

"That's as good a reason as any to work somewhere."

He took his drink and turned from the bar just in time to see Max Blakeman arrive. Eddie's mood immediately lifted at the sight of Blakeman. He'd known what he was in for that night—his classmates with their growing families and easy success, the questions about Martha Martin and his own acting career. The one appeal the evening had held was the chance to see Blakeman. They'd been best friends for years, but it seemed like they hardly spoke these days. Eddie missed him, perhaps more than anything else about his old life. They caught each other's eyes as Luce made his first attempt to call the room to order.

"If I could have just a moment of everyone's time, and then I'll let you get back to catching up with old friends."

Eddie watched with satisfaction as his classmates continued their conversations, barely acknowledging the effort to silence them. George Luce had been a young history teacher when Eddie's class was in school. Eddie's own mother—a secretary at St. Albert's for more than twenty years—had handled Luce's application to teach at the school. Only Eddie knew him in his role as headmaster, and the others seemed not to understand why they ought to be listening to him.

"As some of you know," Luce pressed on, "I'm the kind of man to whom tradition is a very serious matter." Luce was the kind of man, Eddie thought, who liked to tell people what kind of man he was. "Tomorrow, another class will graduate from St. Albert's," Luce continued. "This is the sixtieth graduating class in the school's history, and its members will go on to the finest colleges and universities in the nation. I take pride in having guided the tradition of St. Albert's to this auspicious point." The room came slowly to puzzled attention, as though seeking the source of a faint but persistent buzz disturbing the ambience. Just as Luce secured command of his audience, he seemed to lose the thread of his speech. "I hope you all have as many fond memories of your time here as we who are still here have of you," he concluded. "Now I'd like to hand things over to your class president, Justin Price."

In the days leading up to the reunion, Eddie had entertained the idea of saying a few words himself, offering his insider's view of life at St. Albert's these days. That seemed foolish now. As the only member of his class still connected to the school's daily existence, he'd considered himself a kind of host that night, but he'd played no role in planning the event. Such duties and privileges fell naturally to people—like Justin—in a position to write checks of some significance to the school's endowment and capital needs.

"I'm going to be brief," Justin began, "since I think it's my job to catch Wilky when he passes out."

Justin had come to St. Albert's in the seventh grade as part of the Bootstrappers Program, which matched gifted under-privileged students with private-school scholarships. He'd been one of three black students to graduate in their class, and he now worked at some kind of financial concern—a fund? a firm? a trust?—with an ostentatiously generic name like Redwood or Bedrock, whose primary business so far as Eddie could tell was printing money in sufficient quantities to buy Justin a house on the South Fork and an apartment on Park Avenue by the time he'd turned thirty.

"Most of you know how important St. Albert's is to me, how the opportunity to come here changed my life. And I want that opportunity extended to as many young boys as possible. That's why I'm marking our fifteenth reunion by establish-ing a class scholarship fund. I encourage you all to consider contributing, in addition to your usual support of the annual campaign. To get us started, I'm endowing the fund with a gift of two hundred and fifty thousand dollars."

Luce briefly applauded this number, but he was met only with uncomfortable laughter from Justin.

"I'm also committed to matching every dollar given to the fund up to another two hundred and fifty. So that's a challenge to you cheap bastards. That's all I've got to say, really, except it's great to see old friends."

Two hundred and fifty grand in one shot, Eddie thought as he raised his glass in a toast. Half a million, depending on how things worked out. It was certainly impressive, given where Justin had started. Though neither gifted nor excessively underprivileged himself, Eddie had also been something of a scholarship case, since his middle-class Irish immigrant parents could never have sent him to St. Albert's without the steep discount offered to employees. If his own career had gone just a little differently, he might have had that kind of money to throw around now. After all, the gift was less than Martha made for each episode of *Dr. Drake*.

As the crowd fell back into conversation, Eddie crossed the room to find Blakeman.

"Just the man I've been waiting to see," Blakeman said.

"You, too," Eddie said. "I wasn't sure you would make it."

"I had to show up. Since you won't come down to see me anymore."

In his first years out of college, Blakeman had thrown parties at his place several nights a week, and Eddie had never missed them. At the time, Eddie's acting career had still seemed promising. Blakeman had been struggling to get started as a writer, copyediting on the side for the New York *Interviewer*. Now Eddie was a drama teacher, and Blakeman was on the *Interviewer*'s staff. He still threw the same parties, but Eddie hadn't gone to one in years. He'd tried to keep up for a while, but he couldn't stand in a room of writers and actors and filmmakers—even if most of them were "aspiring" writers and actors and filmmakers—and tell them he wasn't going to aspire anymore. He'd watched himself become less interesting in other people's eyes. Worse, he'd become less interesting in his own.

"Married life," Eddie said. This was unfair to Susan, who

would have been happy to spend an evening at Blakeman's from time to time.

"Talk to me when you've got kids at home," Blakeman said. Everyone knew that Blakeman would never have kids at home. "Unless there's something you're not telling me?"

"Nothing to tell," Eddie said.

They left the building an hour later. Outside, someone made the predictable suggestion that they head to the stretch of bars on Second Avenue they'd snuck into during their last years at school. They stumbled across town until they arrived at an Irish pub that hadn't existed back then but was indistinguishable in look and tone from the places that had. Above the bar a television set that in earlier days would have been showing whatever sporting event could be found now aired a reality show.

"*Pure Bliss,*" Reilly said. "My wife is obsessed with that show."

"Mine, too," Wilkins said as he handed out plastic shot glasses filled with a green liquid that appeared to have toothpaste mixed into it. "I can't say I mind watching with her. Justine Bliss is pretty cute."

"Hey, Eddie," said Reilly. "If you were still with Dr. Drake, you could have one of those shows. We'd all be on TV right now."

Eddie swallowed his shot, which had an odd spiciness that made his nostrils itch.

"If he was still with Martha," Justin said, "he wouldn't be wasting his time with any of us."

"I'm sure a master of the universe like yourself could manage an audience," Reilly told Justin. "But the rest of us would be out of luck."

On the trip across town they had lost all but about a dozen

classmates. Some of those remaining seemed ready to leave after an obligatory first drink. Eddie spotted Blakeman at the bar and thanked Wilkins for the shot before walking over. Blakeman bought a round, which they brought to a table in the corner.

"Catch me up," Blakeman said. "How have you been?"

"What you were saying before," Eddie answered. "About kids at home?"

Perhaps the alcoholic mouthwash had done it, but he felt like telling someone. For all the distance that had grown between him and Blakeman, Eddie didn't have anyone else to tell. He had coworkers and a few couples that Susan invited over for dinner, but he didn't have any real friends anymore.

"Sure," Blakeman said, though he didn't seem to know what Eddie was talking about.

"We've actually been trying for a while."

"I can show you how it works, but I don't think the men's room has a lock."

"It doesn't seem to be happening," Eddie pressed on.

"Aren't there doctors for that?"

"Lots of doctors. Assisted reproductive tecŸology. They call it ART."

"I guess you know it when you see it."

Eddie couldn't even pretend to laugh.

"Sorry to hear it," Blakeman said, once it was clear he couldn't joke his way through the conversation.

"The thing is, for all that pain and trouble, Susan wants to keep at it."

"And you don't think that's a good idea."

"I don't know whether it's a good idea," Eddie said. "I just know we can't afford it. Insurance won't cover most of it. We're out of pocket more than ten grand in the past six months, and we're broke."

Eddie was nearly in tears. He didn't know why he needed to tell Blakeman. There was nothing Blakeman could do about it.

"Do you remember Morgan Bench?" Blakeman asked.

Morgan was an old friend of Blakeman's who used to hang around when Eddie and Blakeman were still close.

"Sure."

"We're having dinner tomorrow night. You should join us."

"I don't know." Eddie was happy to be invited, but he resented the effort to change the subject. "I've got graduation and a reception afterward. But I'll be free by dinner."

"Try to make it work," Blakeman told him. "I don't just mean for the distraction. I think I can help."

"I'm not looking for a loan or anything." This was true, but only because he had no means of paying one back.

"Of course not. I'm as broke as you are." This might also have been true in some tecÿical sense, though money was not something Blakeman had to worry about. "I'm just saying I think I can help."

Eddie wanted to ask what kind of help he could offer, but Wilkins and Reilly descended on the table.

"We were just talking about those Melwood girls from our year," Wilkins said. Melwood was the girls' school around the corner from St. Albert's.

"Do they still hang around the building after class?" Reilly asked Eddie. "With their uniform skirts rolled up?"

Eddie nodded while sipping his drink.

"Not a bad way to end the workday," Wilkins said.

"They're sixteen years old."

"There's no harm in looking," Wilkins said. "That makes them as old as Justine Bliss, and look at the way she gets up on TV."

As he spoke, he settled in across the table. The conversation about Blakeman's help was over. But Eddie couldn't stop thinking about it. After the four of them had closed the bar a few hours later, he walked home with a single phrase in his head: *Blakeman can help*. He dared to say it out loud. Blakeman can help. A couple walking by in the opposite direction— they weren't much older than Eddie's students—turned to look at him and laughed.

TWO

THE GALLERY WHERE SUSAN worked opened an hour after
the start of the St. Albert's school day, so Eddie usually beat
his wife out the door. But she was already dressed to go when
she woke him the morning after his reunion.

"Did you have fun?" she asked.

Eddie tried to piece together the later reaches of the previous evening, but the only fruit of this effort was a throb against
the backs of his eyes. Had his brain been capable of generating
a response, he would still have been unable to break his tongue
sufficiently free from its surroundings to articulate it. He offered instead an affirmative cough.

"Was Blakeman there?"

Eddie remembered with some regret offering Susan as an
excuse for his disappearance from Blakeman's life. In fact,
Susan liked Blakeman, and she didn't understand why they
saw so little of him. Eddie couldn't tell either of them that
Blakeman belonged to his old life with Martha.

"He invited me for dinner tonight," Eddie managed after working his mouth into functioning order.

"That sounds nice. It would be good for you to get out a bit more. Maybe I'll see if Annie wants to do something."

Annie was Susan's best friend from childhood. They'd moved together from Ohio to New York after college, and Annie had introduced Susan to Eddie, with whom she'd worked at St. Albert's until leaving the year before, after the birth of her first child.

"See you this afternoon?" Eddie asked before Susan left.

Each year since their engagement she'd taken half a day off work to join him at graduation. She liked seeing the faces of the boys whose names she heard all year, chatting with the other teachers, feeling fully immersed in Eddie's life.

"I'll be there," she said.

Eddie fell back to sleep after Susan left, and it was almost noon by the time he got across town to pack up his things at school for the summer. Rounding the corner, he saw Stephen McLaughlin sitting on a fire hydrant with his handmade sign propped up beside him. Eddie couldn't read it from where he stood, but he knew exactly what it said. "Make St. Albert's keep its word. Don't evict a disabled man."

Since its founding, St. Albert's had occupied a mansion on Eighty-ninth Street between Madison and Fifth, donated by one of the rich Catholics who'd started the place, mostly third- and fourth-generation Irish who'd finally arrived in the higher reaches of society and wanted their own version of the private schools where rich Protestants sent their sons. The school had eventually expanded into an adjacent building, converting all the apartments into classrooms except the penthouse, where the young headmaster lived with his family. He'd stayed in the job for almost five decades. Shortly after his death, St. Albert's went about taking possession of the apartment and found it still occupied by his fifty-year-old son. For three years now, Stephen and the school had been locked in litigation. For the last two, he'd camped outside the building every day, picketing while parents dropped off and picked up their sons. Despite the message on the sign, Stephen had no disability that Eddie could discern apart from a fairly encompassing pot habit. Since taking up his place outside the school, he'd grown out a thick red beard, as if to appear slightly menacing or to give off a hint of indigence—though he'd refused an offer of three-quarters of a million dollars to vacate the apartment.

"Handsome Eddie," he said. "It's been a slow day."

Eddie's mother had started working at St. Albert's as Mr. McLaughlin's secretary, and Stephen—then in his twenties and unemployed—often babysat the infant Eddie. Apart from Eddie's parents, Stephen had known him longer than anyone alive.

"School's out," Eddie told him. "Graduation starts at the church in a few hours. You ought to set up shop over there."

"Thanks, Handsome E."

Stephen rose from the hydrant and picked up his sign while Eddie let himself into the building. He had a key to the rickety elevator, but he still thought of it as vaguely off limits to him, as it was to students, and he rarely used it. He walked up the back stairs to the faculty lounge on the second floor, which was already stripped almost bare. Most of the other teachers had cleared their things out the day before, while Eddie had been at his reunion. Eddie went through the papers in his small cubby with dutiful care before throwing the entire pile out. He left the lounge and walked up two more flights to the black box theater that held his drama classes.

Looking up at the stage, Eddie imagined himself playing Gayev in *The Cherry Orchard* or Eugene in *Biloxi Blues*. He didn't usually get nostalgic at school. It was the place he worked every day, a fact that generally overwhelmed any memories of that earlier time. But the reunion had put those days in his mind, and with the building empty the weight of the present was not enough to suppress the past. The first time he'd been in that theater as an adult, he'd been shocked at how small it was, since it had seemed enormous when he'd performed there. He'd never felt nervous or excited before the performances, just enveloped in the thing he was doing. The curtain would go up, and for a few hours he felt more real than he did anywhere else.

Before acting, he'd never had something the other boys envied, as he envied their wealth and their easy sense of entitlement. His first years at St. Albert's had not been particularly happy ones, and his unhappiness was made worse by the fact that he could never criticize the place at home. His education had been his parents' second great gift to him, after their prenatal move to America. They'd held out great hopes for the transformative possibility of Eddie's mere presence at a school that had educated the sons of mayors, governors, senators, and one president. At home, they spoke of the place in the respectful tones they usually reserved for Cardinal O'Connor or the Clancy Brothers. When a St. Albert's graduate strangled his girlfriend with her bra in Central Park during Eddie's childhood, even this incident brought an odd credit to the place, since the pages of *Newsday* and the *Post* insistently contrasted the Preppy Murderer's lurid crime with his refined pedigree. When a parochial school kid killed his date, it didn't make the front page.

All this talk about the privilege of attending such a place had accentuated the feeling that he didn't quite belong there. But that had changed when the drama teacher, Mr. Carlton, started casting him in plays. Eddie wouldn't even have audi-

tioned without the twisted ankle that kept him off the basketball court one winter with nothing to do after school. His
success had solidified his long-standing but intermittent friend-
ship with Blakeman, the most popular kid in the grade. The
two of them and Justin Price formed the nucleus of an "artis-
tic" clique—Blakeman the writer, Eddie the actor, and Justin
the musician—that came to dominate their class at St. Albert's
through their high school years. It was then that Blakeman
began calling him "Handsome Eddie," and the name caught
on. Eddie understood it wasn't entirely a compliment, but who
didn't want to be handsome? Another member of their circle,
Eddie Doyle, became "Bright Eddie," because he was in the
honors sections and Handsome Eddie was undistinguished in
the classroom.

Now Bright Eddie was fighting in Afghanistan and Handsome Eddie was a teacher. He expected his old friend to appreciate the irony of this, but no one seemed surprised when he
first took the job. The mediocre student was precisely the one
destined to stay in the classroom, the unspoken assumption
seemed to go. The smart ones earned enough money to send
their sons to the school.

Graduation started at three, and it was after two thirty
by the time Eddie had finished boxing up his papers and the
props he used for acting exercises. He went straight downstairs and crossed the street to St. Agnes Church. Susan had
already found an open pew inside, and she knelt with her
eyes closed. She wasn't ostentatious about her faith—they'd
dated for weeks before he had any idea how important it
was to her—but she couldn't enter a church without saying
at least a short prayer. Eddie always wondered what went
through her head at these times. He didn't much understand
how prayer worked, though of course he could recite various

standards. What Susan did was more in the way of impro-
visation, Eddie imagined, and he'd never had much talent
for that.

As a ten-year-old altar boy at his family's parish in Queens,
Eddie had experienced a single unforgettable moment of what
adults might call transcendence, when his whole body buzzed
with the presence of something other than himself, a moment
he had never talked about to anyone and didn't like to think
about now, because it still seemed unmistakably real to Eddie
and didn't make any sense to him. Something like that feeling
had sometimes visited him while he was onstage, and it might
have been more than a matter of logistics that had led him to
give up altar service just as he started acting in his first play. In
the decade after he graduated from St. Albert's—the years of
his life with Martha and his acting career—he went to church
no more than twice a year, at Christmas and Easter with his
parents. If asked, he would have said he was Catholic, just as
he would have said he was Irish—it was a matter of birth, not
of action or belief.

His teaching career had brought religion back to his life
in a superficial way. School days opened in the chapel on the
second floor, which had stained-glass windows, wooden pews,
and a small pipe organ. The sessions began and ended with a
hymn, but what passed in between was more assembly than
religious ceremony. Each morning a different teacher gave a
"chapel speech," not a sermon or homily so much as a general
didactic pep talk. Every faculty member was required to give
at least two of these a year.

Eddie did the minimum. He didn't think he had much in
the way of advice to give, having come back to St. Albert's
because he'd made such a mess of his life. The best he could
offer were cautionary tales. But he found that the boys appreciated funny stories from his own student days, which he

could shape in a way that suggested some moral, usually not one the events had suggested at the time. He never brought up God or faith in these talks. He didn't have anything to say on those subjects.

He'd been dating Susan for a few months when she invited him to mass one Sunday, and he'd been going with her ever since. He wasn't sure he believed the story the church was selling, but he liked about it the same thing he'd liked about acting: the understanding that someone was watching, that every action had a purpose and a meaning. Like Susan herself, it had come into his life at a time when he needed it. She had brought him back from a desperate place. What's more, she had not even known she was doing so. She'd done it just by being herself. When things weren't going well between them these days, he tried to remind himself of that.

Susan rose from the kneeler and opened her eyes just as the organ in the back brought the crowd to attention. The fifty-three members of the graduating class processed up the center aisle, singing the school song. Eddie watched them take their seats in the front three pews. They had been in seventh grade—little boys really—when Eddie started teaching. They'd been completely altered since he'd first met them. As had he, Eddie thought.

He remembered his own graduation, his mother's pride at the idea that he would be the first in his family to go to college. Many more firsts were expected to follow. After he left NYU as a sophomore to act, his parents used the rest of the money they'd saved for tuition on a down payment for a house in Florida and took to expressing relief, when he called them there, that at least he hadn't killed any girls in the park.

The pastor, Father Seneviratne, gave a brief blessing before welcoming Luce to the lectern. Hungover as Eddie was, he found it mercifully easy to ignore the man's drone while dancing on the fuzzy edge of consciousness. Susan's elbow brought him to attention when necessary. Luce finished by calling up Patrick Hendricks, the class's valedictorian.

Patrick was Eddie's favorite student, the only one in five years to show genuine, if modest, talent for acting. Eddie had tried to encourage him within reason, but he'd been glad to learn that Patrick was going to Dartmouth next year, which seemed far enough away from the temptations of professional work. He would be in a few student productions before finding other interests. After the usual introductory business, Patrick described his pride at representing his class, his love of St. Albert's, which he'd attended since first grade, and his excitement for himself and his classmates as they embarked on the next stage of life. Eddie only came to real attention when he heard his own name.

"When I was a freshman, Mr. Hartley cast me in *The Skin of Our Teeth*. The very night the casting list went up, I went home and saw him on TV, in an episode of *Murder Squad*."

This story was new to Eddie, and he wondered whether it was strictly true or altered somewhat for dramatic effect. His few guest spots on television didn't make the air much, though this was the second time in as many days that someone had mentioned seeing one.

"Here was this real actor," Patrick continued, "a professional actor teaching me how to do this thing. And I thought, I want to be like Mr. Hartley."

By now Patrick had found Eddie's pew, and he was looking at him as he spoke. Eddie smiled weakly back at him before looking down. Patrick was completely serious, in his way. But of course he didn't really want to be like Eddie. He wanted to be the person Eddie had wanted to be at Patrick's age, the person Eddie would have been if things had turned out differently.

Eddie gazed at the worn marble of the floor beneath him. Someone watching might have thought he was simply flattered or moved by pride, but his chest was tightening and he felt suddenly out of breath. The feeling didn't subside as Patrick went on to other things, thanking his family and dropping a few inside jokes for the benefit of his friends, before ending on an earnest note of thanks.

After the ceremony Eddie looked for Patrick out on the sidewalk. He was standing near the corner, with a tall, pretty girl with light brown hair. Eddie thought he'd seen the girl hanging out in front of the school a few times.

"Thanks for the plug," Eddie said.

"I meant it. It's been a great experience learning from you."

"You remember my wife?"

"Nice to see you again, Mrs. Hartley." Patrick shook Susan's hand. "This is my girlfriend, Melissa."

"You must have been proud to see how he did up there," Susan told the girl.

"Melissa's graduating from Melwood next week," Patrick said. "So we're both proud. And she's going to your old school, Mr. Hartley."

"Did you go to NYU?" Melissa asked. "That's so cool."

"For about fifteen minutes. But that wasn't the school's fault. I'm sure you'll have a great time there."

"You know, I really owe you," Melissa said, smiling almost flirtatiously. "I met Patrick through your plays. I mean, I went to go see one of my friends in one, and when I saw him onstage, I made her get me his number."

She laughed a bit as though at her own boldness, though conversations Eddie had overheard in the halls suggested that girls her age were capable of being quite a bit bolder than this.

"I take full credit, then."

"And Patrick really looks up to you. We've watched some

of your commercials and stuff on YouTube. I'm trying to act, too, so it's really inspiring."

"My parents are just getting the car," Patrick said. "They'd be happy to give you both a ride to the reception."

"I'm afraid we're not going to be able to make it," Eddie told them.

"You're not?"

"We've got a family occasion we just can't get out of. But I was really proud to see you up there making that speech, and I appreciate the things you said about me. I hope you'll come by the school when you're home on vacation, so we can catch up and I can hear all about how you're doing." He had a sense that he was speaking a bit manically now. "Congratulations to you too, Melissa. I'm sure you'll stick longer down at NYU than I did."

"WHAT WAS ALL THAT about?" Susan asked when they got back to the apartment.

Eddie couldn't say what it had been about. He had still not quite recovered from the feeling that had locked on to him during Patrick's speech.

"I had some kind of attack."

"You had an attack because a kid complimented you?"

"He complimented a version of me that doesn't exist."

Eddie suspected that Susan might find this beside the point, but she appeared to find it instead precisely the point.

"But you wish that version existed. Because you're not happy with our life."

"And you're happy?" Eddie asked. "You don't wish things were different?"

He shouldn't have said it—not because it was cruel, but

because it invited a conversation they'd already had too many times.

"I do wish our life was different," Susan said. "Because I wish we had a child—together. You wish you were rich and famous so you weren't stuck with me. So you could go win back Dr. Drake."

"Martha has nothing to do with this conversation."

"Isn't she what you think about when Patrick calls you an actor? That's why you get so sick you have to run away."

They'd hardly mentioned Martha before trying to have a child. She hadn't been all that famous when Eddie and Susan started dating, and Susan wasn't impressed by that kind of fame anyway. She didn't watch much TV. She read novels and books about art and what she called "theory," which Eddie took to mean books that belonged on a college syllabus, not in a civilian home. She made it most of the way through *The New Yorker* each week. That a person Eddie had dated was on her way to being a star had interested her only abstractly. What had mattered to her about Eddie's past was that it had ended by bringing them together. This was part of what he'd first loved about her.

All that had changed when they started pulling the money together for their first attempt at in vitro, and the full extent of the debt Eddie had built up while living with Martha became clear to her. After the failure of that first try, he'd made the mistake of expressing some ambivalence about undertaking another. If they couldn't even afford to conceive a child, how would they manage everything that came with it? They lived in a small one-bedroom apartment, and they had no obvious way of getting more space on their current salaries. Not to mention food and diapers and whatever else was involved. If the child was a girl and couldn't go to St.

Albert's, there would be school to worry about. They should have discussed money sooner. They'd avoided it precisely because they hadn't wanted to talk about the past. But it was unavoidable now. Eddie was broke, Martha was extravagantly wealthy, and suddenly the difference mattered. Susan had responded to Eddie's hesitation by suggesting for the first time that Eddie had never quite gotten over Martha, that he dreamed of running off with Dr. Drake.

In the first year of their marriage, it might have been fair for Susan to accuse Eddie of wishing for another life. How could he not? Plenty of people who'd been a lot less close than he had to becoming rich and famous harbored such wishes. And naturally he'd thought often of Martha. But even then he didn't want to win her back. He didn't want to share in her success. He wanted that success all to himself, and he wanted Martha to have his failure. Anyway such wishes could only live so long without sustenance from the outside world. Long before Susan's accusations started, the sheer corrosive force of time had swept away from Eddie any sense that life could be different. These days it would have been fairer to say that Susan dreamed that he could ask Martha for fifty thousand dollars.

"I'm sorry you had that attack," Susan said. "And I'm sorry I made you feel bad about it."

So it always went. The flashes of anger and disappointment were just that—flashes. She was always eager to reconcile, because she took for granted that finally they were in it all together. Perhaps this was the reason she'd only started making these claims about Martha after they had stopped being true.

"I appreciate your taking the day off," Eddie said. "I don't know what got into me."

"Don't worry about it."

She looked at him suddenly with the old appreciative expression he used to be able to find so reliably on her face. She was still capable of showing that expression at any time, but it was qualified now, bestowed as a gift and just as easily withheld.

"I can cancel this dinner with Blakeman tonight. We could do something together."

"That's all right," Susan said. "I told Annie I'd have dinner with her."

"We're going to get this all figured out."

"Sure we will," Susan answered while taking a book down from a shelf. This meant she would spend the rest of the afternoon reading on the couch. Eddie would have to read, too, or else idly browse online; the television distracted Susan while she read, and there was nowhere in the apartment to escape from it when it was on.

"I really mean it. I just have this feeling something's going to happen."

He wanted to tell her that Blakeman was going to help, but it would have sounded ridiculous. Susan sat down and opened her book.

"Let's worry about it in the morning," she said without looking up from the page.

THREE

WHILE RIDING THE 6 TRAIN downtown, Eddie developed some ideas about the nature of Blakeman's help. He assumed it had something to do with Morgan Bench. When Eddie knew him, Morgan had been a gossip columnist at the *Daily News* and briefly notorious for something Eddie couldn't remember, making the lower left quadrant—the bad one—of *New York* magazine's Approval Matrix. The last Eddie had heard, he'd quit the paper and moved out to L.A. to work on screenplays. Perhaps something he'd written was getting made, and he had a part for Eddie. Even if it had nothing to do with Morgan, Blakeman's help might have been in this line. Blakeman had spent several years as a movie critic, and he still knew people in the business.

The address he'd given Eddie was on the Lower East Side, not far from the apartment Eddie had shared with Martha after dropping out of school. He rarely had occasion to come to the neighborhood these days. The restaurant's entrance was below street level, and the place made no effort to advertise itself. Experience had taught Eddie that the easier such an establishment was to walk by without noticing, the more expensive it would be. He hoped that Blakeman planned to pick up the check. Inside, the hostess was dressed like the proprietor of a brothel in a spaghetti western, but she had dark, Asian features and spoke with an accent Eddie couldn't place. She brought him to the table where Blakeman and Morgan were waiting. They both stood up to greet him.

"I'm glad you made it," Blakeman said.

"Of course I did," Eddie answered with perhaps too much eagerness. For a moment he feared that Blakeman had been bullshitting him, or that he'd forgotten his offer to help, remembering only the dinner invitation.

"How the fuck are you?" Morgan asked. "It's been a long time."

"I'm good," Eddie answered as he sat down between them. "How about yourself? Are you still mostly out in L.A.?"

"No, I'm back here full time."

This wasn't necessarily a bad sign. Plenty of things still got made in New York.

"And what are you working on?"

"Have you heard of Jay Rolling?" Blakeman asked.

"Is that a TV show?"

"It's a site I've got," Morgan explained. "Pictures of guys in wheelchairs crossing the street against the light."

"I see," said Eddie. "So you've gotten into photography?"

"No, no, I don't take the pictures." Morgan seemed amused by the idea. "Other people send them to me. I just put them up. I've got some other projects, too. I'm working on one called Big Slurs. It's a clearinghouse for racial and ethnic epithets."

"A clearinghouse?"

"Kind of crowd-sourced bigotry. So say, like, you've got some kind of behavior you want to attach some slur to, like you've got a roommate who washes his balls in the sink or something."

"His balls?"

"You put it up on the site, and then people suggest names. Like, someone calls it 'The Armenian Birdbath.' Then everyone votes on it. It's a democratized lexicon. We're generating memes, you know?"

"I think I get it."

"How about you?" Morgan asked. "Still acting?"

"I'm a teacher. High school drama."

"Right on," Morgan said. "Say, do you still keep up with Martha? She's blowing up right now."

"We're not in touch."

Eddie picked up his menu, which was completely illegible.

"It's Turkmen," Blakeman explained. "Big thing right now. Very hardy. I'll just order for all of us."

The waitress appeared with an unlabeled bottle. Eddie wasn't sure whether this had been requested before his arrival or was simply brought as a matter of course. Blakeman placed their order while the waitress poured shots. After they threw back the drinks, which seemed to be vodka flavored with some kind of mulch, Blakeman excused himself from the table to make a call for work.

"Let me ask you something," Morgan said once they were alone. "Not to be weird or anything. But Blakeman says you and Martha used to film each other."

Discretion wasn't among Blakeman's known qualities, but this particular secret was an old one that Eddie had taken for dead and buried.

"It wasn't anything, really. Just line readings, mostly. We

were both aspiring actors. We made tapes before auditions and watched them together."

"There are people out in L.A. who would pay a lot of money for something like that."

"What makes you think I need money?"

"Everyone needs money," Morgan answered. "I'm not saying you need it especially. All I'm saying is that I'm in a good position to set something up if you wanted."

"I'm not really interested."

"No, of course not. It just came to mind, so I thought I'd tell you. Even for just the two of you reading lines, I could probably get ten, twenty grand. More—a lot more—depending on what else you've got."

"Meaning what?"

"Did you do any fucking around on camera?"

This Blakeman could not have told Morgan, because Eddie had never told it to Blakeman.

"Like I said, it wasn't anything."

"Nothing interesting at all?"

"To be honest, I haven't looked at the stuff in years. I'm not even sure I've still got it. We had a bad breakup, and I tossed most of our old things out."

"If you could find something, it would be worth a lot. Even tame stuff. Still, it's too bad you don't have anything, you know, more explicit. That would be the real deal. Serious."

"Just out of academic interest, what qualifies as serious?"

"It's tough to say without seeing it. Some length, where it's clear that it's her, maybe full frontal, that could be six figures."

"In that case," Eddie said, "it really is too bad I don't have anything. But I don't."

"I understand if this is making you uncomfortable. I just

heard about the videos from Blakeman and thought it made sense to give you the option. I'll give you my card."

The card showed Morgan's name and the title *Meme Evangelist* above an e-mail address and phone number. After accepting it, Eddie felt implicated in something.

"Let's have another shot," Blakeman said as he returned to the table.

"Have you read Finian's memoir?" Morgan asked as he poured out drinks. Finian was another member of the old circle. Eddie tried to remember what he'd experienced that might have justified writing a memoir.

"I've read *in* it," Blakeman answered.

"How have the reviews been?"

"Sickening. Everyone loves it."

"And he was already insufferable."

"The worst part," Blakeman said, "is that he deserves it. The book is great."

"An unfortunate situation all around," Morgan concluded.

The food arrived in a single cast-iron pot, placed in the center of the table along with a basket of flatbread. There was no silverware. Eddie watched Morgan and Blakeman tear strips of bread and drag them through the thick liquid in the pot. They seemed to be well practiced at the method.

"You've done this before?" Eddie asked.

"Turkmenistan's really hot," Morgan explained. "Ever since *Berdimuhamedow Rules* went on the air. It's one of the best things Brian Moody has ever done."

"I don't watch a ton of TV these days," Eddie said apologetically.

"But you know Moody, right? He does *Pure Bliss,* that Justine Bliss show. And *Huffing and Cuffing,* this new one about cops addicted to paint thinner. All the best stuff on television right now has Moody's name on it."

Morgan seemed immediately embarrassed by his own show of enthusiasm, and they all returned to eating in silence. When they'd finished most of the pot, the waitress brought melons for dessert. More vodka was had at each stage. After they'd split the check—as Eddie had suspected, it was more than he'd wanted to pay—Morgan excused himself, saying that he had an early appointment the next morning.

"Did you tell him about the videos I made with Martha?" Eddie asked Blakeman once they were alone. Blakeman gave Eddie the look he often gave when put on the spot, an expression of frustration that he was fated to spend his life being forever misunderstood.

"He came back from L.A. about a month ago. He's had a tough time, to be honest. He started talking about Martha, about when you used to bring her around. Wanted to know whether anyone was still in touch with her. I guess he was looking to get a script into her hands. I told him you guys didn't talk. Then he started asking if I had any artifacts. That's his word, artifacts. Old photos, he said. Shit she'd signed. Anything that could make him some money. Since she's been with Rex Gilbert, she's the most popular paparazzi target in L.A. People go nuts for anything having to do with them. I thought of those videos, but I didn't tell him about them, because I knew you wouldn't want to hear it. When you said that you needed money, the timing seemed perfect."

"So that's your help?" Eddie tried not to sound upset, because it had been his own mistake to invest so much in the idea that Blakeman could save him. "You thought I could sell a sex tape to Morgan Bench?"

"If you don't want to do it, that's fine. I thought I'd give you the option. I wasn't going to make the choice for you."

"Well, thanks for the option."

"You said you were hard up. And Morgan's actually a reliable guy. He's sharp as hell. If he told you he can get something for whatever you've got, I'm sure it's on the level. I'm not saying you should do it, just saying that I wouldn't dismiss it out of hand."

"It's not happening."

"That's fine," Blakeman said. "Let's get another drink and forget it."

FOUR

ON THE WAY HOME, Eddie thought of those videos, which remained on discs in his apartment building's storage room. Hours and hours of footage, at least some of it interesting by Morgan's standards, all of it Martha's doing. She'd bought the digital camera and set it up on a tripod in the corner of their studio on Ludlow Street, and she'd left it running almost all the time. They acted out scenes for auditions or improvised and critiqued each other's performances. But they also went about their natural lives. Later they would watch themselves and try to refine certain unaffected gestures.

She took it all so seriously. She spoke about acting constantly, though not in the pretentious manner of his college professors. People think of actors as egoists, but Martha had the opposite of ego. She'd given herself up entirely. She had always known she was beautiful—the world constantly reminded her of the fact—but she insisted that beauty was worth less than people thought. Her beautiful mother worked the register for ten hours each day at the local grocery store in her hometown upstate before coming home to drink herself to sleep. Martha was attempting to escape this fate by throwing herself into something enormous, and she expected to be challenged. She seemed half surprised that she'd survived as long as she had. Eddie's own passage from Queens to St. Albert's to NYU to his handful of professional roles had been a series of adjacent steps, none quite stretching him to the point of peril. Soon the next step would present itself, he was sure, and he would hop comfortably along. Meanwhile Martha proceeded by great leaps, never assuming safe arrival, always aware that an abyss awaited those who fell short.

He wondered how often she thought now of those days, when he'd been the only certain thing in her life. Did she ever feel bad about walking out the moment she had something else to rely on? She'd never come back to their apartment after the breakup, but he'd put some things in boxes, which her sister eventually came to get. He'd only included items that belonged entirely to Martha, and he hadn't thought the videos qualified. She'd probably forgotten they existed, or for that matter that he did. More than once Eddie had come close to breaking all the discs, but he could never bring himself to do it. As he arrived home, he decided he would finally throw them out the first chance he got, before he was tempted to make anything of them.

The apartment's lights were on when he got home, and a half-empty bottle of wine was on the kitchen counter. Eddie found Susan in bed, surrounded by a tangle of sheets and tissues.

"What happened?" he asked.

"Great news." She looked up now, turned her tear-streaked face squarely to his, and smiled. "Annie's having another baby."

Eddie sat down on the bed and put his arm around her without saying anything. He was a bit drunk, and he wasn't sure he had the energy that the situation required.

"I really *am* happy for her," she added. "I'm not a bad friend."

"Of course you're not a bad friend."

Eddie was sure that she'd put up a properly brave face for Annie and expressed the appropriate levels of excitement and support before coming home to cry.

"I just miss my children," Susan said. "I know that sounds crazy, but it's like they exist out there somewhere—not just the idea of them—and they're being kept from us."

THIS TALK OF LOST children wandering the face of the earth was only the latest variation on a theme that had been playing out for years. They'd both been in their late twenties when they started dating, and though they'd agreed that they wanted children, they hadn't spoken about it with particular urgency. But after the wedding, Susan had made it clear that she wanted to start trying immediately. Eddie had been slightly relieved that nothing happened right away. He suspected that once they had kids they would look back fondly on the brief time when it had been just the two of them. They'd been married for six months when Annie and her husband took them out to dinner and announced that she was pregnant with their first child.

"What's wrong with me?" Susan asked in the cab home. "This is the most basic thing in the world. It's biology. It's what I was made for. Why can't I do it?"

"We haven't been at it that long," Eddie said.

"I'm calling the doctor tomorrow."

The doctor had not been concerned. There was nothing

unusual about these things taking a few months. If they were in the same position after a year, she would refer them to a specialist. In the meantime, she told Susan to measure out her cycles so they could determine her ovulation days. Since they hadn't been timing their sex precisely, they really knew nothing.

"We've been doing it wrong," Susan announced.

"I thought we were doing it pretty well," Eddie answered. When she didn't smile, he added, "That's good news, isn't it? It means we just need to do a little administrative work and we'll be all set."

"But if it doesn't work, we have to wait a year starting now. We've wasted the past six months."

"It didn't feel like a waste to me."

"You know what I mean."

That night after ordering food, Eddie opened a bottle of wine.

"We can each have two glasses," Susan said. She held a sheet of paper she'd taken from the folder the doctor had given her. "No more binge drinking. It's not healthy."

"Splitting a bottle of wine is not binge drinking."

"And you're going to quit smoking."

He'd already promised to do this when they got engaged.

"I did quit."

"You've been sneaking them. You think I can't smell it? You're really going to quit. All of this stuff makes a difference."

When dinner arrived, Susie looked at the bag in disgust.

"No more greasy Chinese food. After tonight we're eating healthy."

"We do eat healthy," Eddie said. "We're both in good shape. It's been a long day, and neither of us wants to cook. I don't think an occasional General Tso's chicken or a third glass of wine is our problem here."

"So you admit we have a problem?"

In this way their life had changed. The day after their doctor's visit, Susan bought a basal body thermometer. She bought ovulation predictor kits. She bought a watch she wore to bed each night that measured the levels of salt in her sweat. She bought a two-hundred-dollar pillow that she placed under her hips after they had sex, when she would lie for half an hour unmoving and silent, with a look of great concentration on her face, as though willing his sperm safely to their destination. The sex itself was always in the missionary position, and it occurred every other day from day ten to day twenty of her cycle. They could have had sex in other manners, at other times. But they didn't. Neither felt much up to it while these command performances loomed.

Susan came to think of the year they had to pass before going to the clinic as a kind of waiting period. The Clomid the doctor put her on after a few months exacerbated her feelings of despair. Being taken off the Clomid after another few months when it had failed to get them anywhere didn't help, either. She no longer had any hope that they would conceive without serious intervention, but they had to keep trying, since the intervention would only come once the trying had failed. Sex went from being merely functional to grim and hopeless. Once in a while Eddie still joked, "At least it's fun trying." But it had stopped being fun a long time ago.

During this waiting period, Susan had found something online about traditional Chinese medicine. For a period she spoke about "qi" and "meridians." She took herbal supplements and went to an acupuncturist. Eddie didn't think they needed any new expenses that insurance wouldn't cover, but he didn't say anything. After the gynecologist suggested that the herbals might be counterproductive, there was no more talk of the matter. At this point, Susan decided she wasn't going to wait for her doctor to acquiesce. She would find a specialist herself.

HOPE SPRINGS FERTILITY CENTER was located on Sixth Avenue in midtown, and its offices might have belonged to one of the white-shoe law firms that occupied the rest of the building. The couches were leather. Expensive paintings covered the walls, by artists Susan recognized. Their doctor, a bald, bearded man named Walter Regnant, exuded a carefully titrated mixture of sensitivity and confidence.

"I have a very good success rate," he said. "Nearly a dozen children have been named after me."

After the first series of tests, he diagnosed Susan with endometriosis. She had scarring on her fallopian tubes, Regnant explained, and he believed this was the source of the problem. The scars were minor and could be removed with outpatient surgery. And so they were, after which it was back to the thermometer and the pillow, this time with a new optimism. Two months later they returned to Hope Springs.

"Now," Regnant said, pointing his finger—literally, pointing his finger—at Eddie, "we need to see how *your* guys are doing."

Their next appointment was at another midtown building, this one farther west, in a neighborhood to which the trains didn't travel. The waiting room inspired less confidence than the one at Hope Springs. The couch had a tear in its upholstery, and the art on the walls didn't even seek to look expensive. Susan sat outside while a lab technician led Eddie to a door marked "Specimen Collection Room 3." The room was the size of a large walk-in closet. There was an armchair and a sidetable on which were spread five-year-old issues of *Playboy* and *Hustler*. These struck Eddie as almost quaint, pornography having long ago evolved past Hefner and Flynt to hidden cameras and point-of-view shots. For the less imaginative there was also a small television with a VHS player and a pile of videos, most of them still plastic-wrapped with pink stickers that read "3 for $20." There was a small sink in the corner. While Eddie washed his hands he noted a sign on the wall: "Do NOT use LUBRICANT of any kind!!"

He set his specimen cup on the floor beside a roll of paper towels, wondering how much time he'd been allotted. In the pile of magazines, he spotted a copy of *CelebNation*, one of the more popular weekly tabloids. Not only was it a different genre than the other materials, it was also of more recent vintage. Eddie guessed that a patient had brought it with him and left it behind. When he picked it up, the magazine fell open to a page that read "Dr. Drake as you've never seen her!" Beneath these words was a series of photos showing Martha in a bikini, making out on the beach somewhere with Rex Gilbert. The page was crumpled and stuck to the one behind it. Eddie closed it to look at the cover. The newsstand date was from the previous week. Within the past few days—perhaps that very morning—another man had been in this room with that magazine open. In nine months a child would be born owing existence to the firmness of Martha Martin's beach body.

"We've found our problem," Dr. Regnant announced enthusiastically at Hope Springs the next week.

Simply put, the problem was Eddie's substandard semen. It was lacking by every metric—concentration, volume, motility, morphology. Regnant seemed pleased by the discovery.

"Where does this leave our chances of natural conception?" Susan asked.

"Not good," Regnant said.

"What does that mean, exactly?" she pressed. "One in a hundred, or one in a million?"

Regnant sighed.

"It's not something I can quantify. What I can tell you is that I've been in the business for twenty years and no couple that has come to me with these numbers has ever conceived naturally. Of course, that doesn't mean it's impossible."

He watched them react to this.

"There's good news here," he said. "Lots of people who come into my office I have to tell them, 'Sorry, I can't help you.' They've got to start talking about surrogates or adoption. There isn't anything I can offer them. That's not what I'm telling you. I can help you. There's nothing here to suggest that you two are chemically incompatible. Your chances with IVF are actually quite high."

The procedure would cost fifteen thousand dollars. Insurance would cover one-third, leaving them a ten-thousand-dollar tab. The number made Eddie queasy. It might have seemed manageable except for the obvious fact that it was far from the final cost. A child was a machine for creating expenses.

All it took in the end was a credit card. Two of them, actually. Eddie was surprised, in an abstract way, that he was allowed to spend money he didn't have on a process that was designed to bring countless new costs into his life. Nobody stopped to ask how he was going to afford it. When it didn't work out, he joked about asking for their money back. Susan had not found this joke funny. Neither had he, really. On some level he'd meant it. At the very least, for the amount they'd paid, they ought to let them try again, if they wanted.

They couldn't put another try on a credit card, because their cards were maxed out. This too had been a surprise. He thought there would always be a way to get more credit, but apparently not. Eddie started to think about all the years he'd wasted. He had never regretted them before, but now he could see that time for what it was. It wasn't just that he had nothing to show for a decade of his life. He had less than nothing. Those years had amounted to a debit on his account.

When told of the situation, Susan's parents had expressed a religious objection to in vitro, though Eddie suspected that this was mostly to cover the fact that they didn't have the money to help. Eddie's parents were blunt: they'd put more than they could afford into their house in Florida and were now in danger of losing it. By the time Eddie had arrived at the reunion, he and Susan were out of options, so Blakeman's offer to help had seemed like an act of God. Instead it had been an offer to sell a sex tape. Sitting next to Susan in bed after dinner, Eddie wanted to join her in tears.

"On Monday I'll start looking for a summer job," he told her. "We can save some money."

"That's not going to be enough," Susan told him. "It will be years before it's enough."

She was right. In the absence of decent credit, it wouldn't suffice to pay off their bills; they would need the money to pay for the procedure itself. A few months of working a second job would hardly make a dent in all that.

"It will be a start," he said. "We'll go from there."

FIVE

ON MONDAY MORNING, EDDIE brought his laptop into the living room to look up job listings. He didn't have high expectations for his search, which he'd actually begun weeks before. He'd hoped to line up something he could start as soon as the school year ended so he could surprise Susan with the news. But he hadn't found anything. If he'd taught a subject that showed up on the SAT or one of the AP tests, he could have spent the summer tutoring his own students, but any St. Albert's parents willing to support their children's acting ambitions sent them to arts camp for the summer. Every time he thought of waiting tables or bartending—the kind of work he'd done on and off throughout his twenties—he imagined a student or parent coming into the restaurant where he worked. What he wanted was an office job that no one would know he was doing. Every temp agency he called began by asking whether he had a degree. When he asked why that was necessary to fill in for a vacationing receptionist, he was told that there were more than enough college graduates eager to do the work.

He'd spent the previous five summers taking classes, in a halfhearted effort to meet the qualifications for his job at St. Albert's, which had been temporarily waived in his case. The effort cost him thousands of dollars a year, but he was still hardly halfway to a degree. After six years of teaching without incident, he couldn't imagine getting fired for abandoning these classes, so he'd given them up. He told the temp agencies that he was a few credits short. He hadn't heard back from any of them, and he didn't expect to do any better on his own.

Eddie closed the job board and searched for "Jay Rolling." Morgan's site wasn't the first thing that came up, but it was on the first page, which seemed vaguely impressive, given the term's more obvious meaning. It was exactly as he'd described it—photos of disabled people crossing streets in wheelchairs. The discovery was at once baffling and strangely reassuring. Not that Eddie had doubted Morgan's veracity. He'd just assumed that there was something about the project he hadn't understood, that it couldn't possibly be as empty as it sounded. But it was exactly that empty. Based on the various comments and "likes" littered throughout the page, it seemed to have some kind of following, so perhaps on some level Morgan knew what he was doing. At the very least, he'd been right to guess that Eddie had something people would want to see.

Around the time Eddie became serious with Susan, he'd transferred the videos to discs and erased them from his hard drive so she wouldn't come across them while using his laptop. That would have been the time to get rid of them entirely, and he'd considered it. As it was, he had not kept everything, but he hadn't been particularly selective, either. He hadn't wanted to look through them carefully enough to decide what was worth saving, or to consider what it meant to say that some part of his past was worth saving while some other part should be discarded entirely.

Instead he'd deposited them all at the bottom of a cardboard box filled with various souvenirs from his acting days. He'd been ready to throw the whole box out when he moved in with Susan, but she'd encouraged him to hold on to some things. They'd want to show their kids one day, she'd said. With black marker and weak irony he'd labeled the box "relics" before locking it in the building's storage space.

The key to that space hung from a magnetic hook on the refrigerator door. Eddie remembered his resolution from the night before, to be rid of these things. He'd bring them straight out to the street, he decided as he collected the key. He'd break them in half and leave them in the trash on the corner. But in the elevator it struck him that there was no harm in getting a last glimpse of his younger self. It might even be cathartic in some way. Catharsis was an idea he held dear and explained carefully to his students, though so far as he knew he had never experienced it personally. He unlocked the storage space and used the key to cut through the packing tape that sealed the box shut.

At the top of the pile was a playbill from an off-off-Broadway show, his first professional job. In the spring of freshman year, a professor named Harold Edmundson had told Eddie about the play, which Edmundson had written. He'd gotten Eddie an audition for a staging on Minetta Lane, where Eddie had earned the part without a head shot or a résumé. The play was called *Midnight with the Lotos-Eaters*. It made no sense to Eddie whatsoever, but it was received well in those quarters that receive such things at all. The write-up in *Time Out New York*—now paper-clipped to the playbill in the box—named Edward Hartley an "attractive newcomer." From those two words came various offers of representation. While his old St. Albert's friends were deciding which major to declare, Eddie was choosing between Talent Management and William Morris. As breaks go, it wasn't so big, but it felt big enough.

He got a part in another play, which was where he met Martha. He asked her out after their third rehearsal. It was shocking to him now that she'd wanted to be with him, but at the time everything just came as it should. He glowed with confidence. It felt natural to him that this beautiful talent should find him so attractive, and he made it feel natural to her. They began to build a life together around acting. He returned to school in the fall and signed up for his classes, but he couldn't force himself to go when all these other opportunities existed. He had to take his chance. He told himself he could always go back if things didn't work out. For a long time it had seemed that things *were* working out. That they finally had not Eddie discovered all at once, after it was too late.

Coming downstairs had been a mistake. Those days were best forgotten. Eddie tried to close the box, but it wouldn't stay shut without the tape, and half-open it seemed to call to him. So much of his life was in there. He didn't want to kneel over it, working through everything until he found the discs, so he brought the box up to the apartment, where he extracted the thin black CD case from it. He picked a disc at random.

There was nothing strange about seeing Martha on-screen, though she was younger than she looked on TV. What was strange was watching himself beside her. They sat facing each other on the edge of the bed. Martha's hair was pulled back in a ponytail, and she wore a red St. Albert's T-shirt from Eddie's school days.

"There's something you need to know about Daniel," he said, reading from a script on his lap.

"I already know," Martha answered. She held her own script close to eye level, but didn't look at it as she spoke. "I've always known."

Eddie had no recollection of rehearsing this scene. Because they were both working off scripts, he couldn't even be sure which one of them was prepping the other. It was strange what stayed with you and what was lost over years spent memorizing other people's words and speaking them as your own. He'd played Quintus in an experimental production of *Titus Andronicus,* and for months afterward, in bed with Martha, he'd ask, "What subtle hole is this, whose mouth is cover'd with rude-growing briers?" And she would tell him, "A very fatal place it seems to me." He still sometimes thought the words while with Susan, though he certainly never recited them to her.

It didn't make sense, what stuck. He'd been in a student horror movie in which he'd had to point off camera, to a collection of theoretical man-eating blobs, and scream, "Get those sons of green bitches." Not "those green sons of bitches," though the objects themselves were supposed to be green, but "those sons of green bitches." He'd never seen the final cut, if there had ever been one, but that line would stay with him forever. He imagined lying on his death bed, surrounded by grandchildren awaiting his last words, a bit of advice or consolation before he shuffled off this mortal coil, and telling them, "Get those sons of green bitches." But the scene they were enacting now was completely lost to him.

Eddie opened the next file. It was longer, more than ten minutes, and once it started he remembered it well. He'd been called in to audition for a sitcom pilot. The part was the star's boyfriend, with whom she broke up in that first episode, but he'd had some idea that if he did well enough they might write him into a recurring role. Just being asked to try out was one of the highlights of his career to that point. The show had not been picked up in the end, which was all the same to Eddie, since he hadn't been given the part. His preparations were difficult to watch, and not just because he knew how it turned out. It was painful to remember how hopeful he'd been, to acknowledge the obvious fact that he wasn't any good.

In the end, the problem had been his face. This was a surprise, since it had gotten him into acting to begin with. He was handsome enough for his appearance to be a distinct advantage in most areas of life, but there were actually quite a lot of good-looking people out there, when it came down to it. Being among that group wasn't nearly enough, if you wanted to survive on your looks. You needed to be one in a million. If you weren't, it was better not to be handsome at all, to be interestingly flawed or even a kind of gargoyle in the manner of a Peter Lorre. This was the route of the memorable character actor, possibly a more inviting one than that of the leading man.

Unfortunately Eddie wasn't ugly. He was good-looking in an entirely conventional way, which turned out to be fatal. He couldn't turn himself grotesque. Casting directors found him blandly inexpressive, and they made no effort to conceal their finding. He overcompensated, and all the subtlety went out of his work. He screamed and pulled at his hair. He could feel himself acting badly, which made him self-conscious, which made his acting worse.

It was entirely different for Martha. She was a real beauty, a rarity. She might have made it somewhere on that alone. But on top of that she could actually act. Perversely, this was a skill that her looks had taught her. Beauty is a kind of cage, she'd told him once, late at night, when they'd been drinking. Real beauty separates you from everyone else, she'd said. He'd wanted to tell her that they were all encaged. Everyone was separated from everyone else. The bars of her cage just happened to look nicer than his. But he knew there was some truth to what she said. The assumption about having such a beautiful girlfriend was that you were constantly in fear of losing her. And he might have been, had she been merely beautiful in the way that he was handsome. But her kind of beauty acted as insulation. When they were out together, guys wouldn't even talk to her, let alone try to take her home. She frightened people.

There were obvious ways a person could respond to this condition. You could become utterly self-conscious all the time, or become utterly unself-conscious and narcissistic, accepting your difference as a prerogative and other people as not quite real. But there was something in between: you could be both self-conscious and unself-conscious at once, treat all these odd standoffish observers like an audience and perform for them in the way they seemed to expect. You could constantly give the impression that you were offering your entire self to the world, while always holding back the bit that mattered, protecting it. In this way, Martha had learned how to act.

That she could act was obvious enough watching the scene in front of him. She made an impression just by giving him prompts. Anyone watching could have known that she would make it and he would not. Had he truly not known at the time? He remembered recognizing that he needed to work to get better. Watching now, he could see that he'd never been good enough. He put on another scene. It was a kind of torture, but he couldn't stop himself.

He'd had just enough success in the early days to keep him going. A few times a year he got bit parts on television shows. He acted in student films, unpaid work to get himself on-screen. He did small, independent theater, nothing bigger than those first two plays. But his agent kept sending him out, which seemed to be what mattered. Martha was clearly doing better, but there wasn't any competition between them. They were happy together. So happy that years passed, and Eddie hardly noticed he wasn't getting anywhere.

Martha started making trips to the West Coast, auditioning for pilots. She got cast in two, and the second was picked up. Over the phone that night he'd spoken with great excitement about all the plans to be made. They'd been living together for almost six years—since they were both kids—and there had been an unspoken assumption that they would marry once one of them really broke through.

"I've found myself a room," Martha said. "With a girl Tina knows."

Tina was a friend of theirs who'd moved out to L.A. a few months earlier.

"A room?" Eddie asked.

"Yeah, you never know how long these shows will last, so I don't want to get overconfident, start spending money I don't have. Everyone tells me that. Save it away for the dry spells."

"Don't you think we should get our own place?"

"Oh, honey. I didn't think it made sense. They'll probably cancel the thing after half a season, and I'll be right back in New York."

But he knew she would never be back in New York. If the show got canceled, she would get another show.

"I just assumed you would want me there with you."

"Of course," she said. "But I'll be so busy, and what would you do out here?"

It took him a moment to understand.

"What would I do? It's L.A. I'm an actor."

"I know you are. It's just . . ."

"Just what?"

"Since I've been here, I've realized how tough it is."

"You don't seem to be having it that tough."

"But that's just it. I'm at a real make-or-break point right now. I need to concentrate on my career. And if you move out to be with me, and you can't find work, it's going to put too much pressure on me. I can't deal with it right now."

"I'm sorry I didn't get cast for a show about a blind detective. I know that's the gold ring we've been chasing all these years."

"Well, if you have such disdain for that kind of work, that's all the more reason you shouldn't come out here."

"Disdain?" Eddie said. "You fucking hate television. You're the one who talks about art, who wants to be doing Chekhov at the Old Vic or whatever. And now you're giving it up because some producer thinks you're the next hot thing."

When she spoke again, she didn't sound angry or hurt.

"The way you're handling all this just confirms that I made the right decision."

"So this was all decided before you even spoke with me?"

"Eddie," she said, and the tenderness in her voice calmed him, brought him to hopeful attention, so that what came next had maximum effect. "You're dedicating your life to something you've got no talent for whatsoever. It's killed me for years to pretend otherwise, and I can't pretend anymore."

For a long time, Eddie had thought that Martha ended his career with this remark, said purely out of spite. But watching the video now, he could see that she really had known all along. It was all over her face as she tried to work with him. If anything, he wished she'd said something sooner. Why hadn't she warned him? Not on her way out of his life, when the truth could only be destructive, but at a time when it was still possible to do something about it.

He continued watching, making no effort to find scenes that would really interest Morgan. There wouldn't be many, he knew. It wasn't something they'd done on purpose. If you spent that much time alternately having sex and being on camera it was inevitable that you would occasionally wind up doing both at once. There had been some excitement to knowing the camera was capturing them, but afterward they forgot about it. They'd never looked at clips, at least not together. In one scene Eddie came across, they were kissing, and he thought he might have found what Morgan wanted. But they stopped and engaged in a discussion of the mechanics of on-screen chemistry. Eddie felt embarrassed for his younger self, trapped in this bubble of dramatic irony, where not just the audience but the other characters knew the simple truth that hadn't dawned on him. And for the first time in years, he even felt some sympathy for Martha.

Perhaps if he'd handled it differently after their conversation, she would have flown back to New York and they would have at least talked it out a bit. After all, they'd been together a long time. You didn't end a thing like this with one phone call. They might have had a few nights together. Who knows what would have happened. Instead, he'd hung up and quickly called back. When she didn't answer, he told her voice mail that she was a shallow, stupid cunt who didn't want him in L.A. because she needed to be free to fuck strangers if she wanted to keep working. Then he drank half a bottle of bourbon and called to apologize, again to her voice mail. A week later her sister moved her things out. Eddie never saw Martha again.

Except, of course, that he saw her everywhere. The blind detective show was canceled before it finished its first season, just as Eddie had expected. But another one quickly followed, also as Eddie had expected. This time Martha was the star. Dr. Drake was the youngest but most gifted member of a team of intensive-care doctors. She had some kind of special power or intuitive gift, could lay her hands on people and discover what was wrong with them, like a human MRI. Since a medical procedural in which all matter of illness could be diagnosed and cured by the laying-on of hands would not make for much drama, the gift was an inconstant one. It was never explained why it worked when it did or why it didn't when it didn't.

The show was an incoherent mess, lacking even the most basic internal logic. The dialogue was occasionally sharp or funny, but just as often sloppy and melodramatic. After watching the first few episodes, Eddie assumed that it too would be gone before it finished its first season. Five years later it was still on the air, the most popular scripted show on TV. To Eddie this was inexplicable. Naturally he'd tuned in every week, in the early years, but he was a special case. It couldn't be that everyone found the show as utterly ridiculous as he did, that they all watched only because of her. Yet the more he saw, the more convinced of this he became. Martha's beauty and charm were sufficient to keep millions of people engaged with a show that wasn't just poorly written or schmaltzy but that on the most fundamental level didn't make any sense. Was she a doctor or some kind of shaman or what?

Even if he avoided NBC, which aired *Dr. Drake,* she was liable to turn up on another network, plugging a late-night spot. The new twenty-four-hour celebrity news channel, Entertainment Daily, seemed to devote more than half its coverage to Martha. He could turn off the TV, but she was everywhere online. He couldn't even read the New York *Herald* in the morning without seeing her in some ad. If he put down the paper and went outside, she was on the side of the passing bus. Phone booths that no longer had working phones seemed now to exist only to taunt Eddie with her image. Eventually he learned to do what everyone else apparently did, which was to believe that she wasn't actually real. In this way, she became for him what she'd already become for the rest of the world—not a human being at all, but a vessel into which could be poured all of his longing and his hope and finally all of his disappointment.

This was the worst part about watching the clips: they made her the old Martha again. It had been seven years since Martha left—he'd now been with Susan nearly as long as he'd been with Martha—and he'd trained himself to look at her on TV without thinking of those days. But here he saw her as he had known her and the public had not, before she was Dr. Drake. Of course this was just what would make the video interesting. Perhaps interesting enough that Morgan would spend some money on one of these innocent clips of the two of them talking. Eddie could already imagine the *Dr. Drake* chat boards filling up with obnoxious comments about what a lousy actor he'd been, but he could live with that if everything else worked out.

He clicked on another file, and there was again the brief blankness of the screen before it started up. The picture was different this time, the view shaky. The camera was off the tripod, presumably being held by Eddie himself, working its way around the room for a few seconds before settling on a scene. When it found Martha she was naked and prone, knees tucked under her body, which was arranged as though in a kind of salutation, her feet and ass hanging off the end of the bed while her arms stretched out in front of her. She seemed to be waiting for him, and he approached with the camera in hand, focused on her unmoving body.

She gave way to him easily and he leaned into her, setting his free hand on the crook where her bony hip gave way to the soft thickness of flesh. Once he'd positioned himself there he didn't move except to run the camera from her splayed ass up the long ellipses of her back to her shoulders and the cropped blond hair on the back of her head. Instantly that hair fixed the scene in time. Eddie remembered that she'd cut it to play Viola in a production of *Twelfth Night*. She rocked front to back on her knees, lazily at first and then with more purpose. The camera followed her for a moment before fixing in place as her head moved in and out of the scene.

After a few minutes of this, the view went sideways, as though he meant to put the camera down, until she looked back over her shoulder at him, and the camera went upright to catch the hungry smile on her face. She stared at the lens and rocked in front of him more deliberately. This went on for precisely two minutes and eighteen seconds, measured at the bottom of the screen, before she pulled herself off him and turned over, showing her whole body. She put a finger in her mouth and then reached down to hook it inside herself.

He had not up until then been aroused by watching the video, but now he was stirred in a sad, desperate way. She was perfect. He had always thought so. If he let this scene out into the world, this was the part that would be played over and over again. She moved with an odd innocence, the only emotion on her face a kind of curiosity. Eddie had the sense now that she was acting. Perhaps he'd understood as much then, because he turned the camera away from her, down to his own erection, as if to bring reality into the matter before quickly returning to her. When she withdrew her hand and brought it to her mouth again, he lowered himself onto the bed and her. The view turned awkward and uninviting—a bit of her shoulder, her jaw and ear, the headboard. Martha took the camera and turned it on him, lowering it slowly from his face to the point where his hips pressed against her thighs. The screen went blank.

Eddie closed his laptop, knowing that the only other option was to watch the thing again. More than once he'd been asked by a crude or drunk friend what it had been like with Martha Martin. He always shrugged the question off, not out of discretion but because he couldn't really remember. Everything about that time—everything about her—had taken on a sheen of bitterness and regret, so that it was impossible to recover from it something so simple and pleasurable as two young people in love, enjoying each other.

He needed to get out of the apartment, to forget about things for a few hours. He ejected the disc and put it back in the case, which he placed on a shelf in the linen closet that Susan couldn't reach without his help. He got in the elevator without knowing where he was going, but he quickly decided to head to Lexington Avenue to see what was playing at the movie theater. He would sit in the cool darkness of distraction. Susan would be home, soon after the movie was over, and they could talk about what they were going to do next. He got to the theater just in time for a showing of *Mantis 3: Slaying Mantis*. Blakeman's review of this installment in the series suggested that it was just the kind of mindless fantasy he needed. He found a spot near the front of the empty theater as previews started. The first was for another movie that also starred Mantis, as part of a superhero collective that was fighting to save the earth from aliens. Eddie thought he might watch that one when it came out. If he didn't find a job and wasn't taking classes, he might go to a lot of movies that summer.

The second preview was for a romantic comedy called *Life After Laura,* starring Turner Bledsoe as a young widower and Martha Martin as the grief counselor who falls in love with him. Eddie hadn't known she'd started making movies. All the effort he'd spent over the years getting used to seeing her on-screen seemed to have been undone by a few hours spent exploring the past. That was his Martha up there, the same one he'd been watching all morning. Everyone thought they knew her, but they didn't. They didn't know that she'd run out as soon as she got her break, that she'd left him behind to start his life over. If they knew, no one would blame him for selling the tape.

He tried to estimate the value of what he had. There was no question that it was Martha. For three minutes she stared right into the camera, and it caught her face many other times throughout. The whole thing was about twenty minutes long, though he would have to cut out four or five that showed too much of him. Perhaps another three or four would go for reasons of quality, though he didn't know how much that mattered in these things. At the very least he had ten full minutes of usable footage. If he was prepared to use it. Assuming Morgan was reliable, it was worth well more than they needed. There had to be some way of doing it so that it didn't come back to him.

As the preview dragged on, Eddie began to laugh at the screen. It might have been taken as laughter at Martha's bad jokes, but he kept it up after the preview ended and another, for a notably unfunny war movie, began. He was still at it during the feature's opening credits, when a woman sitting several rows behind him asked him to stop.

HE WAS BACK IN the apartment when Susan got home.

"How was your day?" he asked.

"Fine," she said. But she didn't look fine. She looked tired. And he was tired of seeing her so tired. "Did you do anything about dinner?"

He hadn't thought about dinner after stuffing himself with popcorn.

"We could order something."

"It's so expensive. We agreed we were going to have some discipline about this stuff this summer. It's the first day of your vacation and we're already fucking up this plan."

"I'll make something."

"Don't bother," she told him. "There's no difference at this point anyway. We're kidding ourselves."

He could just tell her the truth, and they could decide together. She could determine whether one more shot at a child was worth whatever would come out of this. But telling her meant admitting that he'd saved these videos all this time. He could promise her that he hadn't looked at them, which had been true until now, but how could she believe it? Beyond that, how could he force her to make this choice? If he was going to do it, he had to do it himself.

"I *was* going to make something," he said. "But I got some news today."

"Did you find a job?"

"Not quite," he said. "I got a call from Alex at Talent Management. Apparently this stupid horror film I was in years ago has become something of a cult hit. In South Korea of all places."

He didn't know why he'd said South Korea, but he found the audacity of the lie strangely appealing.

"That's fun," she said, trying to generate interest in the matter. "So you're telling me you're going to be huge in Asia?"

"The thing is that the guy who made it couldn't afford to pay us anything. He sold us shares in the movie instead. Now I've got some money coming to me."

"What kind of money?"

"It's tough to say how much it will be in the end. But the agency just got a check for twenty grand. They're going to take out their fifteen percent and send the rest to me. That's seventeen thousand dollars right there. And there might be more coming."

The violence of the sound she let out surprised Eddie. She ran over to the couch and threw herself on his lap.

"It's going to work this time."

"I hope so, too."

"No, it's not hope. I'm certain it's going to work."

"I know how badly you want this," he said. "I want it badly, too. But it can only help to be realistic. That way if it doesn't work out, it won't hurt so much."

She was too happy even to be annoyed by him.

"When was the last time you got a serious residual check, not a few bucks here and there, but enough money to make a real difference?"

The answer was never.

"Probably five years."

"Five years," she nearly screamed at him. "For five years we haven't needed this money, and it didn't come. Now we do need it, and within a matter of weeks a check is in the mail."

He tried to give himself over to the idea.

"You've got a point," he said. "The timing is pretty striking."

"So why would it not work out? Why would God give us this last chance if he wasn't going to make good on it?"

That night they went out for dinner. When they returned home, both a little drunk, they had sex for the first time in more than a year not according to any schedule, not for any end but the pleasure of being together. After guiding Susan onto her stomach and then up onto her knees, Eddie ran his eyes like a lens over the length of her back.

SIX

AS SOON AS SUSAN left for work the next day, Eddie punched Morgan's number into his phone and looked at it on the small screen. He flipped the business card—*Meme Evangelist*—around in his fingers. He put his phone back in his pocket. In an effort to keep himself from watching the video, he turned on the TV. He wanted to find her there, to see her as a television star, like everyone else did. Such a person lived on a screen, didn't really have feelings, and couldn't be hurt by anything he did.

First he tried the basic cable stations, which constantly showed the early seasons of *Dr. Drake* in syndication. When he didn't find anything, he went to Entertainment Daily. The channel's lead anchor, Marian Blair, was talking about Justine Bliss. Eddie had heard her reality show mentioned several times in recent days but otherwise knew nothing about her. From the segment he was watching he gathered that she was a teenaged country singer. Apparently she wasn't eating, and her friends had fears for her life. Eddie had to admit she looked quite thin, especially when the split screen placed her next to her pudgy ten-year-old self.

"Is Justine's life in danger?" Marian Blair asked. "Those closest to her think it is. They staged an intervention, and they've invited our cameras along. Stay tuned for an ED exclusive." Now Marian turned to a different camera, and her expression softened. "Also after the break: reports of on-set canoodling and late night flights to Portugal. Is Dr. Drake in love? Will she leave Rex for Turner? Stayed tuned. I'm Marian Blair, and you're watching Entertainment Daily."

Eddie wondered whether Martha found it satisfying to have her life followed on these shows. Had she gotten what she wanted out of acting? Maybe she still dreamed of Broadway, still hoped to get noticed for her acting instead of her looks. Perhaps everyone nursed a private disappointment.

He turned the TV off and made the call.

"Handsome Eddie," Morgan said. "Good to speak to you."

"You, too. I'm calling to follow up on the conversation we had at dinner."

"That's great. What have you got for me?"

"I'd rather not talk about it over the phone."

Morgan laughed.

"We're doing full cloak-and-dagger here?"

"I'm a little skittish is all. If you drop by my apartment this afternoon, we can discuss it."

"Before I get myself over there, are we talking about real deal?"

"We are."

"I'll be over around one."

Having made this appointment, Eddie realized he'd done nothing to prepare. It had seemed that if he acted without planning, he wouldn't be responsible for what followed. He opened the video and attempted to edit it. He'd become pretty good at this kind of work from putting together video résumés for casting agents. He cut the part where his own face was visible and a few other awkward moments. Eventually he was left with fifteen minutes, which he thought would be enough.

WHEN MORGAN ARRIVED THAT afternoon, he seemed as nervous as Eddie was, though he tried to project a sense of command.

"What have we got?" he asked skeptically.

"Just what you were looking for."

"How long is the footage?"

"A little under twenty minutes."

"That's a good length," Morgan said. Eddie wondered how such things were determined. "Can you see her tits?"

Eddie nodded.

"What about scag?"

Eddie wasn't entirely sure what "scag" was.

"I'm not going to give you the whole director's commentary. Why don't you look at it and tell me what it's worth?"

He didn't want to be in the room while Morgan watched, but he didn't want to leave him alone with the computer. It would be easy enough to put the file onto a zip drive and walk out with it. Eddie opened his laptop on the coffee table, started the clip, and retreated to the corner. He had a sudden fear that Susan would come home, eager to celebrate their good news. He locked the front door and waited there. The scene seemed much longer now than it had when he'd watched it alone. It was certainly long enough for Morgan's purposes.

"Fuck," Morgan observed when the video was done.

"So you're interested in making a deal?"

"Definitely."

"Before we go on, certain points are nonnegotiable." Eddie hadn't planned to say this, and now he considered what those points should be. "If anyone finds out that it's me in the tape, I'm going to tell them it was stolen. I erased these scenes years ago, when Martha and I broke up. Before that, when we were still together, you borrowed my laptop over at Blakeman's place. You stumbled on this file, and you e-mailed it to yourself. Maybe you just wanted to watch it, and you only now decided to sell it. At any rate, I had nothing to do with any of it. That's all if it gets back to either of us. Ideally, it won't."

"You've thought this out."

He hadn't, really. There must have been something he wasn't anticipating.

"Does that work for you?"

"If we plan it right, it won't come back to either of us."

"That's not what I'm asking."

"You're telling me it's not negotiable, so it's not negotiable. Let's talk about the things that are negotiable."

"How much can you offer?"

Morgan sat quietly for a bit, as if replaying the video in his head while making calculations.

"Twenty grand."

Eddie had known it would be a struggle, but he couldn't believe they were starting this low.

"At the party you said you could get me six figures."

"I said six figures depending on what you had."

"What I've got is better than you could have imagined. You see her from the front, from the back, close-up of her face. She practically states her name for the record."

Morgan seemed to concede the point.

"I didn't realize you'd be asking me to risk my reputation."

"Shopping the tape around doesn't risk your reputation, but being called a thief does?"

"There's no shame in porn these days. Might as well be Universal Studios. Listen, you're laying down your terms, which are fair enough, but you can't expect that they won't affect the price."

"So make me a reasonable offer."

"Twenty-five."

"If we don't start talking real numbers," Eddie said, "I'm going to take this thing somewhere else."

"Your story only works with me."

"I can come up with another backup story."

"Are you sure you can trust someone else's discretion?"

"I'll work something out."

"Are you sure you can trust *my* discretion once I don't have a stake in this? Whatever story you want to tell blows up in a hurry if people know you tried to sell it to me and we couldn't agree on a price."

"You're extorting me?"

"It's not like that," Morgan said. "I just don't want to get cut out of something that was my idea in the first place."

Eddie was trapped. Susan had already made the appointment at Hope Springs. He had to strike some kind of deal. But Morgan didn't know that. Eddie recognized on Morgan's face an expression that was painfully familiar to him—the look of a man desperate for something to break his way.

"I'll admit that I can't take this thing somewhere else," Eddie said. "I wouldn't know where to take it. What I can do is erase it with one press of a button, so neither of us gets anything out of it. I'm offering my life up for your profit, and I intend to get something out of it. I'm going to destroy this thing if you even mention to me a number lower than a hundred thousand dollars."

"It's going to take me some time to round up the money. I'll have a bank check in three weeks."

EDDIE TOLD SUSAN THAT it would take a month for Talent Management to send his check. She didn't ask any questions about the money or the movie. All that mattered to her was that things were going to work out. Just as Eddie had hoped, this one bit of good luck had been enough to restore her faith. They went the next week to Hope Springs, where Dr. Regnant greeted them like old friends he'd worried he would never see again. He told them the odds would be higher in the second round. He wanted to give Susan's body a chance to recover, so he suggested putting off the next attempt until the end of the summer. Eddie thought Susan would be disappointed by the news, but she seemed willing to wait as long as it took, now that they had a plan in place. For his part, Eddie was relieved to have some time. Despite Blakeman's promises, he wasn't sure how reliable Morgan would prove to be.

But he didn't need to worry. Almost three weeks to the day, Morgan called to say he had a check. Eddie was surprised that a guy whose main business was posting photos of wheelchairs could get together that kind of money in such time, but he didn't question it. The next day, Eddie gave Morgan the video on a zip drive and erased it from his computer. This last part was only a gesture—the clip still existed along with the others on the disc—but Eddie really felt he was getting rid of it. It wasn't his anymore, which meant he wasn't responsible for what happened to it from there.

At the bank Eddie nearly walked up to the first open ATM. There was no reason he couldn't deposit a hundred-thousand-dollar check right into the machine. Perhaps that's what people like Justin Price did. But he needed to take care of some other things. He'd spent a good part of the past few weeks planning how to break up the cash. He handed the certified check to a teller and asked her to draw two others, made out to two different credit card companies. One was in the amount of

$17,233, the other $19,679. All of his debt, built up patiently over time, through more than a decade of persistent, sustained irresponsibility, was gone in an instant.

He put twenty thousand dollars into his checking account. This was roughly the amount he'd told Susan he would be getting from the horror film, and it would cover the costs of the treatment. He put the rest in a simple savings account. The bank teller tried to talk him into a slightly more sophisticated investment "vehicle," but he wanted something he could move around as easily as possible.

It occurred to Eddie that he could spend this money any way he wanted, since Susan didn't know it was there. For that matter, he didn't have to go back to Susan at all. He could just walk away from everything. Something in him found the prospect attractive. But Susan was the only justification for what he'd done. She'd needed it so badly. The money would go to raising their child. It wasn't all that much for that purpose, but to Eddie it felt like a lot.

THE WEEKS THAT FOLLOWED should have been perfect. For the first time in a decade, he didn't spend a part of every day worrying about money. Once this sense of insecurity was gone, he realized how he'd lived in it. It had become his atmosphere, or a kind of first principle from which every element of his life emerged. Now it was gone.

Susan was happier than he'd ever seen her, happier than she'd been when they first started dating, before all this trouble began. She was convinced it was going to work this time. They had been given this reprieve; it had to have happened for a reason. There was simply no point in their being disappointed again. They decided to enjoy the time before treatments began. They started having sex again—real, spontaneous sex, with no purpose but pleasure. When they went out for expensive dinners, Susan didn't ask how they would pay for them.

Eddie tried not to think about the enormity of what he'd done. The video was going to be traced back to him eventually. There was no way that Martha would let him off the hook. Once it did, would Morgan stick to their story? Would Susan buy it? If Martha tried to sue Morgan, it would come out that he'd bought the tape from Eddie. How could it not? Once lawyers were involved Eddie's cover story about stolen files would be dropped. Either this hadn't occurred to Morgan, which meant that he'd thought this all out no more than Eddie had, or else he didn't care, because he had no particular intention of keeping his promise. Eddie could do nothing to make him. If Susan found out what had happened before the treatments started, she wouldn't let them go ahead. Everything would collapse again. But if the treatment worked out first, she might accept that he'd done it for her.

He called Morgan at the beginning of August.

"I've been wondering how this is going to go down."

"It has gone down as far as you're concerned," Morgan said. "You don't have anything to worry about from here."

"I'm just curious. When do you think it's going to break?"

"It's tough to say, but not immediately. Once it's out, it's very difficult to control, so I've got to be sure to get the most out of the initial blast. Martha is definitely hot right now, but she could get hotter. If this movie she's in does well, or if the rumors are true about this new guy and she really leaves Rex. So I'm going to sit on it for a bit. On the other hand, her stock could drop. Say, if *Dr. Drake* gets canceled."

"Do you think that might happen?"

"I'm not fucking Nielsen or whatever. I'm just laying out the considerations I've got going through my head."

"So when it goes out, how many people do you think will wind up seeing it?"

"If I do my job right, Eddie, everyone will see it. Fucking everyone. I mean, it's going to be everywhere."

"Do you think that's a good idea?"

"Of course it's a good idea. What did you think the point of all this was?"

"I'm just wondering how it will affect Martha."

"Wrong time to get a conscience, Eddie. What did you think you were getting into?"

"Aren't you worried she'll get litigious or something?"

Morgan laughed.

"Is that your concern? We have nothing to worry about. This is going to be great for Martha. At this point in her career, it's just what she needs. She'll be thanking you when it's all over."

"Can you do me a favor?" Eddie asked. "Give me a heads-up before doing anything. Just a few days, so I can work things out on my end."

"Let me talk to my investor."

"It's just one guy?"

"Do you want to know?" Morgan asked.

"Not really."

"I'll see what he says."

Meanwhile, Eddie and Susan returned to Hope Springs, and the process began again.

The Lupron shots were the easiest ones. The needle was small, and the drugs came from the pharmacy already mixed. Each morning before Susan went to work, Eddie took the vial from the fridge and filled a syringe. He brought it to their bed, where Susan waited with her shirt pulled up. During the first round, they'd experimented with ice cubes to numb her skin, but Susan said the cold was worse than the shot, so now Eddie just wiped a bit of her belly with rubbing alcohol and pinched a quarter of pink skin. When he'd finished pushing the needle, he covered the syringe and put it into the red hazardous waste barrel that now sat in a corner of the bedroom.

As far as Susan knew, Eddie was still looking for work, since their financial problems were far from over. But Eddie knew there was more money, and he was too anxious to go job hunting. He'd started following Martha more closely, looking for developments in her public life that might send Morgan into action. He turned on the TV as soon as Susan left each morning. He bought all the gossip magazines and read them at coffee shops, throwing them out before coming home. There was a lot to follow—Entertainment Daily and half a dozen other channels; *Star Style, Peeper,* and *CelebNation.* Martha had definitively split from Rex, and her publicist confirmed that she was dating Turner Bledsoe.

She had left Rex just as his status as Hollywood's leading heartthrob was coming into doubt. His big summer movie was a box office disappointment, and his new girlfriend, Carla Lender—the head chef on the cooking-and-dating show *Butter Me Up*—was an obvious step down from Martha. Meanwhile, Martha's romance with Turner had helped make *Life After Laura* into a hit. She was bankable now. According to *Star Style,* she was considering half a dozen new projects, and the upcoming season of *Dr. Drake* would be her last. Eddie found dozens of message boards dedicated to predicting how the series would end. Would the true nature of Drake's gift finally be revealed? Would she marry the hospital administrator with whom she'd alternately flirted and fought through the duration of the show? Serious consideration was being given to alternate theories that Drake was either an angel or a space alien. In either case the final episode would close with her ascension into the skies. Eddie spent entire days on this, and there was always more.

When he wasn't following the intricacies of Martha's career, he was watching the two of them together on his computer. He didn't watch the clip he'd sold to Morgan, just the everyday images of their old life. At times he would watch a scene that reminded him of something, and he would go into the closet and search the relics box for an old photograph or script. He would emerge eventually to find that an hour had passed. It had been a mistake to bring the box upstairs, to invite her back into his life. He'd thought it would be harmless to remember from a safe distance what it had been like to be in her thrall, but there was no safe distance.

And he wasn't just following Martha. Justine Bliss had admitted her problem and agreed to check herself in to the hospital. Entertainment Daily had exclusive access to her first days there. They reported every meal she ate and every morning weigh-in. Meanwhile Sandra Scopes, three-time winner of *Scavenger: Urban Adventure Edition*, had been diagnosed with breast cancer.

"There's a lesson here," Sandra told Marian Blair. "If it can happen to me it can happen to anyone."

"Anyone who watched Sandra in the roller derby challenge of *Scavenger Detroit*," Marian assured her viewers, "knows she's not a quitter."

"Burt Wyman got a DUI," Eddie told Susan one morning while flipping through a copy of *CelebNation* that he'd found in the Hope Springs waiting room.

"Who on earth is that?"

"He was the runner-up in the last season of *We Drink Too Much*."

"You watch that show?"

"It's very popular."

"Put that thing down."

She laughed as she said it, but Eddie followed her command. More and more she addressed him in this imperative mode. Clean up the kitchen. Turn off the TV. Be gentle with that needle. They moved from Lupron to Menopur and Follistim, which was a good sign, except that the drugs made her angry and manic. She needed constant reminders of why they were doing all this. Eddie considered it a good day when she was too tired to be mad at him.

Otherwise everything seemed to be working out. On the morning that Eddie told Susan about Burt's relapse, Regnant announced that they had a good number of suitable eggs. They needed to get ready for retrieval.

Two days later the nurses brought Susan to the room where her follicles would be removed. She was put under general anesthesia for the procedure. For once Eddie had his own job to do. This time he didn't have to go off site, to the farthest reaches of the West Side. It amazed him how much nicer a room you were given for this business once you paid five figures. The array of auxiliary materials provided was astonishing. A few months from now, he imagined, the Martha Martin tape would be included in the Hope Springs library.

Regnant called the next week to say that things looked good, though it didn't sound that great.

"It's not the ideal scenario," he admitted. "But I'm honestly pretty happy with where we are. We've got three fertilized embryos, which is a lower number than I'd hoped. None of them have developed into blastocysts yet, but that's not necessarily a problem. I'd like to go ahead and implant all three of them. I think that's our best bet."

This mixed news already put them further along than they'd gotten the first time around, and Susan seemed entirely encouraged. The next morning, they went back to Hope Springs. Given all they'd been through and the importance of this next step, it was a remarkably simple procedure. Susan was put into stirrups in the surgical room. Eddie held her hand, but he looked away as Regnant brought the catheter between her legs. There was a sloppy, squishing sound while it entered her, and Susan squeezed Eddie's hand. After it was over, she smiled. There were embryos inside of her, little babies waiting to be born. They would have to wait about two weeks for a test to tell them if any had implanted themselves.

In the recovery room, Susan was punchy from excitement. She looked at Eddie with a silly, loving smile. Once she had regained some strength, he stood her up and helped her to get dressed. Halfway to the elevator, she pointed at a magazine on the coffee table.

"Look, honey," she said.

Eddie picked up the copy of *CelebNation*, a new issue he'd somehow missed. "Dr. Drake Baby Bump?" the cover headline asked. There was a photo of Martha and Turner walking hand in hand. Martha's midsection had been magnified within a red circle in the middle of the page. It might have just been the loose shirt she was wearing, but it did look like her belly was bigger than usual. Eddie looked over at Susan, waiting for her reaction. She laughed and put her arms around him.

"I guess we're not the only ones having a baby."

PART TWO

SEVEN

INTRODUCTION TO DRAMATIC ACTING was Eddie's first
class of the year, second period in the theater. Nearly a third
of the sophomore class—about twenty students—had signed
up, making it the most popular elective. Eddie was under no
illusion about this popularity. The creative impulse was meant
to be encouraged and critical judgment understood as finally
subjective, so any student who showed up in Eddie's classes
and gave some sign of having done the work could expect an
A– or, at worst, a B+. The same was true of some of the other
electives—fiction writing and art studio—but there were ad-
ditional advantages to "DramAct," as the boys called it. Eddie
was a lousy disciplinarian, and he was easily led into digres-
sions that took up much of the fifty-minute period. At some
point word had spread that you could get away with attending
his classes while stoned. He didn't believe in his own authority, which made it impossible to project it to the boys. At heart,
he didn't care whether they learned anything. His first goal

was keeping himself out of trouble by avoiding any student complaints. His second was making sure he didn't accidentally inspire one of them to a vocation, which could only end badly. With the exception of Patrick Hendricks, he seemed to have succeeded so far.

"If you've ever smiled in appreciation after opening a present you didn't want, you've been an actor," Eddie announced to the boys by way of introduction. "If you've ever told your mother you were cleaning your room when you were really watching the game, you've been an actor. If you've ever made up an excuse to get out of going out with a girl whose feelings you didn't want to hurt, you've been an actor."

This was the speech his predecessor, Mr. Carlton, had made at the beginning of this class, and Eddie performed it more or less verbatim, though the examples were hopelessly stale. These boys were not required to put on a smile when they didn't like something they were given. They told their mothers what they actually wanted and got it the next day. As for cleaning up their rooms, the best of them were minimally polite to the household help. Nor did they care about sparing feelings, based on what Eddie heard in the hall. The attitude seemed to be that the less attractive you made a girl feel, the more accommodating she would be.

But the examples hardly mattered, since the entire speech was wrong. Eddie didn't know whether Carlton had ever believed it, but Eddie himself certainly did not. He remembered Martha telling him how she had learned to act by being encaged in her beauty, holding herself apart from the world. This conceit had appealed to him so long as he thought he was in on the act, not just another member of the crowd. But what she'd done wasn't acting. You weren't actually supposed to lie to the audience. It wasn't acting when you told a stranger that you were a Russian aristocrat. Acting was when you told a stranger, "Tonight, I will be playing the role of a Russian aristocrat," and proceeded to make that stranger believe you in the role anyway. Lying credibly, Eddie had learned, took no talent at all if you were telling a lie that the other person wanted to believe.

He repeated the speech nonetheless, because nothing else he thought to say seemed any better. If he told them that acting wasn't the same as lying, without telling them what it might be instead, that only confused matters, which wasn't supposed to be a teacher's job. Most of what people said about acting was wrong. There was a truth to be learned, but it could only be experienced, not named. You arrived at it through trial and error, and that process couldn't be taught. This obviously wasn't a great attitude for an acting instructor to have, which was why Eddie kept it to himself.

When he'd finished, he took a moment to measure the class's reaction. The boys looked blankly at him, except for a pair talking in the back of the theater, who made no effort to lower their voices.

"Why don't we go around the room and introduce ourselves. You all know each other, of course, but I don't know everyone. Say your name, and tell us your favorite actor."

"I'm Paul," the first boy said. He was familiar to Eddie, because he'd auditioned for the spring play the year before. "My favorite actor is Rex Gilbert."

A few of the others laughed at this.

"I'm Peter," said the boy next to Paul. "My favorite actor is Turner Bledsoe."

More laughter.

"I'm George, and my favorite actor is Martha Martin."

Now the entire class laughed.

"Is it true?" someone said.

"Is what true?"

"That you dated Dr. Drake?"

Eddie wasn't sure how this had first reached the students a few years back. One of the other teachers might have mentioned it; one of the boys might have had an uncle or cousin who'd overlapped with Eddie at the school. Maybe some document linking him to Martha existed in those dark corners of the Internet that they accessed so easily. However it had come into circulation, the story had been reliably passed down each year. Eddie could measure the boldness of a new class—their willingness to cause him trouble—by how soon they mentioned it.

"We're not going to talk about that," he said, though he knew they would talk about it nearly every day. In previous years, such conversations were a mild nuisance, but now he felt she was recapturing every corner of his life. He had two more classes that day, and Martha's name came up in each.

ON THE WAY HOME, he called Susan to see whether he should pick up something for dinner.

"There's still no blue line," she said.

Regnant had told them not to bother with home tests, which wouldn't be accurate yet. These things took time to develop, and the clinic's technology would answer the question well before anything over the counter. Susan was going in to Hope Springs the next day, but she'd been peeing on plastic sticks all day.

"It doesn't mean anything," Eddie said.

"I don't think I can survive if it doesn't work out this time."

"It's going to work out."

He had come to believe this with certainty. It had to work out. It was the only thing that could give meaning to what he had done.

After he got off the phone, Eddie ducked into a deli on Second Avenue to pick up a salad and a couple of pieces of roasted chicken. At the register, he saw the cover of *Celeb-Nation*. Amid the confusion of colorful typography he read, "Our Spies Say: Dr. Drake Sex Tape?" It was written in small letters at the bottom of a cover otherwise dedicated to Justine Bliss's release from the hospital.

Eddie picked up the magazine and found the Our Spies Say feature, a repository for gossip even more poorly sourced than the rest of the magazine's stories. Items appeared there about celebrity tipping habits, e-mailed in by unhappy waiters. Dramatic, life-altering news was floated that would never be mentioned again. Eddie read the first "dispatch."

Martha Martin may be planning her future with Turner Bledsoe, but our spies say she should get ready for a visit from the past. Whispers have it that a sex tape from before the TV hottie's Dr. Drake days has found its way out into the world. This is a story our spies will be following very closely!

Eddie flipped through the rest of the magazine. Martha was featured in both Why Did She Wear It? and Stars Have Zits! There was a two-page spread of speculations about her bump. But there were no other mentions of the tape. Before checking out, Eddie took a copy of each magazine on the rack. He paid and found a stoop outside, where he sat with the deli bag between his legs and skimmed through pages. None of the covers mentioned the tape, and he couldn't find it discussed anywhere inside *Star Style* or *Peeper*. He threw the magazines out and called Morgan.

"Did you do it?" he asked.

"No time for pleasantries, I guess."

"You said you'd give me a heads-up first."

"Relax, it isn't out yet."

"I saw the thing in *CelebNation*."

"Just priming the pump, Eddie. I gave them an exclusive tip. Now that they're spreading the word, people will debate it online for a while—whether or not it's real, how much it will show, who else is in it. It's just like any film, you want to get some prerelease buzz. Then we go out with it."

"Can you hold it a bit longer? I think my wife is pregnant."

"That's great news, Eddie. I'm happy for you. But if you think I can sit on this for nine months you're kidding yourself."

"Not nine months. Just a little while."

"This is our big shot right now, and we paid you good money for it. I wish you and Susan all the best. But you need to prepare yourself for the fact that this thing will be out there soon."

Eddie hung up and went home. Upstairs, he heard Marian Blair's voice before he entered the apartment.

"Burt Wyman says he's back on the wagon and ready to talk about his journey. Next on Entertainment Daily."

Susan was sitting on the couch, half watching the TV, which she muted when the show went to commercial.

"What are you doing?" he asked.

"I'm watching crap on TV," Susan said.

"You hate those shows."

"I wanted something mindless to distract me. I'm so nervous."

"Can we watch something else while we eat?"

"I'm actually weirdly enjoying it," Susan said. "It's sort of addictive if you give yourself over to it."

Eddie sat down on the couch and put their food on the table.

"I'd really like to watch something else."

"Let me just see one more segment."

The show came back, and Susan turned the sound on.

"In a candid, touching interview, Burt Wyman opened up to Entertainment Daily's Terri Reese about his recent relapse, how faith has helped him recover, and what's next for the *We Drink Too Much* fan favorite."

Now the screen showed Wyman, a fat, bearded man in early middle age, who was crying as he spoke.

"I don't remember getting into the car," he said. "I was just having a beer in my trailer, and the next thing I knew the cops had me in cuffs. That's when I thought to myself, I've got a real problem on my hands. And the first thing I did was I just prayed to Jesus. I said to Jesus, I got a real problem here."

Susan turned off the TV.

"You're right," she said. "This stuff is gross. You forget that these are real people you're watching."

"I know what you mean."

Susan smiled.

"I did get some news about your old girlfriend, though."

"Really?"

"Apparently, she's confirmed that she's pregnant. And this Turner guy has proposed. There was a whole segment where people argued about what designer she should choose for her dress. God, that channel is really obsessed with her. Could you imagine if we had to have some publicist talking to the media after we got the call from Regnant? Why do people think this stuff is their business?"

"People like Martha make it everyone's business," Eddie said. "She didn't have to tell Entertainment Daily that she was pregnant. It helps her sell movie tickets. Shows like this have made her very rich."

"But from what you've told me, she was never into this

stuff. She just wanted to be an actress. It seems too bad that she can't just act without all the other bullshit."

A few weeks before, he wouldn't have imagined Susan defending Martha on any grounds. Now things had changed. Eddie was tempted to keep pushing back, but what did he want to convince her of, really?

"I guess you're right," he said.

Eddie wanted to join Susan at Hope Springs for the test, but they agreed it was better for him to save his personal days. If all went well, there would be many more appointments to make. Anyway, they wouldn't be getting the results of the test until that evening at the soonest.

On his way to school, he picked up the daily papers. In the *Post,* Page Six had an item about Martha's pregnancy and her engagement, but nothing about the tape. Eddie tossed it out and opened the *Daily News.* The gossip page was still written by Morgan's old boss, Stanley Peerbaum. He also led with Martha's engagement, but he added more: "It may not be all good news for Martha Martin, though. *CelebNation* is reporting rumors of a sex tape making the rounds, dating back to Martin's early days as a struggling actress in New York."

The magazine had never mentioned New York. It only said that the tape was from before the start of *Dr. Drake.* The rest must have come to Peerbaum directly from Morgan. It was all going to get back to Eddie a lot sooner than he'd thought. He'd been with Martha the entire time she lived in the city, and it wouldn't take long for some devoted fan to figure that out. But there was nothing to be done. Morgan hadn't even broken their promise, really. What he'd told Peerbaum would be obvious at first sight to the people who followed Martha's career obsessively on the message boards. Eddie hadn't thought any of this out.

He was already late for school, and he handed his paper

to Stephen McLaughlin on the way inside before rushing to chapel. He arrived there just as the opening hymn drew to a close. A long silence followed. Some of the faculty in the back looked at Eddie. He'd come in a bit late, out of breath, but that shouldn't have been the cause of such attention. One of the history teachers, John Munroe, bumped Eddie with his elbow.

"You're up."

Eddie had completely forgotten about his chapel speech. Only veteran teachers were assigned to speak this early in the year, but somehow he had become one of the veterans. At the lectern, he cleared his throat and waited for the boys to quiet down. He never had their attention in this setting, but he didn't blame them for that, since he hadn't been inclined to give his attention when he was in those seats himself. Now he found that his silence had more effect than his words usually did. The boys looked at him expectantly, almost hopefully. What could he tell them that would mean something to them? What had he wanted to hear at that age?

"I graduated from St. Albert's more than fifteen years ago," he said. He cleared his throat while considering where to go from there. "Just last June, after you guys all left for the summer, I had my fifteenth reunion. Sixteen years ago, I sat where you seniors are sitting now. Thirteen years before that, I went to kindergarten here. Some of the people I saw at this thing I've known for almost thirty years."

He could see how smoothly things might go from here. Say a few words about lasting relationships, about treasuring your time, be done and sit down. But he was on the edge of something that some of these boys might actually remember. He started over.

"Those of you who have been in my classes know that I was an actor before I came back to St. Albert's. That is, I was trying to be one. And in fact I continued to try after I started teaching. Or I thought I would continue to try. The point is, I assumed that I was just passing back through here. I suspect now that this isn't the case. Most of you probably are just passing through. As most of my classmates, the people I saw last June, were just passing through. You won't think all that much about this place after you leave, though ten or twelve years is a long time to spend somewhere. But one of you might come back, like I did. And maybe you'll think you're just passing back through. But probably you will not be."

They were listening now, if only because they were curious where he could possibly be going. Even some of the seniors in the back had quieted down. He was getting close. He was right there, looking at it.

"What is my point here? A question I've asked myself occasionally is why I thought I was just passing through. That is, why I thought I might still be an actor when I had not had any success at it. Something you have no doubt been told at some point, perhaps even in this very chapel, is that you can do anything you really set yourself to doing. I know that I was told this many times when I was your age. Although it should be obvious enough to all of you that this isn't really true. I mean, supposing there are fifteen of you in this room who want to be president of the United States. And you all really set yourself to this task. Well, how many presidents are there going to be in your adult lifetime? Ten? Most presidents wind up getting two terms, but let's just make it simple and say they're all single-termers. So let's say twelve presidents. That's forty-eight years. You can't be president until you're thirty-five. That's in the constitution. It doesn't matter how hard you try, or put your mind to it. It's the law. And then no one gets elected in their eighties. So then let's say that for an unprecedented string of fifty years this country only elects presidents who are in this room right now. That's still, what, thirteen at the most. I don't know if I'm doing this math right, but you get the idea. So two of you, who really, really set your mind to it, don't get what you want.

"But of course that's even taking it to logical extremes. The reality is that none of you are going to be president. Not one. I mean, let's be serious. Because it's not really up to you or how hard you work. It's up to voters. It's not in your control. Acting is like that. You could be Robert De Niro, but if the casting director and the producers don't want you, it doesn't matter. Plus, needless to say, I wasn't De Niro. In fact, I understand now that I was pretty terrible."

Some boys laughed uncomfortably, until the look on Eddie's face silenced them. They were a little frightened, and that made him happy.

"It wasn't because I didn't want it," he continued. "I wanted it as badly as anyone wants it. A lot of the people I went to school with, they did get what they wanted. So it's not all bad news. But mostly what they wanted was to be rich. Which it turns out isn't that hard, especially if you were born rich to begin with, which most of them were, and which I guess most of you kids were, but which, as it happens, I was not, so maybe even if that had been my big goal I still wouldn't have been able to make it happen.

"So anyway, that doesn't mean you shouldn't try really hard. I don't regret having worked so hard at acting. At least, I don't think I do. Sometimes I do, but not most of the time. I guess I just wish I'd quit a little sooner than I did, when there were still some other options available to me. Not that I'm sorry I wound up back at St. Albert's, exactly. So I think you should put your mind to whatever you want, but also be realistic about the fact that, depending on what it is, you probably aren't going to get it, in all honesty."

Everything went silent as he walked away from the lectern.

The closing hymn was supposed to start, but even the music teacher at the organ had stopped to watch Eddie walk down the aisle. Finally he reached the back of the chapel, the music started, and everyone stood.

Eddie wasn't sure how his performance had gone over, but he had other things to worry about. When he left the chapel, he headed straight for the faculty lounge. Most of the other teachers had class first period, so Eddie found the place empty. He sat at a computer that faced away from the door, so that he could close his browser if anyone came in, and he searched for "Martha Martin Sex Tape." The first site that came up was CelebretainmentSpot.com.

"Dr. Drake Sex Tape is for real," Eddie read at the top of the page.

> On the same day that pregnant Dr. Drake star Martha Martin announced her engagement to her *Life After Laura* costar Turner Bledsoe, rumors swirled of the existence of a sex tape featuring Martin, apparently taken by an ex-boyfriend while both were struggling actors in New York. Now, a CelebretainmentSpot source has confirmed the existence of the tape. They say it is clearly Martha Martin in the tape, and that it is HOT! "I'd rank it three jalapeños," our source said. "It's definitely her, and it's definitely steamy." He said that Martin's partner, who has yet to be identified, can't be seen in the tape. "That's okay," he added. "No one will be watching it for him." That's for sure! Stick with CelebretainmentSpot for more on this developing story.

The door to the lounge opened, and John Munroe appeared, bringing in a waft of the cigarette he'd likely just smoked on the roof. Munroe had been teaching there since

Eddie was a student, and his graded papers had always given off the warm scent of the Tareyton 100s he smoked from a soft pack.

"That was quite a performance," he said.

Eddie liked Munroe, had always liked him, and he felt uneasy under his skeptical stare.

"I guess I was a little unprepared."

Munroe laughed.

"Kids could stand to hear a bit of reality. Anyway, they'll all forget it soon enough."

This seemed to be his philosophy of teaching—the boys would forget it all anyway. As Munroe crossed the room, Eddie clicked the browser closed and stood up from the computer.

"I've got a few things to take care of in the theater before second period," he said as he left the lounge.

The mentions of Martha and the general level of misbehavior seemed much increased in class that day. It might have been related to the talk he'd given that morning, or it might have been a natural process of boundary testing, but Eddie worried that some of the boys had already heard about the tape. They would be among the first to see the thing once it was released. High school boys were probably the target audience. It was another thing Eddie hadn't considered. He gave the boys scripts and ran them through line readings onstage while he sat in the back of the theater, working out what he would say to Susan that night.

He had his own script pretty well prepared by the time he got home. First he would mention the rumors about Martha in the paper and wait to see Susan's response. Eventually he would admit that the rumors had reminded him of some videos he'd made with Martha. They couldn't be the ones in question, of course, since those had been destroyed years ago.

Although, come to think of it, he'd only destroyed the ones he had. He couldn't be sure that Martha didn't have some herself. Susan wouldn't like any of this, but he couldn't see how she could blame him for it.

"How was the appointment?" he asked first.

"It was good," Susan said. "But I'm nervous."

"I'm sure we're going to get great news."

He couldn't see how to make the transition from there. Neither of them spoke for a few minutes, until Eddie said, "You know, I read something funny about Martha in the paper today."

"Oh, let's not talk about her right now," Susan said. "We've got our own things to worry about."

They fell back into silence, which persisted until the phone rang. Susan jumped from the couch to pick it up.

"Hello," she said. Eddie watched her face. "Yes," she said. She repeated this word three or four times mindlessly, and Eddie couldn't tell what it meant. Then she started to cry, and still Eddie couldn't tell. Finally, she said, "Thank you, doctor. Thank you for everything." She hung up the phone, ran back to the couch, and wrapped her arms around Eddie. "I knew it," she said. "I knew it, I knew it, I knew it."

"I guess we're having a baby."

He could barely hear Susan's response through her tears.

"Based on my blood numbers, he thinks all three embryos attached."

"What does that mean?"

"It means we're having triplets." She was still crying, and it didn't seem entirely from happiness. "It's so overwhelming," she said. "How are we going to afford triplets?"

She looked helplessly around their one-bedroom apartment. Eddie wanted to let her know about the rest of money— not that it would be enough on its own to solve the problem, but at least it would take some pressure off. In a few weeks, maybe a few months, he'd say that another check had come from Korea. But he couldn't do that too soon if he wanted the story to have even a modicum of credibility.

"We'll make it work."

This seemed to be what she was waiting to hear.

"It's a blessing, really," she said. "It's going to be great."

EIGHT

STILL SHOTS FROM THE video, cropped and strategically blurred, filled the front pages of the *News* and the *Post* on Sunday morning. "The Doctor Is In!" read the *Post*'s headline. The *News* had gone with the more esoteric "Martha Tart-in'."

Eddie didn't look through the papers before going back to the apartment with the breakfast sandwiches he'd gone out to buy. He needed to get to Susan before she heard from someone else. He'd tried several times in the preceding days to mention the tape to her, but everything had been so busy, and she'd been so happy.

"There's a big story about Martha in the papers," he said after they sat down to eat.

"These days I'd be shocked if the paper didn't have something about her," Susan said. "I have to admit that I'd have a hard time hearing about her pregnancy if things hadn't worked out for us. But now I just wish her the best."

"It actually isn't about the pregnancy."

"What's it about, then?"

"People are saying there's a sex tape floating around with her in it."

Susan cringed.

"I hope you don't have anything to do with that."

"Why would you think that?"

"I'm kidding. Of course you don't have anything to do with it. Is it Turner or Rex?"

"No one seems to know."

"People are so gross. Who even makes these tapes to begin with? And why would they pick now of all times to release it?"

"When I read about it," Eddie said, "I remembered something."

Susan put her sandwich down.

"What did you remember?"

"When Martha and I were together, we made a lot of tapes. I don't mean those kinds of tapes. Just, you know, rehearsing. Preparing for auditions. Line reading. But we may have taped some other stuff once or twice."

"You *may* have?"

"It wasn't something we were into or anything. I never even looked at them. It just sort of happened while the camera was on. I never mentioned it to you because I didn't see the point. I didn't think they even still existed. But I guess she might have kept it, and someone could have stolen it off her computer or something."

"Is it you in that tape? Is that what you're telling me?"

"I don't know," Eddie said. "I haven't seen it. Martha was the one who set up the video camera. She was the one who was constantly taping everything. She probably did it with other guys. And why would this ten-year-old video just be surfacing now? But I saw this in the paper, and I remembered. So I thought I should tell you."

"Isn't there some way you could find out? By going online or something?"

"I guess so."

"Don't you want to know?"

Eddie opened his laptop and did what he would have done if he were really looking for the video. When he searched "Martha Martin sex tape," thousands of hits came back.

"It's all over the place," he said. Susan got up and left the room.

The video itself was harder to find than he would have imagined. Most sites that claimed to have real footage just linked to other pages. Those that advertised free access actually showed a staged scene featuring an actress who resembled but clearly wasn't Martha. It might have been made for the purpose or just pulled from some stock of celebrity look-alike videos. Pop-up ads crowded Eddie's screen. He found sites that weren't selling the video outright but included it with annual subscriptions. Bits and pieces could be had for ten or fifteen bucks. Finally, he bought the whole fifteen minutes for $49.99. Thousands of dollars must have already been spent that day. He wondered how much Morgan would make. Moments after entering his credit card number, Eddie was watching himself.

Someone had added opening credits, subtitles, and a soundtrack of bad electronic music, edited so that it seemed that they'd been listening to it at the time. Otherwise it was exactly as he'd cut it. He tried to imagine Martha watching the video. Would she feel any emotions besides anger or embarrassment? He watched only a few minutes before closing the computer and calling Susan back into the room.

"It's me," he told her, nearly in tears from embarrassment. His shame was real, which at least made it convincing. "You can't see me in the video, though. I don't think anyone could trace it to me."

"We've got to do something. People can't just steal things and put them on the Internet, can they?"

"Probably not. But I don't think it was stolen from me. I mean, who hacks into a high school teacher's computer, looking for something like that?"

"I thought they weren't on your computer."

"Exactly," Eddie said quickly. "So they couldn't have taken them from me."

"It doesn't matter whether they took it from you. If it's you in the video you have some right to stop it. Don't you? Call Alex and tell him to do something about it."

Alex was Eddie's agent at Talent Management. They hadn't spoken in years. Eddie almost told Susan this, but he remembered that he was supposed to have received a royalty check from the agency only a few weeks before.

"I don't know how much he can do about it," he told her instead. "Once something is out, you can't really make it go away."

"So we're completely helpless?"

"We'll wait for it to blow over. Something more interesting will come along, and everyone will forget about it. In the meantime, we'll just hope that no one connects it to me."

This seemed like a real possibility to Eddie. There was no mention of his name in the papers, and no one online seemed all that interested in knowing the identity of the other figure in the tape.

"She probably leaked it herself," he said. "These things are actually good for people's careers."

"Do you really think she would do that?"

"Who can say? I don't think she's the same person she was when I knew her."

WHEN THE WEEKLIES HIT the newsstand on Tuesday morning, Martha was on the cover of every one. Eddie wasn't mentioned anywhere. In his first class of the day, the boys didn't seem any more distracted or disrespectful than usual. Near the beginning of his second class one of them raised his hand. This in itself was a bad sign, since the boys just spoke out when they had something to say.

"What is it?" Eddie asked.

"Do you have any advice about acting in sex scenes?"

The entire class burst into laughter before he'd even finished the question.

"That's not appropriate," Eddie said. He could have sent him to the headmaster's office, the last resort for dealing with bad behavior, but he wanted the matter dropped. He didn't need to bring it to Luce's attention. He took out a few copies of *Twelfth Night* and set them to reading aloud for the rest of the hour, which was what he did when he wasn't interested in teaching.

"If there are no more questions," he said at the end of the second act, "I can let you go now."

He watched the boys deciding between getting out of class early and staying to provoke him. They opted to file out of the theater.

"I hope I'll see some of you at auditions after school," Eddie called out as he watched them leave.

But there were no auditions that day. Luce was waiting when Eddie returned to the theater that afternoon.

"Mr. Hartley," he said. "I wondered whether you might come to my office for a talk."

"The boys will be arriving any minute," Eddie said.

"I instructed the other teachers to let their students know during last period that auditions for the fall play have been postponed."

They walked to the headmaster's office, where Luce closed the door behind them.

"Have you seen this week's St. Albert's *Canticle*?" he asked as he positioned himself behind his desk. He didn't invite Eddie to sit.

"I haven't," Eddie said.

Luce passed a copy of the student magazine across his desk.

"It seems that some of the boys made some last-minute modifications after Mr. Munroe gave final approval of the issue. The part that might interest you is on page seventeen."

Eddie opened to a page that read "St. Albert's Celebrity News":

Our Arts and Entertainment correspondent is recommending the latest viral video, featuring St. Albert's own Mr. Hartley. It must be seen to be believed. Luckily, it can be seen almost anywhere online this week. Take a tip from us, and watch it.

"I hope you're going to harshly discipline whoever is responsible for that," Eddie said.

"We'll certainly take care of that," Luce told him. "But that's not why I've asked you for this chat. You understand this puts me in a very bad position?"

"I'm sorry, sir. I can explain."

"That would be gratifying. To be honest, I found the item slightly obscure, but I've had some calls from parents, who have clarified the reference for me and described the video mentioned here. I'd like you to begin by explaining whether you are, indeed, the person in that video."

Eddie didn't know what evidence connected him to the tape, but something would come out eventually. Better to help Luce with damage control.

"It's from years ago."

"So you acknowledge that you made this tape?"

"I was in a committed, monogamous relationship with the woman. It wasn't like I worked in pornography. Someone stole it from me."

"That's all very unfortunate," Luce said. "I sympathize with you in many ways. But you have to understand where I'm coming from, which is the position of having fielded more than a dozen calls today from parents whose twelve-year-old sons have paid money to watch one of my teachers have sex on the Internet."

"I can see why that's a problem."

"Yes, I should hope you can. Please understand that I'm the kind of man who holds the well-being of the students in my charge above everything else."

"Maybe I can draft some kind of letter."

"A letter?"

"Explaining to the parents what I've just told you. The extenuating circumstances. I can write it this evening, and the boys can take it home to their parents tomorrow."

"I'm afraid a letter isn't going to cut it here. This is a Catholic school. That might not mean anything to some people who work here, who treat ceremonies like our morning chapel as jokes, but parents pay a lot of money to send their children to a place where they'll be instilled with certain values."

"Don't you see that I'm the victim here? I'm being exploited."

"There's a lot to be said for that," Luce told him, though his voice suggested there wasn't much at all to be said for it. "But the safety of the boys has to come first."

"No one's in any danger here," Eddie said. "This will blow over soon. I'm sure of that."

"I'm not the kind of man who spends his time on the Internet, but my understanding is that things don't just blow over there. It's all permanent, yes? To put it differently: every student, every current or prospective parent, every alumnus considering making a gift will be able to find this video forever. It will be searchable. It will be the first thing that comes up when they search for your name. It may be the first thing that comes up when they search for *our* name. Is my understanding correct?"

"It's an algorithm," Eddie said.

"Am I correct?"

"Yes, I suppose you're right."

"I've spent some time this afternoon speaking with the board, and we've already made our decision. I'm not here to negotiate with you, only to explain what will happen from here. You're going to take a paid leave of absence for the rest of the calendar year, until the semester is over."

Eddie thought he could live with that, especially if he kept getting paid. He could use the time to help Susan and manage the damage from the video.

"That sounds reasonable."

"At that point, your tenure at the school will be over."

"You mean I'm fired? For something I did before I even started working here?"

"As I said, we didn't see how we really had a choice."

"At the very least, you've got to pay me through the end of the school year. I've got a contract."

"It's the opinion of our board that we have plenty of standing to terminate that contract based on the personal character and conduct clause. Frankly, there was a lot of sentiment to simply get this all over with now, since we'll have to start paying your replacement right away. But as you well know, you have your supporters on the board, and they were able to persuade others to pay you through December. I promise that you won't do any better than that. We have had to give some of the parents reassurances that you won't have any contact with their boys, so I'd like you to leave the building quickly and quietly."

"Jesus, I'm not contagious. For God's sake, I was having sex with a grown woman. They should be relieved that my proclivities run in that direction. It puts me ahead of most Catholic school teachers."

"I really don't think there's any reason to be nasty at this point."

"Nasty? I've spent the majority of my life in this building, since before you'd even heard of the place. Now you're cutting me loose over something that's not my fault. If you had any decency, you'd be circling the wagons. You'd be supporting me."

"If it makes you feel better to continue yelling, go ahead, but nothing can be done at this point."

Eddie needed a different approach.

"Listen, Mr. Luce. I just found out my wife is pregnant. She's having triplets. I've got three kids coming in the spring. I can't be unemployed right now. I don't know what I'll do."

Eddie watched the news pass over Luce's face. He seemed to be considering the possibility that Eddie was lying in an awkward ploy for sympathy.

"I'm sorry," he finally said, and he almost seemed to be. He continued in an unguarded tone that Eddie had never heard from him. "Of course I didn't realize that. But you've got to know that the board and the parents call the shots. They're paying a lot of money to send their boys to a place where they expect them to be protected. To be sheltered. And if they don't want you teaching their kids, then you're out of here. I serve at their pleasure just as much as you do, trust me on that. If they wanted me gone, I'd be done just as quickly."

Outside, a single photographer stood talking to Stephen McLaughlin. When the photographer noticed Eddie he started taking shots of him. It seemed a good sign that only one person had come. Nothing connected him to the video besides the imaginative minds of some of his students and his history with Martha. Perhaps the story really wasn't that big. It might all be over soon. If Eddie couldn't get his job back, there would be something else. In the meantime, his salary would be paid for three months. But all this hopefulness disappeared when he got home and found a dozen more photographers waiting on his block. They charged him as he approached his building.

"Can you confirm that it's you in that tape?"

"When did you make it?"

"How did it get out?"

"Do you have a message you want to send to Martha?"

"Is it true that your wife is having triplets?"

The terror that came over Eddie's face in that moment would be captured from every possible angle and sent around the world within minutes. He dropped his chin and pressed through the crowd.

"When are they due?"

"Boys or girls? Or both?"

"Did you lose your job today? What are you going to do to support the kids?"

"Are there any other tapes?"

"Why do they call you Handsome Eddie?"

He pushed through the door and stood in the hall, catching his breath while they took pictures through the glass. Luce must have gone to the press the moment Eddie walked out of St. Albert's. Not just about firing him, but about the babies. He might have done it in exchange for some protection for the school, but he could have just as easily done it out of spite. Eddie walked past the elevator and took the stairs to their floor, trying to imagine as he went what he would say to Susan. He wasn't sure how much she knew, or how much anyone did. Inside she sat on the couch with her head in her hands.

"You did this," she said without looking up. "You made this happen."

"I'm so sorry," he told her. "Luce fired me today, and I was begging for my job back, and I told him about the babies, because I thought that would make him reconsider. I didn't know what else to do."

Now she looked up.

"They know about the babies?"

"It never occurred to me."

"You did this," she said again.

"I'm trying to explain," he said. "I didn't think he'd go telling people. What a hypocrite. He talks about instilling values."

"Alex called."

"What?"

"Your agent called the house."

"What did he have to say?"

"For starters, he said you never talked to him about the video. He also said that there isn't any fucking movie playing in South Korea."

Eddie sat down on the couch beside her, but she immediately stood and crossed the room.

"South Korea. Honestly, you must think I'm such an idiot. And the worst part is, you were right. I wanted this thing so badly that I didn't ask where the money was coming from. South Korea. I should have known right away. Do you know why?"

"Why?"

"Because you can't act, Eddie. You couldn't act sweaty if they sent you on a ten-mile run. People would think it was a rainy day. You couldn't sell anything to anyone but me."

"I just wanted to make you happy," he said. "I couldn't do it myself. And then I saw this chance, and it all seemed easy and harmless."

"Get out."

"Let's talk about this. Try to see where I'm coming from."

"You had your chance to talk about it. You've been lying to me every day for weeks. For months. Probably for years."

"Not for years."

"I'm going to be a laughingstock. There are camera crews staked outside our building. Is that what you think I wanted? You may have wanted that. Martha Martin might want that. But I don't want that. Get out, Eddie. Get out right now."

"It will pass."

"Get out," she told him.

"We've got to stick together on this."

"Get out."

He wasn't sure where he was going when he left. Coming out of the building, he prepared for the flashes and shutter clicks, but the cameras were all pointed upward. He couldn't help looking in the direction of whatever they were capturing. Susan was hanging out the window, calling down to the street.

"He did this," she said. "Eddie Hartley sold that tape. If he tries to tell you otherwise, he's lying."

When he looked up, she stopped for a moment and disappeared from the window. Eddie thought the onslaught might be over. But she returned with something in her hand. She set it free, and Eddie watched it briefly take flight before beginning its descent. It was one of his old head shots. In the moment it took Eddie to understand the photo's significance, Susan picked up the entire box of relics and emptied it into the street. The cameras didn't follow Eddie's things as they fell or take in his reaction as he watched them hit the ground. They stayed fixed, every one of them, on the woman inflamed above.

NINE

THE NEXT MORNING THE cover of the *Daily News* showed Susan leaning out the window like a madwoman, throwing old photos into the air. "Three Tykes—And You're Out!" the headline read. "Drake Tape Wife Expecting Trips, Sends Bum's Stuff for a Fall." Eddie found the paper in the lobby of the Metropolitan, a cheap hotel above a parking garage just off First Avenue. He'd often passed the place but hardly noticed it, except occasionally to wonder what kind of person stayed there. When he checked in, the man behind the front desk was watching an Entertainment Daily segment about the Drake Tape on a small black-and-white TV. Eddie worried about being recognized, but the man didn't turn his attention from the screen while accepting the cash and passing over a key.

The calls had started almost as soon as he left the apartment, mostly from blocked or unfamiliar numbers. After settling into his hotel room, Eddie turned off the phone. He stayed in bed until noon the next day, when the same man who'd checked him in—he seemed to be the owner, or else the place's only employee—called up to say he needed to pay for another night or else leave. Eddie had no other place to go, but since he didn't have anything to keep in the room he just left.

He read through the rest of the paper at a diner across the street. Stanley Peerbaum reported that Eddie had been fired, quoting a statement from Luce: "Given the circumstances, we decided it was best for the entire St. Albert's community, and especially for our boys, if we parted ways with Mr. Hartley." Peerbaum described St. Albert's as an "elite private academy on the Upper East Side." On the facing page there was a brief history of scandals at the school, dating back to the Preppy Murderer. They had dug up random bits of biographical detail about Eddie and still shots from commercials, which might have been collected from the street after Susan emptied the box. The most recent one was eight years old, but Eddie was easily recognizable in it. He closed the paper and put it down on the table. Looking at Susan on the front page, he tried to make sense of what had happened. It wasn't her anger that puzzled him, but the performance of it. She was not the type for dramatic gestures, but a few cameras seemed already to have changed her. He considered calling the apartment, but he wasn't sure what he could say, except that he was sorry. He'd already left an apology on Susan's voice mail the night before. Thinking of it now, he turned his phone on to see if she'd responded. His mailbox was full, but none of the messages were from her. Almost as soon as he turned it on, the phone rang. The call came from a blocked number, but he picked it up. It was more than curiosity; he wanted someone to tell him what was supposed to happen next.

"Is this Handsome Eddie?" a cheerful voice asked.

"Who is this?"

"Eddie, this is Geena Tuff from *Star Style*. I'm calling to see if you'd like to sit down with me for an interview."

"No thanks."

"Think of it as a unique opportunity to get your side of the story on the record."

"I don't really have a side of the story."

"We're willing to pay ten thousand dollars for the exclusive."

"Ten grand just to talk with me?"

"You're a hot commodity right now. But it would have to be an exclusive."

"I'm afraid I'm still not interested."

"Can I leave you my number, in case you change your mind?"

"I'm not going to change my mind," Eddie said.

A text came soon after he hung up: *Just in case ;) -Geena*, followed by a phone number and an e-mail address. Eddie thought of all the calls that had come in already. Ten thousand dollars was just a starting offer. Once he got them competing with each other, it might become a lot more, and he and Susan needed that money. But he couldn't go to the press without talking to her first.

HE LEFT THE DINER and walked a few blocks, until he passed an empty bar that didn't seem like the kind of place where news of Dr. Drake traveled. It might be a good spot to spend the afternoon while he decided what to do with himself. Apart from the bartender, the only person inside was an old man with a pickled pink face. A muted TV above the bar played a tampon commercial. Eddie took a seat and ordered a beer.

"Turn the sound up," the old man said. "Show's back on."

They were watching Entertainment Daily.

"Just a week after her release from the hospital," Marian Blair announced, "a collapse in the studio has friends again worried about Justine Bliss's weight. Now there are whispers about an addiction to pills as Justine's father rushes to her side. Meanwhile, executives at the 2True Network discuss canceling *Pure Bliss,* Justine's Moody Productions reality show."

"She's got to eat something," the old man announced before swallowing the rest of his drink. "It's not a healthy lifestyle she's got."

"I blame the father," the bartender said. "He pushed her into music at such a young age, and now he enables her. No one gets into that kind of mess alone."

Eddie put money down for his drink as the show moved on to a story about Rex Gilbert breaking up with Carla Lender. They would get to Martha eventually, if they hadn't already. He was curious to see whether anything had changed overnight. He wanted to know where the story stood. After a few more words about Rex, Marian said, "Turning now to Drake Tape news, Turner Bledsoe is standing by his girl, but he has a few harsh words for Martha's onetime costar."

The screen flashed to Bledsoe, walking alone down an L.A. street as cameras approached.

"How is this affecting your engagement?" an off-screen voice asked.

"As far as me and Martha go," Bledsoe said, looking straight into the camera, "everything's great. This was something she did a long time ago with someone she trusted. But I'd like to give a message to Hartley."

"What would you tell him?"

"I wouldn't use words. Let's just say if I ever run into him I'll leave an impression."

"That guy sounds like a real dirtbag," the bartender said.

"Bledsoe?" Eddie asked.

"That Hartley guy."

"Well, he got his," said the man at the bar. "Out on his ass." His sharp laugh turned into a lengthy cough.

"If Turner is really looking for Eddie Hartley," Marian Blair told the camera back in the studio, "our spies might have found him. Reports have the erstwhile actor spending his first night away from his pregnant wife at the Metropolitan Hotel just blocks from his home."

A picture of the hotel appeared on-screen. Eddie hadn't noticed anyone following him from the apartment the night before, or anyone waiting outside when he left that morning. But apparently he was easy to find.

"That's right around the corner," the bartender said. "I know the guy who runs that place."

Eddie stood up, leaving his half-finished beer. Back on the street, he took out his phone and called the only person he could think to ask for help.

"Congratulations on the triplets," Blakeman said by way of greeting.

"What have you gotten me into?"

"I gave you an option. The last I heard you weren't even going to take it."

"Well, I took it, and I'm in trouble now. I need a place to crash until everything calms down."

"Sure thing," Blakeman said. "I'm at the office now, but I don't imagine you'd want to come here to pick up keys, unless you want to give the *Interviewer* an exclusive. Just drop by the apartment any time after eight or so."

FOR A FEW YEARS Blakeman had shared a house on Washington Square with his cousin Charlie, but they'd been thrown out over an incident with the owner's fish tank—an incident in which Eddie had played a small, forgotten part. After that Charlie left town, and Max returned to the loft on West Broadway where he'd lived right after college. In those days, Eddie and Martha had spent several nights a week there, but Eddie had hardly visited since Blakeman moved back. That evening, he arrived a bit later—and drunker—than he'd intended, having worked his way downtown by stopping in bars.

A men's clothing boutique had replaced the tobacco shop that once occupied the storefront downstairs. Eddie pressed the buzzer outside and the front door clicked open without a question. A key in the elevator unlocked the button for the second floor, and the elevator opened directly onto the apartment, where a party appeared to be in full swing. Blakeman hadn't mentioned that he was expecting company, but it shouldn't have surprised Eddie. Blakeman always expected company. One of his roommates, whose name Eddie couldn't remember, stood near the door.

"Handsome Eddie," he said, as if Eddie were still a regular. "Grab a drink."

Eddie gave a casual nod and walked into the room. The apartment was large and entirely open apart from three small bedrooms in the back, separated by a thin wall of Sheetrock and plywood that Eddie had helped install a decade earlier. There was a kitchen area not far from the elevator, with a wooden butcher block that served as the bar, just as it always had. It was nearly ten o'clock, which felt late to Eddie, though it was barely time for a Blakeman party to be picking up. The place was packed, and even the crowd looked the same as always. Eddie felt the passage of time pressing in on him, just as he had when Patrick spoke about him at the church.

His bouts of chronophobia had begun when he still lived with Martha. Whenever a new actor made a name on television or in the movies, Eddie would look up his date of birth. So long as these rising stars were mostly still older than Eddie, the habit gave him some satisfaction. He could almost see the years that separated them, and he could fill those years with all the things he needed to do to catch up. It all seemed possible. But the span of years slowly shrank, until the day when most new stars were younger than Eddie. Out of habit, he kept looking up actors' ages even after he'd abandoned his career, and the rare occasion when someone older suddenly gained some attention could still excite him briefly. Then he remembered that it meant nothing, since he wasn't going anywhere.

Eddie fixed a drink and struggled to find some thought with which he might fight back the passage of time. He remembered the call from the reporter at *Star Style,* who'd called him a "hot commodity." He hadn't become "hot" in the way he'd wanted, but who ever did? Martha wanted to be doing Broadway instead of playing Dr. Drake. You didn't always get to choose. Perhaps it would be possible to get some real work out of this. Susan wouldn't like it, he knew, but why did it have to be up to her? He remembered the feeling he'd had after depositing the money, that he might do anything now. He had dismissed it at the time, he'd gone straight home, but now Susan had thrown him out. Didn't she lose some rights for doing that? In the past two days, he'd lost a job he'd never wanted and a marriage that had never been as happy as it should have been. Perhaps life was telling him it was time to start over.

He was still standing in front of the drinks when Blakeman approached, bringing along a small crowd.

"Guys, this is my oldest friend, Handsome Eddie."

Eddie wished he hadn't used the nickname, which had already found its way into the press. As he shook hands and introduced himself, he measured the level of recognition on each face. Blakeman had probably told them all that the Drake Tape guy was coming over. Perhaps he was the reason they were there. Eddie could almost tell from their looks which ones had seen the tape and which had only heard about it. It was strange when people you'd never met knew intimate details about you. He'd long imagined the feeling but didn't much like it now.

It was possible that he really did know some of these people from the last years when he was still in Blakeman's circle, but that time was a bit hazy for him. He'd been drinking a lot. He wasn't going out on auditions, because they made him sick. He vomited before each one, and when he got into the room he couldn't remember his lines. The only words that kept any purchase in his head were Martha's about his dedicating his life to something for which he had no talent.

Her departure had created other problems, like making his rent, which had doubled when she moved out. More than doubled, in fact, since she'd been covering his shortfalls all those years. For that matter, she'd been paying for groceries, utilities, Internet, and cable. Years of working odd jobs, temping a few weeks at a time while trying to keep up with friends who had proper careers, had left him in bad financial shape. His debts had never worried him while they were piling up. He had the money he was spending, he just didn't have it on him. It was stored someplace in the future. One of them—admittedly, more likely Martha—would be breaking through at any time, and a few thousand dollars would be trivial. It had never occurred to him that he wouldn't be brought along when the breakthrough happened.

A few months after Martha left, he got the job at St. Albert's, through the intervention of Blakeman's father, who was on the board of the school. He accepted it out of necessity, not thinking that he was giving up his acting career. But the job had led him to Susan, and Susan had made him feel that he didn't need to keep trying to act in order to be happy. Another life presented itself. It would be quieter, but it wouldn't be such a struggle. In the end, of course, it had turned into its own kind of struggle, one with no prospect of making him a star.

But now Eddie felt like a star. He could see it in their faces, in the eagerness with which Blakeman introduced him. He was just making small talk, but people looked at him as though every word was fascinating. They crowded around, and he was hardly surprised when one drunken girl called out, "I know you."

It took Eddie a moment to realize he really did know her, because he couldn't immediately connect this figure, in her dark makeup and short leather skirt, to the girl Patrick had introduced to him outside church last spring.

"Melinda, right?"

She laughed.

"Melissa."

"Right. Sorry about that. How's Patrick?"

"We broke up."

"I'm sorry to hear that."

"It's cool. It just wasn't working out. He's so serious, you know?"

Eddie hadn't found Patrick particularly serious.

"Sometimes that can be good," he said. "Maybe I should have been a bit more serious when I was your age."

"How are things at St. Albert's?"

"Not so hot," Eddie said, suspecting that she already knew. "I got fired yesterday."

"That's a bummer," Melissa told him. "I got fired from

my internship this summer. My boss caught me doing blow in her office."

"You seem to have recovered all right."

"Totally."

There was a lull in the conversation until one of Melissa's friends approached.

"Let me get a picture of the two of you," she said.

Melissa handed the girl her phone and put her arm around Eddie.

"Get closer," the girl said.

Melissa squeezed up against Eddie. He didn't mean to move, but her weight unbalanced him and he wrapped his arm around her shoulder to straighten himself up.

"It's totally cute," the girl said after taking the picture. "I'll text it to you."

Eddie told her his number and the girl sent him the photo. He took out his phone to look at it.

"You're right," he said. "Totally cute."

Melissa put her head next to his and looked at the screen.

"I like the way you fuck," she whispered to him.

"Excuse me?"

"I like the way you fuck in that video."

She was the first person that night to have mentioned the tape directly, and that fact briefly overshadowed the manner in which she'd brought it up.

"I didn't really mean for people to see it."

"You don't have to act all embarrassed. It's hot. I'd like to be fucked that way."

Eddie tried to remember whether girls had spoken this way when he was Melissa's age. Certainly they hadn't spoken this way to him, but perhaps they did to the older men who hung around at parties. Under the circumstances he seemed to have lost any grounds to protest.

"Well, I'm sure you'll meet a nice guy who can, you know, take care of that for you."

"The world is crawling with nice guys," she said. "Patrick's the nicest guy I know. But I'd like to be fucked that way by you."

"I'm married," Eddie said, somewhat irrelevantly. "And twice your age. And your boyfriend is a student of mine."

"He's not your student anymore, or my boyfriend. It's not like I'm some kid. I'm nineteen years old. Anyway, didn't your wife throw you out?"

"Did you read that in the paper?"

"Good one. 'Cause I'm some lame who reads the newspaper. It was on Teeser. You've got your own threadhead and everything. 'Mr. Drake.' I hear she threw all your shit out on the street."

"She did." It still didn't seem quite real to him.

"That sucks."

"It sucks," he agreed.

"But so do I."

It occurred to Eddie that being propositioned by beautiful nineteen-year-olds was another part of the fame he'd once wanted so badly.

"It's a little weird talking with you. I mean, knowing you just watched that thing."

"Because I've seen you but you haven't seen me?"

"I didn't mean it like that."

"You can see me if that will even the score."

"I guess you're not too hung up on privacy."

Melissa laughed.

"Just to be clear, I'm getting a lecture about privacy from a guy who sold a sex tape for a hundred grand?"

"How did you know how much I sold it for?"

"Morgan told me."

"You know Morgan?"

"I met him here a few weeks ago."

"That son of a bitch."

"If you want my opinion," she said, "you got ripped off. You could have sold it for twice as much."

"You should have been my agent. Maybe we can go into business together."

"No, I'm serious. I wasn't kidding when I said it's superhot. I'd watch it again even if there wasn't anyone famous in it."

Eddie was surprised at how reassuring it felt to hear this. In spite of himself, he was enjoying talking to her.

"So what are you going to do from here?" Melissa asked. "I mean, what are you going to make of all this?"

The obvious answer was that he was going to convince his wife to take him back. That he was going to find a way to return everything to normal as soon as he could. But he knew that answer would disappoint her, and he couldn't bring himself to give it.

"I have some ideas," he said. "But I don't want to talk about them. It's private."

"Private," Melissa said, and she laughed again. "Suit yourself. Do you want another drink?"

TEN

WHEN HE WENT TO make a pot of coffee in Blakeman's kitchen the next morning, Eddie found a note on the counter.

Off to work. Make yourself at home. Aspirin in the cabinet beside the fridge. I left the paper, thought it might interest you. —Blakeman

Beside it was a copy of the *Daily News*. "Who Is Handsome Eddie?" the headline asked. It showed a still shot of the video, Eddie's body leaning into Martha's. Some parts of the shot had been blurred, but it revealed a lot for the newsstand. Where Eddie had carefully cut out his own face, the paper had superimposed an image from a commercial he'd done years ago. In it, he wore the expression of a man eagerly accepting a stick of cinnamon chewing gum. It was a grotesque contrast, the forced smile on top of the thrusting body. He should have known that he would become part of the story. Now that he had, his efforts to conceal himself were damning. He would have been better off just leaving his face visible.

Below the picture the front page read "Details Emerge of Dr. Drake Tape Bum: See Pages 9–10." Eddie flipped to the spread, which attempted to tell the story of his life. It was filled with old head shots and playbills—most of them, it seemed, from the box that Susan had emptied out onto the street. But there were also more personal items, including a photo of Eddie, Justin, and Blakeman standing on a corner in their school uniforms, their arms over each other's shoulders. It looked to be from about seventh grade.

"At the Upper East Side's elite St. Albert's School, where he earned the nickname 'Handsome Eddie,'" the caption read, "Hartley's friends included Justin Price, now a megarich hedge fund manager and prominent philanthropist, and longtime lit scenester Max Blakeman." This might please Blakeman, Eddie thought, but Justin wouldn't be happy to see it. Although he was a familiar figure from charity boards and benefits, Justin kept his personal life out of the news. He had a very simple metric for success—money—and he didn't need public approval. He didn't even want public attention.

But Eddie had wanted attention. Now that he had it, he wasn't sure what to make of it. Did the quality of the attention matter? He remembered Melissa telling him that he could be a star, wondering what he planned to make out of all this. He set the paper on the table and called Talent Management.

"Where were you yesterday?" Alex asked when Eddie got through to him.

"Were you trying to reach me?"

"Are you kidding? I called ten times."

"I turned my phone off. I was getting a lot of calls."

"No shit you were getting calls. We've got a real story on our hands."

"I know. I was hoping you could help me with that."

"Before we go any further, what's this shit about a movie in China?"

"Korea," Eddie corrected him. "It's a much smaller market."

"Now you're a funny man?"

"I'm sorry. I shouldn't have lied about that."

"What do I care if you lie? Wouldn't be the first time I've been asked to help out with some domestic deception. But come up with something semi-plausible. Then tell your fucking accomplice, so I don't have your wife asking me about checks I don't know about. That's Bullshitting 101."

"I was going to tell you. Everything got out of hand so quickly."

"Water under the bridge. This story has real potential. We've got not one but two wronged women, both pregnant. And triplets! The tabloids love these multiple births. I'm going to have a lot of opportunities for you."

"That would be great. I need some opportunities right now."

"The first thing we do is get you and Susan on the morning show circuit. Tell your side of the story and whatnot."

"She threw me out."

"Don't I know it. I read the paper. What are the chances you two patch things up?"

"We'll straighten it out eventually."

"Eventually is great, but how about right now?"

"I'm guessing it's going to take a little bit of time. She seems pretty hurt by things."

"You aren't going to get many invitations to appear by yourself. People want Susan. They want those triplets. I could get you on one of the twenty-four-hour entertainment channels, but if you want the *Today* show or *This Morning Live*, you're going to have to get her on board."

"I don't want to go on talk shows and talk about Martha or the tape or my triplets or any of that. That's not the kind of opportunity I'm looking for. I want to act, Alex. I think this is my chance to have a real career."

"How about celebrity strip poker?"

"Do you hear what I'm saying?"

"You can't act, Eddie. That's the truth. You've never been able to. You've got a shot at fame here, but it's not going to be Stanislavski or whatever the fuck you're hoping for. You want to make something of this, I'm telling you, you've got to get Susan to go along. Once she's in, sky's the limit. Brian Moody wants to talk about a reality show. He's the best producer out there. You're not going to do any better than Moody."

"We don't want our own show."

"Everybody wants their own show."

"Not everybody."

"Great, so I've got a client who doesn't want to be on television? What am I supposed to do with that?"

"I want to be on television, just not like that. I don't want to talk about Susan's pregnancy on *This Morning Live*. She's embarrassed enough about this whole thing as it is."

"All right," Alex said, the energy gone from his voice. "I'll see what I can do in a more traditional line. I'm telling you now it's going to be a harder sell."

"I thought hard sells were your job," Eddie answered.

Once off the phone, he sat on the couch with his cup of coffee and turned the TV on. He wanted to see if there was anything about him on Entertainment Daily. Despite what Alex had said, he still thought he could get real work out of all this. After a commercial, *ED Morning News* came on, hosted by a woman named Coco Kalman.

"Just a day after leaving his triplet-expecting wife, Drake

Tape star Eddie Hartley was seen out on the town, and even canoodling with an apparently underage girl." The screen cut to Eddie leaning toward Melissa's face, his eyes half closed in drunkenness. "This photo was Teesed out last night by a user named SweetMelissa1987," Kalman continued. "Along with the message 'Spent the night with Mr. Drake.' No word yet on SweetMelissa's real identity or where Hartley's night with the young hottie went from there. Entertainment Daily will be all over this story as it develops."

Eddie turned off the TV and called Blakeman at work.

"How do I get on Teeser?" he asked.

Blakeman laughed.

"Where have you been hiding? All the best stars know how to work social media."

"St. Albert's always wanted us to be careful about this stuff, with all the students on it and everything."

"That worked out pretty well for you."

"I know. So explain what I'm supposed to be doing."

Blakeman told Eddie where to find his laptop and walked him through opening an account.

"You might as well just use your own name, since no one will believe it's really you."

Eddie typed in the user name "EddieHartley" and was told it already existed. He tried "HandsomeEddie" with the same result. Then he tried "HandsomeHartley," and that worked.

"She said I was a threadhead? Mr. Drake. What does that mean?"

"Go in that search box there and put in an asterisk and then type 'MrDrake.' One word, no period."

The page's layout confused Eddie. There looked to be about a dozen hits, which didn't seem so bad, except that when he scrolled down more appeared. He reached the end, and it did it again. He kept going until he was in the hundreds. Who were these people? What could they possibly have to say about him? "Honey, gonna do you like *MrDrake," one read. Another said, "Shaping up to be a two rub out mornin *Drake-Tape *MrDrake." Every few seconds another appeared. He searched for the user name SweetMelissa1987, and he found Melissa's feed. At the top was the post from the night before: "OMG Spent the night with *MrDrake. Photographic evidence." A link in the message brought up the photo he'd just seen on TV.

"She's got 5,352 names in her tease circle," Eddie told Blakeman. "Is that a lot?"

"It's more than I've got."

Eddie continued scrolling down the page, which showed replies to Melissa's message. "Thatzz shit hot grrrrrl" was the first, from a user named NoNocaine. The one next said, "Dudes a creep but I'd get on it." Beneath that was a message that read "Lulz that guy was my drama teacher!" Eddie clicked on the user name, but nothing in the profile immediately established whether it was really a boy from one of his classes.

"By the way," Blakeman said, "I'm having some people over tonight."

"Again?"

"More or less always, as you might recall. You might want to clean up a little bit. And try not to get quite so banged up this time. You know I don't stand on formalities, but I mean more for your own benefit. From an image-management standpoint and all."

"Is Melissa going to be back?"

"I don't know. I don't think I'd met her before last night."

"Maybe I should just go somewhere else."

"If you're going to wind up in the paper either way, you might have to learn not to worry about it. You can't control what they write, so just relax. And like I said, make yourself presentable."

But Eddie wasn't listening. While scrolling through another *MrDrake thread, he'd found a link to a poll on CelebretainmentSpot:

Should Susan Take Eddie Back?
*Yes, it's for the kids!
*Maybe, but make him sweat first!
*No! She doesn't need the jerk!
Click to see results.

"I'll call you later," he told Blakeman.

Yes, maybe, no. Eddie hesitated, as though weighing the pros and cons. Did people honestly believe they were in a position to form an opinion about the relationship of two people they'd never met, never even heard of a week before? Of course they didn't. It was just for fun. Eddie wasn't sure whether this made it better or worse. He guessed there would be a lot of maybes. That seemed fair enough. He clicked "yes" and was brought to the page that showed results. Eight percent of respondents agreed with him. Another 15 percent thought she should make him sweat. The other 77 percent said he should be gone for good.

He returned to the home page and clicked "yes" again. This vote wasn't enough to change the results, which either meant that the whole system was fake or that the participation rates were higher than he'd thought. He didn't know how many times he'd need to vote to change the answer, but he couldn't bear Susan coming to this page and seeing that number. After three more clicks, "yes" ticked up to 10 percent. He kept clicking and refreshing until it got to 15. If Susan could see that at least some people in this world thought he deserved her mercy, it might make some difference for him. Once he'd accomplished that, he called her. He wasn't surprised when she didn't pick up the phone.

"It's Eddie," he said to her voice mail. "I don't know if you've seen this thing about the girl, but it's not what it seems. I went to Blakeman's last night, because I didn't know where else to go. And there was a party going on. There's always parties going on here. It's not like I went out somewhere looking for fun. Patrick Hendricks's girlfriend was here, and some people took some pictures. It's like I was a celebrity or something. It was weird. Anyway, I definitely didn't 'canoodle' anyone or anything like that. So, just call me when you can."

Now that this photo was floating around, he didn't imagine she would be taking him back too soon. If he wanted things to quiet down, the first thing he needed to do was make sure he wasn't still at Blakeman's when people started arriving that night.

NO ONE WAS WAITING outside when he left late that afternoon. But the tabloids didn't need to send photographers after him when so many readers were prepared to do the job themselves.

Eddie walked a few blocks to the Cue Hotel on Thompson Street. It was a celebrity favorite, and he thought it could be trusted for discretion. At the front desk they told him that a luxury suite was the only thing available on short notice. Eddie was shocked at the price they quoted, but he could afford it, for now. The fact that his windfall wasn't nearly enough to raise triplets made it seem strangely dispensable. And Susan wouldn't want this money to support their children. He was like a man in a screwball comedy, obliged to spend all he had and come out of it with nothing. Only then could he return to his family, cleansed. With this in mind he felt a kind of satisfaction when he handed over the cash for three nights in a stack of hundred-dollar bills.

The flat-screen TV on the bedroom wall was as wide as the king-sized bed facing it. A laptop computer sat on an ornate writing desk in one corner. In another was a wooden bureau, but Eddie had nothing to put in it. Beyond the bedroom a separate sitting room was filled with a leather couch and a starkly modern coffee table piled with the kind of expensive photography books that Susan actually liked to look through, here meant to sit untouched to suggest sophistication.

Eddie had once thought that such rooms would be a regular feature of his life. Perhaps he'd wanted that as much as he'd ever wanted to act. In those early days the flush future had seemed as real to him as the actual life he was living. The worst part about giving up, when it had come time to give up, was knowing that all those years had been wasted. That time would never be turned into the story of early struggles leading to success. He should have quit years before, when it would still have been easy to go back to school, before his parents bought the house in Florida, before he'd acquired credit card debt it would take him decades to pay off.

But maybe it would amount to something after all. Those years had left him in debt, but they had also left him with that video, which had erased the debt and then some. Those years had paid for the procedures that conceived his children. Eventually all this business would pass, and he would return home. Susan would take him back, because she would do whatever was best for these kids. Even if they never got back what they'd had before, they would have something new.

But was this what he wanted? He would not have chosen for things to have gone this way, but was it really so terrible? Here he was in a luxury suite in the Cue, and people were talking about him on TV. If he could make everything go back to how it had been, he wasn't sure that he would. He sat on the bed and turned the TV to Entertainment Daily. He was almost surprised that they weren't talking about the tape.

"Justine Bliss was picked up on the streets of Silver Lake just hours ago," Marian Blair intoned. "Police say she was incoherent and had been wandering the Los Angeles neighborhood for hours. Friends tell us they are praying for her recovery. But they say she won't get better until she fixes her toxic relationship with her father." She turned to look into another camera. "That leads us to today's Entertainment Daily U Decide poll question: Is Tom Bliss part of the problem or part of the solution? Text one for 'yes' and two for 'no' to EDUDECIDE. Standard messaging rates apply.

"Now for some happier news. Fans who have been calling for more of Susan Hartley are about to get their wish. Tomorrow morning she'll be appearing on *This Morning Live*, where the pregnant gallerist will open up to Sandra West about her future as a single mom and rumors that she's about to sign a reality deal."

Eddie turned off the TV. His immediate reaction was a sense of betrayal, though he couldn't say in exactly what way he'd been betrayed. He had spent a lot of time in the past few days thinking about what he could make of his new fame, but he hadn't imagined Susan having similar thoughts. And he'd been waiting to hear from her before doing anything. He'd turned down his own chance to get them on *This Morning Live*. He wondered what Alex would think when he found out that Susan had gone ahead on her own. Why had she agreed to do it? She didn't want that kind of attention. She'd said as much when she threw him out of the apartment. But he knew she was scared about paying for these kids. He couldn't blame her for taking a shot that might make her some money. Instead, he blamed himself for passing up the chance. If he'd known she was willing to do the show, he would have asked her himself. They might have been on it together.

Before going to bed, he dialed down to the front desk and asked for a wake-up call to get him up before the show began.

ELEVEN

HE WATCHED THE FIRST hour of *This Morning Live* with the volume turned down while he searched online for stories about Susan. CelebretainmentSpot and half a dozen other sites reported that she would be making a "major announcement" on the show. Several commenters guessed that she had lost the babies. Some of them took an inexplicable glee at the possibility, and there was speculation that she'd never been pregnant at all. Others shouted this speculation down. Within fifteen minutes and fifty comments, the conversation had moved beyond Susan to what appeared to be long-standing arguments between pseudonymous opponents. Eddie kept reading after it had all stopped making any sense to him. It was strangely absorbing in spite of its uninviting tone. He became so immersed, in fact, that he almost missed the beginning of Susan's segment.

"The celebrity world has a new darling," Sandra West said, coming back from commercial. "Susan Hartley was re-

luctantly thrust into the spotlight when an explicit video sur-
faced showing her husband getting intimate with *Dr. Drake*
star Martha Martin. Then the stylish art world veteran
showed her fierce side, sending her husband out the door—
and his things out the window—just as news arrived that she
was pregnant with triplets. Now, for the first time anywhere,
Susan sits down to discuss what comes next. Thanks so much
for being here, Susan."

The camera turned now to show Susan sitting next to Sandra in the studio.

"Thanks for having me," she said.

Her face was bright and inviting, and she neatly fit the part
Sandra had described—a stylish art world veteran.

"First of all," Sandra said, "I want to ask what went
through your head when you first saw that infamous video."

She talked as though Eddie had cheated on his pregnant
wife. No one hearing the story for the first time would know
that the video was a decade old.

"To be honest," Susan said, "I still haven't looked at it.
I'm not sure I could stand to see it. I'm trying to keep positive,
not just for me but for the babies. I think they can feel that, if
I have a negative experience. It's like, if I watched it, they'd be
watching it, too. And I don't want them to have to see their
father that way."

Her hand shook lightly as she reached for her water. Otherwise she seemed entirely calm. Eddie understood how appealing
she would be to the morning audience. She appealed to him, too,
more than she had in a long time. When she spoke, she kept her
face at the right angle to the camera and the host, something that
Eddie knew did not come naturally. She had obviously been given
some training. Her poise seemed the product of more than a few
hours' work. She might just have been a natural, but Eddie knew
that such people were rare.

"That's such an inspirational attitude," Sandra said. "It seems like your husband has only gotten himself into more trouble in the past few days, running around with young girls."

"I'm trying to keep positive, but Eddie just isn't a very mature person. I hope for his own sake he gets there eventually, but he's not there now. I don't think he's ready to be a father. I think that's a lot of it. That's why it's best for both of us if I go through this process by myself."

Eddie had never expressed doubts about being a father, just about how they would afford it. Having these kids was the reason he'd done what he did, and Susan knew it. She was telling a story about him, making him fit the idea the audience already had. Whose story was it? Had she been told to follow this line, or was it her own idea? He found it all hard to watch.

"Speaking of this process," Sandra said, "I understand you might have a bit of news to share this morning. There have been some rumors about a reality show. What can you tell us?"

"I just finalized a deal yesterday with Moody Productions. We've already got several networks interested, but I can't say more than that."

"That's very exciting news. Can you tell us what viewers can expect from the show?"

"It's just going to be me," Susan said. "My work at the gallery. My life preparing to be a single mom. There's been a lot of stuff out there the past few days. Some of it is true, some of it isn't. I just want to show people what I'm actually like."

"Before we finish up," Sandra said. "Let me say how brave I think you are."

"Thank you for that. And thanks so much for having me on the show."

"There you have it. If you're as fascinated by Susan Hartley's story as I am, I know you're going to be eagerly awaiting this show. I hope you'll come on again when there's more news about that. We'll be right back after this break with a report from Afghanistan."

Eddie turned off the TV and called Talent Management. When they told him Alex wasn't in, Eddie called his cell phone.

"I just watched *This Morning Live*," he said.

"Wasn't she great? I'm in the greenroom now, she'll be out in a second."

"You're with her?"

"Of course I'm with her. I set the interview up."

"Why didn't you tell me?"

"I did tell you. I said I'd get you on *This Morning Live*, I'd get you a reality show with Moody, the whole deal. You said you weren't interested."

"That's because I thought Susan wasn't interested."

"She's interested now. It's going to be a great show. Moody says we may get Bliss's old spot on 2True. And I got Susan some serious money. In case you weren't aware, kids aren't cheap."

Of course Eddie understood the appeal of making some money. Susan didn't know about the remaining cash from Morgan, so their situation seemed even more desperate to her than it was. Still, she'd made the choice so quickly, as if acting on an impulse Eddie had never seen in her before.

"If she's on board," he told Alex, "then I'm on board."

"I'd like to get you involved, Eddie. But Moody wants Susan. A single mother with triplets is a great story. You're sort of a complication at this point."

"A complication? No one would even have heard of Susan if I hadn't sold that tape."

"It doesn't matter how they heard of her. The point is, people like her. They're interested. Pretty soon the tape is going to be old news, but if she plays it right, Susan's going to stick."

"You're just going to cut me out of the story?"

"I offered you these opportunities, Eddie. You said you can't do this, you can't do that. I called Susan, and she was ready to go. So we're going. Give it some time, and I'm sure they'll find a way to work you into the story. Listen, here she is now. I've got to go."

"Maybe I could talk with her?"

But Alex had already hung up. Eddie called Susan's cell phone and left a voice mail, his tenth in the past three days. He doubted that she was listening to them.

"It's Eddie," he said. "I saw you on TV. You looked really great. I just want you to know you don't have to do this reality thing if it makes you uncomfortable. I'll find a way to get us some money, something that keeps you and the babies out of the spotlight. I think we could figure all this stuff out, just the two of us, if we had a chance to talk. Give me a call when you can. I love you."

Eddie knew it was useless. Who would turn down what Susan had been offered? Besides, she'd hardly looked uncomfortable. In fact, she'd looked made for the part. This producer knew exactly what he was doing. Alex hadn't been exaggerating when he called Brian Moody the most successful reality-show producer in Hollywood, as Eddie learned from a quick search on his laptop. Moody's imperiled Justine Bliss show was only one of more than a dozen currently on the air. One Web site called him "the genius behind *Baby Pageant* and *Dog Swap*." He seemed to be taken in the press as something more than a simple producer. A strange kind of legend had built up around him. His Wikipedia page reported that he was a former priest who'd left a contemplative order to work in television. Other, less reliable sites made more elaborate, even baroque claims about his mystical inclinations.

The man made TV shows, Eddie thought. That was all.

Though if it was true that he had some religious background, that might explain how he'd convinced Susan to sign on. He would have spoken a language that she understood. Eddie preferred this idea to the alternative, which was that he didn't know his wife as well as he thought he did. Long ago, Eddie had asked Susan if she'd ever dreamed of being a famous artist herself. It seemed a natural question. He hadn't set out to teach acting, he'd come to it by way of trying to do the thing itself. He imagined that curators and gallerists and art critics similarly began as failed artists.

He remembered the conversation now. It had come on their very first date, the second time they'd met. They'd been introduced during Eddie's first year back at St. Albert's, at a dinner party held by Annie, who was still teaching then. Eddie had noticed Annie and another female teacher whispering and laughing when he was introduced on the first day of school that year. After years of disastrous auditions, being held to a standard that didn't apply to the rest of the world, he'd become handsome again.

When Annie invited him over early that fall, he assumed she was interested in him, but the man who answered the door that night was obviously Annie's boyfriend. There were about ten people at the party. Apart from Eddie they all seemed to know each other. The whole thing puzzled him until dinner, when he found himself seated next to Susan. She was very pretty, Eddie thought. Not Martha Martin pretty, but no one was, except for Martha herself. Susan had light brown hair that she wore pinned up and a full, freckled face. She had high, round cheeks and a wide mouth that was quick to form into a smile. But Eddie didn't think of her physical appearance when he remembered that evening. He didn't really picture a person at all so much as a hazy, warmth-conferring glow. The overwhelming impression she gave was that of kindness, generosity of spirit. Not until he recognized this did he realize how conditioned he'd become to being regarded with skepticism, measured and found wanting for the purposes for which he was presenting himself. He'd come to anticipate disappointing people.

"Annie tells me you're an actor," she said while serving herself from a large bowl of pasta. Before passing the bowl along, she filled Eddie's plate without asking him. "What kind of stuff do you do?"

"Mostly theater."

"It must be exciting."

He'd become used to exaggerating his few accomplishments in such situations, or even lying outright, which he could do convincingly, since he'd seen a successful career up close and knew all the relevant details. But the combination of that warmth and the sense that there was nothing much at stake led him to say, "I'm not having a great time with it right now, which is why I've taken this teaching job."

"Doesn't every famous artist have these stories about the odd jobs they took before they made it big?"

"That doesn't mean that everyone who does odd jobs goes on to make it big," Eddie answered, having considered the point at some length. This wasn't an attractive response, but for the moment he felt no need to be attractive.

"When you do make it, it's going to be that much nicer to know that you worked for it. I see it with the artists at the gallery."

After years of work at an auction house, she explained, she'd recently moved to a gallery in Chelsea owned by a dealer named Carl von Verdant. She hoped the change would let her work directly with artists, instead of just rich collectors.

"Some of them have been struggling for years. But they're just so committed to their art. And then Carl discovers them, and like that their lives are changed. Maybe that will happen to you."

"Do you represent anyone I might know?" Eddie asked, though he didn't know any contemporary artists at all.

"Have you heard of Graham Turnbough?"

"I'm afraid not."

"His work is very painterly."

Did this just mean he was an actual painter? Eddie wondered. What made one painter more painterly than another?

"He's going to be in a group show going up next week," Susan said. "You should come by to check it out."

The previous year had treated his confidence so badly that he might not have taken up Susan's offer had it not been so obvious that he'd been brought to the party for the purpose of meeting her. At the opening, Susan found him drinking a beer he'd taken from an ice-filled trash bin and looking at an installation piece made of string and melted crayons, presumably not the work of the painterly Turnbough.

"I like it," he told her.

"Do you?" she asked. "I think it's kind of empty and dumb. But Carl doesn't care what I think. I'm hoping once I've been here longer that will change."

She laughed nervously, and Eddie could tell she'd had a few drinks in advance of his arrival.

"What kind of work do you like?"

"I guess this seems old-fashioned," she told him, "but I like art with real belief behind it. Stuff that isn't just about provoking people."

"That doesn't seem old-fashioned," Eddie said. "When I was growing up, my parents didn't take me to museums or anything like that, so the only art I saw was in churches."

"That's just it," Susan answered, as though he'd said something very profound. "When I studied art history in college,

I specialized in the Renaissance, when all the great art was religious. Of course I knew that things had changed a lot since then, but I wanted to find that strain in contemporary art. Then I got out of school and started working in the art world, and I can't even tell people that I believe in God. They find it ridiculous. But look at the ridiculous stuff that they believe in." She waved at the piece in front of her, then laughed again. "I guess I shouldn't be saying this so loudly."

Her face was bright now, as if illuminated by wonder, and Eddie felt again the warmth he'd felt at Annie's apartment. He hadn't gone to the gallery that night with any particular expectation, but seeing that look on her face made him ask, "Can I take you to dinner when this thing ends?"

At dinner he'd asked the question about whether deep down she'd wanted to be an artist herself. In retrospect, it might have been an insulting question, since it suggested failure, but after all, he was unapologetically a failure himself. Susan hadn't seemed offended. She'd spoken passionately about what art had meant in her life and her desire to live around it. She was in awe of great artists, and the idea that she could be one herself simply hadn't occurred to her. She wanted instead to help great art get out into the world. She'd taken some studio classes in college, because she'd wanted to know more about the process she planned to spend her life thinking and talking and writing about. She hadn't been very good at it, but that only gave her more respect for the people who did it well.

It was painful for Eddie to remember this side of Susan, mostly because remembering it meant admitting that he'd forgotten it for a time. Perhaps he'd just stopped seeing it, but it seemed at least as likely that it had been worked out of her over time. By years of menial treatment from Carl at the gallery, years of living with Eddie's disappointment. She had turned from these things to the prospect of motherhood, which had only brought more disappointment. The girl he'd sat at dinner with that night years before was on track to become the art world veteran of Sandra's depiction. It had never occurred to Eddie that this might be another part of Susan's disappointment. And now it seemed there might be a remedy to it. She didn't have to play the part of long-suffering assistant. She didn't have to play the part of childless wife. She could play whatever part she wanted.

PART THREE

TWELVE

AT THE BEGINNING OF his third week at the Cue, Eddie
went to the lobby newsstand to buy his magazines. This trip
was already developing into a kind of weekly ritual, a way of
marking the passage of days that were mostly spent alone in
his room. He could follow Susan's life—to some extent, he
could even follow his own—hour by hour online or on TV,
but there was something more meaningful about these pages
held in his hand, which told only those stories that had risen
above the daily chatter and solidified into something slightly
more substantial.

He took the magazines from the rack and paid without
looking at them, eager to get back upstairs before being
caught on his errand. There was no sign that anyone in the
lobby recognized him, but he had already learned that someone was always watching. On his second morning at the
hotel, having realized he'd be staying a while, he'd gone shopping for clothes. No photographers waited when he left the

hotel, and no one stopped him outside or even paid him any particular attention that he noticed. But the next morning, a report on CelebretainmentSpot documented his slide into shopping addiction, complete with a list of every purchase he'd made the day before. An anonymous friend expressed worry that Eddie's new lifestyle was ruining him.

When he finally left his room again a few days later, the seeming normalcy of the world outside was enough to lull him back into complacency. That evening his entire day was documented online, in bits and pieces, videos Teesed out, eyewitness accounts on gossip sites. He'd responded politely to a flirtatious barista at the coffee shop, but in the photo he was leering at her. A sneeze at the lobby bar became a drunken scowl.

All the magazines spoke of their "spies" in the streets. They used the word self-mockingly, but it was exactly right. Eddie felt like a man awaiting trial in a police state. None of the evidence would be falsified, because if you followed someone everywhere you eventually found something real you could use against him. Actual police states, he knew, hardly needed spies. Instead, they taught their citizens to spy on each other. This was how it seemed to him—he was constantly being watched, but there was no one doing the watching. In such a world, no one could be trusted. So he stayed in his room. Ignoring it all might have been easier than locking himself away. They could write what they wanted; no one was making him read it. But these magazines and gossip sites were his only sources of information about Susan, who still wouldn't answer his messages. So long as he kept up with them, he had nearly as much access to her as he'd had when they were living together. She'd become a top story. CelebretainmentSpot's Bump Watch tracked her belly on a daily basis. On *This Morning Live,* a celebrity obstetrician held up an artist's rendering of the fetuses and recited a long list of possible developmental complications.

The New York *Herald*'s Art & Entertainment section, keeping slightly above the fray, profiled Carl von Verdant. Susan had always complained that Carl didn't let her do anything besides answering the phone, but now he told the paper that he supported his "protégée" completely. He only hoped that the show wouldn't be a distraction, because he depended so much on her talents. The paper had interviewed half a dozen artists represented by the gallery, including Graham Turnbough, who said that Susan had one of the sharpest eyes in the business. The *Herald* wondered whether her show would raise the level of the conversation on television, introducing viewers to serious artists. "A funny thing happened on the way to tabloid infamy," the article concluded. "It turns out Susan Hartley is the real deal. She might even prove to be that rarest thing: a reality television heavyweight." Eddie knew better than anyone that this was a concoction, but he found himself looking at Susan through the eyes of all the fascinated onlookers. Maybe she really was a "heavyweight," or could turn out to be one. Maybe he'd actually given her a gift, the chance to put her life on the track she wanted for it. He wanted to be on the track with her.

Back in his room, Eddie took the magazines out of the brown paper bag and looked them over. The cover of *Celeb-Nation* showed Martha walking down the street in dark glasses, with a shawl over her head, looking as mournfully dignified as a widow at a state funeral. The getup was not actually meant to conceal anything. Instead it announced her as herself in disguise. She so captured every bit of attention in the frame that Eddie didn't immediately recognize his apartment building behind her.

"Dr. Drake Makes House Call," he read. "Martha goes in person to comfort Susan."

He flipped inside the magazine to find a story about the two women banding together, showing solidarity.

"We had a great talk," Susan told CelebNation after her meeting with Martha, which those in the know said lasted nearly an hour and included plenty of tears. "It meant so much that she would travel all this way just to see me." But as for the deets on her convo, Susan was tight-lipped. "You're going to have to tune in to the premiere of Desperately Expecting Susan, only on the 2True Network."

The one mention of Eddie was a poll question at the bottom of the page—*What do you think Martha and Susan talked about? A) Prenatal care; B) What it's like to be in the spotlight; C) Life after Handsome Eddie.*

How many times had he dreamed of seeing her again? Though they'd lived together for years, Martha had since become as unreal to Eddie as she was to everyone else, and he couldn't quite believe that she'd been in his apartment. Whatever she was doing there, he knew it had nothing to do with "comforting" anyone. Perhaps she'd gotten jealous of Susan's popularity and wanted to remind everyone who had the real star power. Eddie called Susan almost reflexively, expecting to hear her voice mail, as he had dozens of times in the past few weeks. When she picked up he responded with panicked silence.

"Is that you?" she asked.

"It's me."

There were countless things they might have talked about, but the only one that came to his mind was Martha's visit, and he didn't want Susan to think that Martha was the reason he'd called.

"Where are you?" she asked eventually.

"I'm at the Cue Hotel in SoHo," he said. "I didn't think staying at Blakeman's was such a great idea."

"That didn't turn out so well." She seemed almost amused.

"Nothing happened with that girl," Eddie said.

"Of course. I give you that much credit at least."

"I don't like living this way. I've barely been outside in a week. I want to come home."

"Not now," Susan said. "I'm not ready yet."

This seemed to suggest she'd be ready eventually. It was the first bit of hope she'd given him. Somehow progress had been made.

"I've been watching you on the talk shows," Eddie said. "You're really good at it."

He tried to keep the edge of bitterness out of his voice. He couldn't justify blaming her for this star turn. The best he could do was keep the feeling from her.

"I didn't ask for it," Susan said with a laugh. "But I'll admit I'm enjoying myself."

"So you're going to do this show?"

"It just seems to make sense. It's like I'm discovering a side of myself I'd lost for a while, and I really like it. Besides, they're not that bad."

"The people from the show?"

"For starters. But everyone, really. The press, the photographers and all. They've got a job to do, but they're actually sort of friendly if you're nice to them. I've gotten to know some of the guys who hang around all the time. They run errands and stuff for me, help me carry things upstairs if I agree to give them good shots. Of course you know all about that. I'm sure you're getting hounded the same way I am."

"It takes some getting used to," Eddie said.

"Martha gave me some advice for dealing with it."

Eddie was glad she'd brought Martha up, so he didn't have to do it himself.

"I read about her visit," he said dumbly.

"We wondered what you would make of it."

The idea of Martha talking about him pleased Eddie, no matter what they might have said.

"There must be something in it for her. She wouldn't just come without an agenda."

"She actually seemed really nice. For the first time I understood why the two of you were together for so long."

"We were different people back then."

"She said good things about you, as crazy as that might sound. She was surprised that you hadn't leaked the tape years ago, the moment she walked out the door. She's been waiting for it ever since, and she's kind of relieved. This baggage from her past is out there, and she doesn't need to worry about it anymore. Now she can go about the rest of her career. It wasn't that bad, she said. It would have been worse if it had happened sooner, when she was just getting started. Or later, once she was married and her baby was born. The timing worked out well. It's just like you told me, it's good for her at this point."

"Everyone seems to have come out all right except me."

"Don't sound so bitter," Susan told him. "You deserve to suffer a little. And she helped you out, too. She's the reason I picked up the phone when you called. She's the reason I'm starting to think about taking you back. She told me to give you another chance. I think she's felt pretty guilty all this time about the way things ended between you. Now you guys are even."

"However it happened, I'm glad you're thinking about it. I love you."

"Stay out of trouble," Susan said.

EDDIE WANTED TO TELL *CelebNation* or Entertainment Daily or even the people on Teeser that he'd been forgiven. They'd both forgiven him. The story was over, and everyone could leave them alone. But it didn't work that way. The story would only be over when people got tired of it. Martha wasn't going to let him off the hook, wasn't going to go to the press and tell them that she'd deserved it, that he wasn't such a bad guy. She had said these things to Susan, which was more than she'd had to do, but she wasn't going to tell the rest of the world. Even if she did, it wouldn't end the story. Martha lived to have the story told about her. It was her job. Soon it would be Susan's job, too.

He called Talent Management, and he was put straight through to Alex.

"Did you see Martha going to my apartment?"

"Isn't it great?" Alex said. "There's going to be a big dramatic reconciliation scene to begin the show."

"Susan's going to take me back?"

"Not you and Susan. Martha and Susan."

"You're going to *reconcile* them? This is the first time they've even met."

"Poor choice of words. The point is they hugged and they cried, all that. The business with the tape is behind them."

"You sent Martha there?"

"Not me, Moody. Everything they say about the man is true. He's some kind of genius."

"How did he get Martha to agree to it?"

"It wasn't all that hard, to be honest. She's got a big celebrity wedding to plan, and this will help make her more relatable. Martha can come off as a little cold, you know, especially after the way things ended with Rex. But Susan's got relatable to burn."

"Listen, Alex, you are still representing me, too, right?"

"Sure thing, Eddie."

"So do something to get me back into this story."

"I'll try my best."

How could he have thought for a moment that the visit had been spontaneous? He'd made the mistake of imagining that Martha was still a human being, not a carefully marketed product. But Susan wasn't a product, and he was surprised that she'd kept the truth from him. Perhaps she already took it for granted that everything that happened to her was planned for the show. This almost certainly meant that her encouraging phone call was also staged. But maybe it wasn't such a bad thing that Moody wanted him to be encouraged. And Susan might still have meant what she'd said, even if she was saying it for other reasons. Each event could mean two things at once—one for the cynical producer who orchestrated it, and something else for the people who experienced it.

HE WAS STILL CONTEMPLATING these possibilities a few hours later when he heard the knock. A glass of melted ice sat on his chest, and it spilled as he sat up from bed and pulled his Cue bathrobe shut.

"Room service," a voice on the other side of the door announced.

Eddie had no memory of ordering room service, but he knew his memory was not entirely to be relied upon at that point.

"What is it?"

"All of our extended-stay guests get a free meal for each month of their stay."

Had it been a month? He wasn't sure. It had been close, certainly.

"Just a second," he called out.

He stood up, put on his slippers, and pulled his robe shut. When he opened the door a great burst of light filled his eyes. The man in the doorway lowered his camera and they stood face-to-face.

"Motherfucker," Eddie said as he lunged. But the cameraman was already running down the hall. In his robe and slippers and drunkenness Eddie couldn't keep up with him. He tripped and his robe came open as he hit the hallway floor. The camera clicked another half dozen times before the man disappeared down a stairwell. Eddie picked himself up and returned to his room, but the door had locked behind him.

He'd lost his belt somewhere, perhaps back in the room, so he held his robe shut with one hand as he waited for the elevator. In the lobby the woman at the front desk smiled.

"Hi, Aimee," Eddie said, reading her name tag. "I've locked myself out of room 341."

"It happens all the time," Aimee answered, seeming unfazed by his appearance. "I just need to see some photo ID."

Eddie waited for a second.

"I'm in my bathrobe."

"Of course," she said. "Here's what we can do. If you tell security where your wallet can be found in your room, they can go get your ID. They'll bring it down here, and I'll print out a key card for you."

"You're serious?"

"We are committed to security here at the hotel. It causes some slight inconvenience at times, but our guests appreciate it."

He could tell she had been trained to say just these words in just this way, and there was no sense arguing, but he couldn't remember where he'd left his wallet.

"I think it might be on the bedside table," he told her. "Or else on the floor near the bed."

"That should be sufficient."

"Do you think I could speak with a manager?" Eddie asked.

A few moments later a tall, thin man in a double-breasted suit appeared at the desk.

"How can I help you?" he asked with a vaguely European accent.

"Did somebody tell the press about my presence in the hotel?"

"Sir?"

"I just opened my door to someone claiming to be room service and a fucking photographer started taking pictures of me in my underwear."

"I'm sorry to hear that, sir. It sounds very unpleasant."

"That's great that you're sorry, but I'd like to hear what you're going to do about it."

"Have you been drinking, sir?"

"As a matter of fact I have, but that isn't relevant right now. This woman has been telling me about all your security, but then I've got paparazzi stalking me."

"I see," the manager said. "That's a real problem, sir."

"Do you have any idea how that could have happened?"

The manager seemed to consider possible answers to the question.

"To whom am I speaking?"

"Eddie Hartley, from room 341."

Now the man looked carefully at Eddie, as though he might recognize his face.

"I don't believe that anyone here at the hotel was responsible for alerting the press to your presence. But I promise you I will look into the matter very seriously."

They waited together for the security guard to arrive with Eddie's wallet.

"It was right where he said," the guard told them. He withdrew Eddie's license and passed it to the manager, whose face was brightened by a flicker of bemused recognition. He passed the ID to Aimee, and she smiled. It was clear that neither had known until that moment that Handsome Eddie was staying at their hotel. The manager handed over the wallet while Eddie's new key card was being printed.

"I'm terribly sorry for your inconvenience," the manager said. "I promise to look into the matter. In the meantime, would you like us to move your room?"

Eddie knew they could find him if they wanted to.

"I don't really think it matters," he said.

"IS HANDSOME EDDIE HEADED for a breakdown?" *Celeb-Nation* asked when the photos of Eddie spread out in the hallway hit the Internet. "Attacking photogs, making scenes in hotel lobbies—Hartley is hitting rock bottom just as Susan moves on with her life." "This latest outlandish behavior came just hours after a tearful call in which he begged Susan to take him back," Marian Blair told Entertainment Daily viewers. "Sources say she was even considering it, but now she worries he'll be a danger to her pregnancy."

He'd told Susan where he was staying, and immediately they'd come for him. He remembered what she'd said about making friends with the photographers. You helped them with certain things, and they made deals with you. Martha had given her advice about dealing with things. Was this the advice? Did she want him to look like a fool? There was a cruelty to it that was entirely unlike her, as though she wanted to punish him a bit more before accepting him back.

Eddie considered moving hotels—and not just for the privacy, which wouldn't last in any case. He was running through the money that he'd thought could change his life forever. In another month, his St. Albert's salary would stop coming in, and the payment for the video would disappear even more quickly. He'd liked in theory the idea of leaving himself with nothing, as a kind of penance for what he'd done. But now he was faced with the real problem of what to do then. He might easily run through it all before Susan took him back.

The person he needed to help him through all this was Susan. After their one conversation, he'd imagined they would talk regularly again. But he called every few days after that, and she never picked up. Their brief conversation—and the visit from the photographer that followed—felt like some special message to him. But he didn't know what the message meant. So he waited where he was.

THIRTEEN

SUSAN'S SHOW PREMIERED ON the Tuesday after Thanksgiving with an hour-long episode, which Eddie watched from his king-sized bed. The episode began with Martha's arrival at the apartment. The scene seemed designed to signal to viewers who Susan was and why they were supposed to be interested in her without the work of lengthy exposition. Something had happened that brought Susan's life into contact with the likes of Martha Martin, and this was enough to demand the world's attention. Martha was a stand-in for all the events that had precipitated this premiere. All of this heartened Eddie somewhat. Even if he wasn't included on the show, the story still required him to connect these two women now hugging each other on his TV. Soon they were both crying. Alex had been right: it humanized Martha. She seemed so caring, like a real person.

"I can't believe you're having triplets," she said, running

her hand over Susan's belly. "Carrying just one around is hard enough for me."

"It's a bit overwhelming," Susan admitted, though she didn't look overwhelmed. She looked beautiful, even next to Martha.

After a commercial break, an exterior shot established a new location, which Eddie recognized as the gallery. Inside, a camera ran across a series of small works in charcoal hanging on one wall. They were more inviting than Carl's usual tastes. Eddie assumed this was by design. He knew the gallery was meant to be important to the show, but he was surprised that Martha would take the time to go into work with Susan. As the scene progressed, he realized that their visit was in fact over. It had already done its job, without any mention of Eddie. Anyone watching would have known that he was the thing connecting these two women, but they hadn't even said his name. Martha's presence was apparently enough to tell viewers everything.

"Carl von Verdant is one of the most highly respected dealers in the city," Susan explained to the camera. "I've been working with him for five years now, and I'm currently the gallery's associate curator."

Eddie had never heard this title before. Susan had always been one of Carl's assistants. In the past, she'd described him as brusque and condescending, but in the half hour that followed he asked her advice about everything—where to hang a piece, what to look for at an upcoming fair. The friendly conversations Susan shared with the other assistants—now presumably her subordinates—didn't at all match her long-standing complaints about the gallery's atmosphere. Eddie couldn't be sure the depiction was false. Perhaps Susan had been exaggerating her problems at work. What Eddie saw on-screen was entirely believable.

Susan left the group to take a call from Richard Oh, a young artist whose debut show she was organizing.

"It's going to be great," she told Richard. "You'll be the toast of New York."

After the call, Richard spoke to the camera from a nondescript room somewhere. He was an Asian American in his early twenties. The right side of his head was shaved, the hair on the left pulled into a long pigtail.

"I'm so excited to be working with Susan Hartley," he said. "She's the reason I chose Von Verdant to represent me."

Later in the show, a shipment of Richard's work went briefly missing, creating the episode's only real bit of drama. Carl yelled at two of the young assistants while Susan went about locating the lost packages. She was the calm center around which the gallery revolved. She advised Carl with confidence, and the answers she gave him were smart and knowledgeable, which didn't seem to Eddie something that could be faked. Her job bore no resemblance to the menial frustrations she'd so often described to Eddie at home.

Had everything really changed for her so quickly? Their jobs had long been a shared source of disappointment in their lives. Perhaps Susan had been all along doing better than she'd let on. Perhaps she had persisted in presenting herself as a failure out of a sense of solidarity, or because she thought he wasn't capable of appreciating her success. She'd probably been right to suspect this, if in fact she had suspected it.

There was a simpler explanation: he was watching a fictional television character, based only loosely on his wife, and he was wrong to compare the particulars of this character's life to those of the Susan he knew. This seemed comforting at first, but it was ultimately troubling in its own way, because this fictional Susan already seemed so real after less than half an hour. More than that: he wanted this Susan to exist. He liked her better this way.

After work, the assistants Carl had berated took Susan out to a bar, where they gossiped while she sipped on club soda. It was obvious that the others looked up to her, but there was also a sense of camaraderie. They joked about naming one of the babies after Carl. The scene was broken by an interview with Tomaka, the gallery's youngest employee. She'd been working at the gallery for just a few months, but she was the prettiest of the assistants, and she'd been given the most screen time.

"Susan is the happiest we've seen her in years," she said. "I think all these changes in her life have been really good for her."

The show's tone changed in the second half. Susan sat in a doctor's waiting room while in a voice-over she explained that she was getting her first ultrasound.

"I'm scared to be doing this alone," she said. "It makes me think how hard it's all going to be."

You don't have to do it alone, Eddie wanted to say. The doctor took Susan to an examination room and talked in an understated voice about the risks presented by multiples. Susan pulled her hospital gown over her belly, where the nurse applied a layer of gel. The doctor set down the transducer, and a picture came on the screen. It wasn't clear to Eddie exactly what it showed, until all of a sudden it was. Those were his children. He was seeing them for the first time, alongside a million other people.

The picture was replaced on-screen by a close-up of Susan's crying face.

"They're so beautiful," she said, looking into the camera. "I can't believe they're inside me. I've never been so happy. But it's scary, too, knowing I have to go through all this by myself."

Eddie was sorry not to be there, sorry to see her scared, but he felt something else, too. She needs me, Eddie thought. She can't do it by herself. Everyone said that Brian Moody knew what he was doing. He must have created this tension— between professional confidence and personal uncertainty— for a reason. To satisfy it, they would have to bring Eddie back. Susan had nearly said as much. I'm not ready yet, she'd told him, which he took now to mean: we have to establish the story first.

As the credits ran, Eddie searched for his name online and found a post titled "Take Him Back!" on what appeared to be a Christian television blog. It said that Moody would be sending a "strong message about the importance of the traditional family" if he reunited Susan and Eddie. The post compared Susan's situation to that of Justine Bliss with a logic that struck Eddie as somewhat imperfect, though he was happy to read it. A small but persistent movement existed in his favor.

But that movement could only be found by looking for it. Most pages that Eddie read had nothing good to say about him. In fact, the majority of commenters didn't mention him at all. They talked about the visit from Martha, about the gallery, about the babies. Most of all, they talked about Susan. She seemed human and "relatable," an ugly word that came up in nearly every post. Relatability was, apparently, the gold standard for a character, and Susan possessed it. The term connoted precisely the things about Susan that had made her suffer in Eddie's eyes when compared to Martha. She was pretty but not overwhelmingly beautiful. She was smart but not intimidating in her intelligence. She was confident but not domineering. Vulnerable but not needy. Kind but not desperate for approval. She was just Susan, and everyone loved her. I loved her first, Eddie wanted to say, though he understood that in some sense he'd seen this Susan for the first time just when everyone else did.

IN THE DAYS AFTER the premiere, more stories emerged about Susan's need for help, her struggle to make it through alone. With each one Eddie felt closer to being back in the fold. Her situation had to change in some way to keep viewers interested. The question was how long the producers would play things out. He held off calling Alex, because he thought he would be in a stronger position when they came for him if he didn't seem desperate to get back.

The next week's show began at the gallery, where Susan prepared for Richard Oh's opening. His work had been safely shipped to the gallery, and the assistants helped Susan install it. Most of it had the appearance of melted wax in various vomitous shades.

"Susan has really been Richard's champion," Carl told the camera. "She's the one who turned me on to him, and she's the one who brought him in to the gallery."

It was an atypical bit of selflessness on Carl's part, but it also seemed to suggest that the blame would be on Susan if the show didn't succeed. After a few more shots of Richard's work, they cut to her.

"The medium is melted-down G.I. Joe figurines," Susan explained. "It's such a haunting evocation of the horrors of war. This one is called *Fallujah*." She pointed to a hardened brown blob fixed to the wall. "It's amazing how something so seemingly abstract can have such an emotional impact."

Now they cut to Richard, who had let the pigtail down from the unshaved side of his head.

"It's incredibly exciting to have someone like Susan Hartley embrace your art," he said. "Everyone thinks so highly of her taste."

In Eddie's memory, these openings had always been casual affairs, with garbage cans full of PBR and a few bottles of white wine on a table near the door. People came in for a free drink and took a lap around the show before moving on to the next gallery. But now they were setting up something rather more elaborate. There was a brief bit of phony drama when the caterers called to say they were stuck in traffic.

"I'm launching a career here," Susan said dramatically. "Everything has to be on time."

Later they showed her back at the apartment, picking out a dress that would elegantly handle her growing bump.

"It's times like these when I really wish I had someone going through all this with me," she said. "I've got a lot riding on this. Not just for my own career. I really believe in Richard, and I want this night to be perfect for him."

So much of their life in the past two years had been wrapped up in their failure to conceive that a failure at work hardly seemed to register. But now he could see how badly Susan wanted this show to succeed. She had a whole emotional life attached to her work that Eddie had never known. Eddie felt himself rooting for Susan, as he imagined most viewers would, and he was relieved to see people waiting around the block to get inside the gallery. A velvet rope kept them in a line more in keeping with a movie premiere than the first exhibition of an unknown artist. Inside, Susan eloquently explained the importance of Richard's work to various well-dressed people who were labeled by way of subtitles as prominent collectors or socialites or art critics. The only name familiar to Eddie was that of the lead art critic at the *Herald*. Susan had mentioned her in the past mostly to complain that she never came to their shows. As the evening wound on, all of the works were sold, checks for thirty or forty thousand dollars were written on the spot.

The cameras cut back outside, where a black car pulled up to the curb. A driver emerged to open the passenger door. Eddie could tell from the response of the people still waiting in line that whoever came out of the car was famous, but it took a moment for him to recognize Rex Gilbert. As Rex walked up to the gallery door, the screen cut to Tomaka.

"I'm like, oh my God, Rex is in our gallery," she said. "We're all trying to keep ourselves together."

She was replaced by Susan, who looked at the camera more calmly.

"Rex is famous in the art world as more than just a dilettante with some money to throw around," she said. "He's a great collector. So it's a real honor for him to come to this show. Mostly, I'm just happy for Richard."

Susan was waiting at the door when Rex came inside. She introduced herself and showed him around.

"Unfortunately, our major pieces have already sold," she told him. "But Richard is working on a very exciting new series. I could arrange a private showing if you're interested."

"I would love a private showing," Rex said.

Susan handed him a business card, and the camera turned to capture Tomaka and another assistant looking on.

"Rex Gilbert is flirting with Susan," Tomaka said. "I'm totally going to die."

Susan walked Rex back to the door.

"I'm sorry I couldn't get here while there was still more work available, but I certainly like what I saw."

He passed his eyes over Susan and smiled.

"Some of it is still available," Susan said. She kissed him

on both cheeks and stood watching in the doorway while he walked back to his waiting car.

Eddie turned off the TV as the credits ran. They might have picked Rex, of all people, just to torture him. But really there was nothing to worry about, he assured himself. It was a cameo, like Martha's appearance the week before. A star of Rex's caliber wouldn't get himself stuck in this story. He just wanted to look like he was serious about art. His last three movies had been disappointments, and his popularity had been declining since he'd split with Martha. Establishing some high culture credibility would be good for him. It was easier than getting involved in politics or directing an indie script.

Every site Eddie checked had Rex and Susan on its home page. CelebretainmentSpot ran a story that had obviously been waiting to post the moment the episode ended. "Hollywood's worst-kept secret is out. Rumors have been swirling for weeks about Rex and Susan spending time together. Our spies say the two have been privately inseparable since the visit to her popular Chelsea gallery depicted on tonight's show. Rex's friends are hoping that the prospect of a family might be enough to finally tie down Hollywood's most notorious bachelor."

Eddie closed the computer and called Talent Management.

"What the fuck is this?" he asked Alex. "Rex Gilbert wants to start a family with my pregnant wife?"

"It's quite a story, isn't it?"

"I thought you were supposed to be getting me on the show?"

"Let's be honest, Eddie. Between you and Rex there's a bit of a difference in interest level."

"Isn't that supposed to be my agent's job?"

"You're not exactly doing me any favors."

"What's that supposed to mean?"

"You don't *do* anything. Granted, you spread out naked in the hallway once, which wasn't bad. But since then you don't even leave the fucking hotel room."

"I was trying to stay out of trouble."

"Who told you to do that? If you want to get on this show, you need to get yourself *into* trouble. No one gives a shit about you right now."

After he hung up with Alex, Eddie searched through the messages on his phone and found the number of the reporter from *Star Style*.

"This is Geena Tuff," she said.

"Hi, Geena, this is Eddie Hartley."

"Right, Eddie. How are you doing?"

"Listen, I've been thinking about it, and I'm ready to give you that exclusive interview."

"I'm afraid the window has sort of closed on that."

"You don't have to pay ten thousand dollars. I'll give it to you for free. I've got some juicy material."

"What kind of juice are we talking about?"

Eddie paused.

"I'll tell you during the interview."

"Why don't we call this the interview, and you can just tell me now?"

"I just need a little more time to prepare."

"If you've actually got a story to tell, call me back. Right now I'm on deadline for a piece about Susan and Rex."

He'd already missed his chance. If he wanted to get on the show, he couldn't just wait until their story needed him. He needed to make a story for himself. He continued looking through his phone, as though the answer to his problem could be found there. After two minutes of mindless scrolling he came across the photo from Blakeman's party, and he called the number that had sent it to him.

"Is this who I think it is?" Melissa asked. "I didn't expect to hear from you again."

"I've got a job offer for you," Eddie said. "It's an acting job, and it will pay pretty well."

"What do I have to do?"

"For starters, I want you to come to the SoHo Cue and ask for my room. When you get here, I'll tell you the rest."

FOURTEEN

AN HOUR LATER, EDDIE answered a call from the front desk.

"Mr. Hartley, there's a young woman here to see you."

"Send her up," Eddie said. "Have room service bring us a bottle of champagne. Just leave it outside. We don't want to be disturbed."

When he opened the door, Melissa stood in the hall wearing a short, high-waisted skirt and leather boots that came up to her knees. Her hair had been light brown the last time he'd seen her. Now it was dyed black, and her eyes were made up darkly to set off her pale skin. She was perfect for the role, Eddie thought.

"So you've got a job for me?" she asked. "What have you got in mind?"

"We're going to have an affair."

"You don't need to pay me for that."

"I don't actually want to sleep with you," Eddie explained,

though it wasn't precisely true at the moment. "I just want it to look like there's something going on between us. I need to get my wife back."

"You want to get your wife back by pretending to sleep with me?"

"We're going to create a scandal. It's the only way the producers will let me on the show."

"You want me to go out with you, hold hands, kiss in public. That kind of thing?"

"That's the idea."

"I'll be famous for sleeping with a married man whose wife is pregnant with triplets?"

"More or less."

Melissa smiled.

"This is amazing."

"I can't offer you much money. But if it works out I'm sure you could turn it into something."

"The money isn't the important thing. Just tell me how you want it to work."

"I think we'll just hang around the hotel at first, until someone tips off the press. Once the cameras get here in a day or two, we'll start going out together and pretend to be surprised."

"I can get cameras here a lot quicker than that," Melissa said. She handed Eddie her phone, pulled her skirt up half an inch, and undid a button on her shirt. "Take a shot of me."

"What are you going to do with it?" Eddie asked as he handed back her phone.

"I've got twenty thousand people in my Teeser circle now. A lot of tabloid people are still following me from when I sent that last photo out."

She posted the photo Eddie had taken with a message: "Wearing my best to meet *MrDrake at the Cue on Thompson."

"Give it half an hour," she said.

"Maybe we should do something with both of us in it?"

"Not yet. People will want to break the story themselves. We've let them know where to find us. The idea is that you're trying to keep things under wraps, and I'm a little overeager."

"You seem to have thought this out already."

"I've been waiting for a chance like this for years."

FOR WEEKS EDDIE HAD been expecting a crowd to appear in the lobby looking for him, and every time he came downstairs he was disappointed, even as he was infuriated to get back to his room and see his latest outing documented online. He seemed to be losing all his privacy without getting any of the attention in return. This time he imagined things would be different, and he was disappointed all over again when he stepped out of the elevator with Melissa into the empty lobby and no one was waiting there. They were in the revolving door before he saw the photographers out on the sidewalk, and the cameras caught a genuine look of surprise on his face.

"Don't say anything," Melissa whispered. "Duck your head and turn for the corner."

"Does Susan know what you're doing?" someone shouted as they stepped outside.

Eddie did as Melissa said and walked on without responding, but Melissa stopped and yelled back.

"It's none of her damn business what we're doing."

She took Eddie by the arm and hurried him down the street while the photographers followed, shouting questions. They'd never bothered following Eddie before. Melissa led him on for two blocks before they stopped at a dimly lit Thai restaurant with loud electronic music playing inside. The photographers stopped at the door as Melissa approached the hostess and asked for a table in the back.

"Shouldn't we be closer to the window?" Eddie said.

"If we sit in the window, they'll take a few more shots before getting tired of us and leaving. If we sit in the back and make out, people at the other tables will e-mail our dinner order to StalkTalk, and the photographers will wait outside to catch us coming out."

She didn't even need to think about it. She just followed her instincts. Eddie had needed a guide like Melissa all along. When she'd said at graduation that she wanted to be an actress, this was what she meant. This was what she aspired to be. She'd never breathed air that hadn't first been filtered by CelebretainmentSpot and Entertainment Daily. She kissed his neck for a minute while a woman at the next table took out her phone to record them. When Eddie felt a tongue edging into his mouth, he stopped.

"What are you doing?" he asked Melissa.

"People are watching us," she whispered. "Don't break scene."

Throughout the meal, diners approached their table to catch a glimpse of them and take pictures. But no one spoke to them, even to ask for an autograph. They behaved as if Eddie and Melissa weren't actually present, as though they were being projected on some screen. Eddie imagined Susan being treated this way. Had she learned to like the attention? How long did it take to get used to it?

For now, Eddie enjoyed his dinner. He'd been alone for weeks, separated not just from Susan but from everything, watching his own life on TV or reading about it online, waiting for the viewing public to decide whether he could see his wife. Eating curry with Melissa, he inhabited a scene again. He was playing a part, and he had an audience.

Melissa seemed to be enjoying his company, but this could have been good acting. Watching her across the table, Eddie saw her for what she was—a beautiful nineteen-year-old girl. He pictured her in a dorm room as the school year began, telling her roommate, "That guy in the Drake tape was my boyfriend's high school teacher." He imagined the odd satisfaction the tenuous connection offered her, and the sense of opportunity to build on that connection she'd felt when she saw him at Blakeman's apartment. All that talk at the party had been part of her act. She'd never really wanted to sleep with him. She'd wanted exactly what she was getting now—to sit in a restaurant and know that every other table was talking about her. To know that there were people across the country she'd never met and never would meet who would read at some point tonight or tomorrow about what she was now wearing or eating and would take these facts as matters of interest to their own lives. He guessed she would have slept with him to get all that if it had been necessary, but it hadn't been. Things had gone better than she could possibly have hoped.

The photographers were still outside when they left, just as Melissa had predicted. If anything, there seemed to be more of them. The night had turned cold, and they were wrapped in scarves and gloves. They followed Eddie and Melissa, getting three minutes of access for the hour they'd spent waiting. Eddie wasn't sure what to say when they got back to the hotel. It seemed like they'd done enough for one night to get the story under way.

"Take your shirt off and get in bed," Melissa told him.

"What have you got in mind?"

"Just trust me."

With his shirt off and the covers pulled up above his waist,

Eddie appeared naked. Melissa lay down next to him. She took off her own shirt and pulled one bra strap down her arm. She leaned toward Eddie until he felt her firmness against his shoulder.

"Sit back and close your eyes," she said. "Like you're sleeping."

Eddie heard the click of her phone taking a picture. When he opened his eyes, she was sitting up, typing with her thumbs.

"How's this for a start?" she asked, showing Eddie the Teeser post on her phone: "I wore out *MrDrake."

HE SLEPT ON THE floor that night and woke to the sound of Melissa snoring lightly in his bed. He stood up and looked around the room. The bottle of champagne he'd ordered sat empty on the bedside table, along with two glasses. Melissa had slept in nothing but a Cue bathrobe, which had come open in the night, leaving her body exposed. Eddie walked over to the bed to cover her up. As he reached for the robe, she opened her eyes.

"Easy, perv. You didn't pay for that."

"I'm sorry," Eddie told her. "I wasn't, I didn't mean to—"

Melissa laughed.

"Just fucking with you. I was awake the whole time."

She closed her eyes again, and the soft snore started back up. She still hadn't covered herself. Eddie couldn't help looking at her bare body, though he knew she could open her eyes at any moment, so he went to the bathroom, hoping she'd be dressed by the time he got out. His back hurt from sleeping on the floor, and he let the hot water in the shower pour over it.

If they kept this up, Eddie thought, they would need a better sleeping arrangement. He didn't want to call down to the lobby for a cot, which would become its own story. Perhaps the leather couch would be more comfortable than the floor, though it looked too short for him. He wondered how people managed to live entire lives built around deceptions of this kind. They probably just shared the same bed.

When he came out of the bathroom, Melissa was sitting up with the paper open and the TV on.

"How does it look?" he asked.

"Not so good," she told him. "Justine Bliss is in a coma."

FIFTEEN

THAT MORNING, MARIAN BLAIR hosted the Entertainment Daily news hour from the emergency room. There didn't seem to be anything to report about Justine's condition, but there was no possibility of reporting anything else. Every fifteen minutes, Marian listed all the drugs that had been found in Justine's system after she collapsed at the top of a staircase in her father's house. In the absence of other information, she put a microphone into the faces of waiting patients, asking what had brought them in. Eddie and Melissa were mentioned only in the ticker running at the bottom of the screen, which every few minutes read "Lower East Side Lolita Steps Out with Handsome Eddie, More @ EntertainmentDaily.com."

"I read that book for class," Melissa said as she sat down at the computer to look them up. "Lolita was twelve. I'm not even a minor. And I don't live on the Lower East Side. I'm in student housing on Mercer Street."

Nonetheless she seemed pleased.

"This girl is in a coma," Eddie said.

"We can wait it out. Her condition will stabilize in the next day or two. She'll get better."

"What if she doesn't?"

"Either way, there won't be much else to report after a while."

Melissa clearly admired the daring of the dark story line. She acted as though Justine were offstage somewhere, drinking a Diet Coke and watching the coverage, waiting to be called back into a scene. The bruises on her face on the cover of the *Post* were the work of an expert makeup artist. The tube parting her lips into that oddly alluring oval didn't continue down her throat and into her lungs. She could spit it out at any moment to ask a friend how her performance had gone.

For the first time since she'd come over to the hotel, it struck Eddie how young Melissa was.

"Do your parents know you're here?" he asked.

"My parents, *qua* parents, aren't superinvolved," Melissa said. "But I'm sure they're happy for me."

"What makes you so sure?"

He'd never seen her look uncomfortable before.

"My mother was this beautiful model," she said, "and all she ever wanted was to be a big star. But it didn't work out for her. She says getting pregnant kind of fucked that up. My dad's some big deal out in Hollywood, but they didn't really stick, and I don't know him. Anyway, my mother didn't make it, but she married my stepdad, who's superrich and actually a pretty good guy. They split up, but he's raised me on and off. He's the one who paid for me to go to Melwood, and he's paying for college and all that. My mother is still kind of back and forth to the West Coast trying to do shit, so I don't see a ton of her. But she'll be thrilled to hear my name on Entertainment Daily."

"Speaking of college, don't you need to go to class today?"

"I'm dropping out."

"Don't do that," Eddie told her. "Even I made it through a year."

"Kidding, Dad. Today is Saturday."

"I kind of lost track," Eddie said.

By the end of the day Justine's condition was stable, but she was still comatose. The doctors had lowered her body temperature to counteract the lack of oxygen going to her organs, and medical experts on every channel explained the significance of this process. Respiration and pulse were at safe levels, but the fall had damaged her cerebral cortex, and these same medical experts couldn't come to any consensus about her brain functioning or her chances of recovery.

"Don't you think this will tire people out on the whole celebrity thing?" Eddie asked Melissa. They were seated together at the desk in the corner, looking at the open laptop as they browsed through gossip sites.

Melissa laughed.

"You mean like Princess Di did? Or Anna Nicole Smith? The *Herald* will get a good op-ed out of it. There will be a full day of hand wringing about what's 'really' responsible. Then we'll all move on. You know what people will be asking next week?"

"What?"

"Who's fucking Handsome Eddie?"

"You think we'll get picked up?"

"This Justine stuff is fascinating, but it's depressing as hell. People don't want to go overboard with the sad stuff. Mostly, they want to be able to judge people, and they can't judge a girl in a coma. If she was older and had some kids, they could judge her for being selfish and irresponsible. But she's too young for that. Maybe they can judge her father for a little while, but that's his daughter in the coma, so that will only last so long. They can judge, like, the culture at large, but that means judging themselves, so that gets tiresome, too. And there's another episode of *Desperately Expecting Susan* to watch on Tuesday. Everyone will want an excuse to return their attention to the usual entertainment. We give them a nice opportunity."

"So what do we do?"

"I need to run some errands. Get some stuff from my dorm. I'll come back tonight. Tomorrow during the day we'll go out—brunch at Balthazar or something. Then you take me shopping. Buy me a nice piece of jewelry. Don't worry, you can take it out of my pay. We come back here, we hang out for the night. I've got a media studies class Monday morning. You can drop me off at school. That image is going to drive people crazy."

JUSTINE WAS STILL ON all the front pages the next week, but on Tuesday Stanley Peerbaum's column included a photo of Eddie dropping Melissa off for class. Peerbaum had interviewed some of her Intro to Media Studies classmates, as well as the professor, who said he was writing a scholarly article about the Martin-Hartley tape.

"She was real stuck up from the first day of class," a girl named Edwina Gart was quoted as saying. "Like because she grew up on Fifth Avenue and goes to hot parties she's better than everyone."

"I don't even know who that girl is," Melissa said. "This is so amazing."

The weeklies—not just the tabloids but the newsmagazines— were devoted almost entirely to Justine. "Have We Finally Gone

Too Far?" *Time* asked on its cover. "We Did This," *Newsweek* announced. Both showed Justine inert in her hospital bed.

"I bet these are their biggest sellers in years," Melissa said. "They must be thrilled."

Speaking after a round of chemotherapy, Sandra Scopes from *Scavenger: Urban Adventure Edition* told Marian Blair that Justine was a fighter and her inspiration. Burt Wyman admitted that the collapse had set off "larm bells" for him.

"I thought, Jesus, this ain't a joke," he said. "I'm walking the straight and narrow here on in."

Tom Bliss gave a press conference to address rumors—Eddie had not heard these rumors himself, and he was following the story as closely as one possibly could—that he planned to take Justine off life support.

"I love my girl," he said. "And she's going to be back better than ever."

That night the new episode of *Desperately Expecting Susan* began with a brief tribute to Justine, in which Susan, Carl, and Tomaka stood arm in arm to wish her a speedy recovery. The rest of the show went on as usual. Near the end, Susan went in for another ultrasound. This time Rex came with her.

"We're just friends," Susan insisted to the camera. "But he's so sweet to come support me. It makes everything a little bit easier."

Susan and Rex waited alone in the examining room. The doctor appeared, and Eddie learned that his wife was expecting three girls.

SIXTEEN

MELISSA WAS RIGHT: PEOPLE could only take so much of Justine. So long as she was unconscious, the story had nowhere to go. Everyone seemed ready to move on to other matters. But those matters didn't include Eddie. *CelebNation* dedicated its next cover to Martha and Turner, whose wedding would take place on New Year's Eve. Martha was likable again, and her marriage to another Hollywood star was just the kind of story to displace Justine for a few days. There were even whispers that she missed Rex, that she felt betrayed by Susan, as if they were old friends. This was all to the good as far as Eddie was concerned. Once people were talking about Susan, it was just a small step to start talking about him. Eddie didn't expect to compete with Martha, but he didn't need to be that big. He only wanted enough press to get Moody's attention. So it felt like an act of God when the egg came.

It sailed from nowhere one morning as he stepped out of the hotel alone. The day was beautiful, cold but dry and bright, a day that demanded you look up to the sky with some measure of gratitude, whatever your troubles were. This Eddie did. He squinted at the naked sun, and the egg seemed to sneak in behind it. It might have been a trick of the light, a dust mote, or something dropping from the sun itself. By the time its true nature was apparent to Eddie, the thing was already upon him, breaking on his chin and splattering on his shirt. The impact of the shell carried more force than he would have expected, and he bit his lip as he recoiled.

The scrum of photographers who'd been waiting outside separated, as if by common decision, allowing his accuser to face him. She was a woman of early middle age, dressed in torn clothes, her face darkened by dirt. He thought she might have been a random attacker until he heard her call, "You monster. You pervert. You predator." The photographers turned, and Eddie expected her to keep screaming. But she seemed only to want their attention. Now that she had it, she went quiet. She had more eggs in her hand, and she fired one straight at Eddie's chest. A third broke on the ground in front of him, splattering on his shoes. The fourth flew over his shoulder, and Eddie went into full retreat.

"Who was that?" he said out loud in the lobby.

Eddie had heard stories from old friends with parts in soap operas, about being accosted on the street by women asking why they hit their wives or neglected their parents. They had to explain that they were actors reading lines off pages. It was just a television show. Standing in the elevator, Eddie wanted to say the same to the egg-throwing woman. Eddie Hartley was a character, not a real person.

Back in the room, Melissa sat in front of the TV.

"You're going to want to see this," she said.

"I need to shower first," Eddie told her. "I got attacked out there."

"I know."

"You know?"

"I read about it."

"That was fast."

"There's a great photo on Teeser. But I think you should watch this first."

Melissa took the TV off mute.

"Does Susan want Eddie back?" Marian Blair asked. She turned to another camera before continuing. "As Eddie Hartley parades around town with teen tart Melissa Westlake, his pregnant wife fumes at home. Sources tell Entertainment Daily that *Desperately Expecting Susan* star Susan Hartley is scared to go it alone as she prepares for the birth of the couple's three daughters. Rex is ready to step in, but Susan wants Eddie back. It may be too late, as the infamous other in the Dr. Drake sex tape is enjoying his new role as boy toy to the teacher's pet. We'll have more on this developing story later in the show. But now, here are Justine Bliss's daily vitals. Body temperature ninety-one point three degrees. Her pulse is holding steady."

"Teen tart," Melissa said after putting the show on mute. "It's kind of clunky, but I like it."

As Eddie washed the egg off his face and neck, he wondered what would happen to Melissa when Susan took him back. Would she find some way to drain every drop of this notoriety? He imagined watching her in a year on a new season of *Scavenger: Urban Adventure Edition* or *Celebrity Sex Addict*. Eddie was grateful to her, but he was already tired of playing this part. He didn't want people throwing eggs at him.

The call came from Talent Management the next day.

"Jesus," Alex said. "I'm looking at the front page of the

Post, and there you are with egg on your face. Literally, egg on your face. I love it."

"I'm just trying to get myself back into the story."

"Well, it worked. I talked with Moody's people, and they want you in. They're drawing up the contracts now. Boiler-plate stuff. I'll be in town tomorrow, and you can come to our New York office to sign. I'm setting up a meeting with Moody himself. You're going to be in very good hands."

"That's great," Eddie said.

"You should know that there's going to be some serious nondisclosure language in this contract, so I wouldn't say too much to anyone."

"That's all fine," Eddie said. "So long as I get to see my wife."

"Still working on that."

"I thought you were getting me on the show."

"They don't want you with Susan. They want you with the girl. Same show, but a separate story line. On one hand, we've got the single mom struggling through pregnancy, try-ing to decide what to do about these overtures from Rex. Will she or won't she, that sort of thing. On the other, we've got the cad and the nymphet."

"The only reason I'm even with Melissa is so I can get Susan back."

"You're in danger of making me very disillusioned," Alex said. "It looked so real from where I was standing. In any case, you're going to have to keep it up if you want on the show, because that's what they're looking for. And once you sign this contract, you can't go around telling people this thing with Melissa isn't on the level."

"Does Susan know about this?"

"She doesn't have much choice, if it's what Moody wants. It's going to be great for the ratings. They're talking about a special when the babies are born. Live from the delivery room."

"Will I be there for that?"

"Let's worry about keeping people interested for a few more months. Right now, they want to see you with Melissa."

"I'm going to have to ask her if she's all right with it," Eddie said, though he knew Melissa would be thrilled.

"She's already on board," Alex told him. "She's represented by the agency now."

"You spoke with her before you spoke with me?"

"I knew we needed her for it to work, since I've already tried to pitch you to these people solo. And she's been really proactive about things. To be honest, you owe her a lot. Moody loves her. You've got some kind of gift, Eddie. People don't want to put you on TV, but when you fuck someone, they want to put her on TV."

"I didn't fuck Melissa."

"For our purposes, you did. If you say that out loud two days from now, you're in the hole five million."

"I don't have five million dollars."

"That's why you're not going to go telling people you didn't fuck Melissa."

"I'm not sure I want to do this."

"What do you mean? Isn't this the reason you started this bullshit with the girl? So people would get excited about it and put you on TV?"

"I thought I'd be on TV with Susan."

"You'll probably get there eventually."

"Probably?"

"Do you think people are going to be interested in all this nonsense forever? You should take some advantage of it all while you can. You've been living in a luxury hotel. How much money do you have left?"

THE NEW YORK OFFICES of Talent Management were in midtown, not far from Hope Springs Clinic.

"Glad we've got you involved," Alex told him in the office's conference room. "This is a great opportunity for you. Brian Moody is a real pro. I've done lots of deals with him. I hardly ever get involved with scripted work anymore. Ninety percent of an actor's job is maintaining a public image anyway. If you can cut out the acting part, it really simplifies things."

"I wish I'd figured that out sooner," Eddie said. "The acting part was always what gave me trouble."

"Well, it was a different time then," Alex assured him. "You couldn't have known."

Alex had first contacted Eddie after reading a review of *Midnight with the Lotos-Eaters*, but so far as Eddie knew he'd never actually seen him act. He now handed Eddie a copy of his contract, and they went through it point by point. It all seemed fine to Eddie until they got to the part about payment, which was a thousand dollars an episode.

"A grand a week doesn't seem like that much," Eddie said. "It's less than I got for teaching. And it's not like I'm just on a set for a few hours. They're asking for complete access to my entire life. Shouldn't that be worth a bit more?"

"Moody could *charge* people a grand a week to follow them around with a camera," Alex said. "Most of the time giving complete access is the whole point. Plus you've got to think long term here. There will be other opportunities. Appearance fees, things like that. This is about exposure. Building your platform. How you monetize it is up to you. In the meantime, you won't have to pay your hotel bill anymore."

The Cue had agreed to put Eddie and Melissa up free of charge for the remainder of the show's season. They'd be moved to something called the imperial suite, which was large enough to provide the crew their own room, so that their living space would be unobstructed.

"Does that mean she's moving in?"

"Well, it simplifies matters in a lot of ways. They won't need a separate crew for her dorm room. The university offered full access, but the hotel's deal seemed better. And Moody says as far as school goes he only needs to show her walking into a classroom once in a while, just enough to remind people that she's still a child."

Once living expenses were covered, the deal didn't seem so bad to Eddie. In any case, it was the only deal being offered. They moved on to the nondisclosure agreement.

"This is very important," Alex said, "so I'm going to read all of it to you. Then we'll discuss it to make sure we're on the same page."

"Okay."

"'The parties enter into this agreement for the purposes of preventing the unauthorized disclosure of confidential information. For purposes of this agreement, "confidential information" shall include any information about the show's production process not already publicly acknowledged or described by Moody Productions, as well as information about the show's characters or story arcs that conflict with the depiction of said characters and story arcs on the show or in other works by Moody Production or with public claims made by Moody Productions. This agreement further bars the receiving party from publicly questioning the veracity of any element of the show in a way that will be detrimental to the show or to Moody Productions. If the receiving party is found to be in breach of this agreement, he shall be liable for a minimum of five million dollars in addition to any damages Moody Productions suffers as a result of the breach. Moody Productions does not need to prove any damages in order to enforce the terms of this agreement. The nondisclosure provisions of this agreement shall survive the termination of this agreement. Receiving party's duty to hold confidential information in confidence shall remain in effect until Moody Productions sends the receiving party written notice of release from this agreement.'"

Alex looked up from his recitation.

"Do you understand any of that in English?"

Eddie nodded. "No spilling trade secrets."

"It's a bit more than that. What it means, basically, is that this story is your story. Not just now, or through the end of this season, or the end of the show, but for as long as Moody is doing business. To take an obvious example, say a few years from now you're tired of having a reputation as a dog. So you go on TV to say you never touched Melissa, you just did it to get on the show. You never once cheated on your wife. Now they're into you for five million bucks. Doesn't matter if the show's long gone and forgotten. You get it? As far as you're concerned, whatever story this show tells is the truth, forever and ever, amen."

"Did Susan sign one of these?"

"Of course Susan signed one. Everyone signs them. I had to sign one just to negotiate these contracts. Moody probably signed one himself. And he'd sue himself if he broke it."

Two days later, Eddie met Brian Moody for the first time. Only when he saw the man in person did he realize that in all the time he'd been reading about Moody he'd never seen a photograph of him. Someone in the business of manufacturing celebrities had managed to keep his own image entirely under wraps. He was tall and thin, with shoulder-length blond hair and a long, creased face at once undeniably ugly and strangely compelling. Greeting Eddie, he smiled widely to reveal a gap between his two brown front teeth. He thrust a cigarette into his mouth, but it stayed unlit through the length of their conversation. He wore a cheap, ill-fitting business suit—not ill-fitting in a stylish way, but in the manner of a man who didn't care how he looked. Eddie remembered what he'd read about Moody being a former priest. When Eddie extended a hand, Moody pressed into it a green rubber bracelet with "Justine Justice" printed along its edge.

"This is my new thing," he said by way of greeting. "In honor of Justine Bliss. Every bracelet sold raises money for—what, Lisa?"

He didn't turn as he spoke his assistant's name. Lisa stood behind him trying not to be noticed. She might have been a shy child protecting herself with a parent's leg, if that child also carried a clipboard and a six-pack of Diet Coke.

"Head trauma," Lisa said.

"Right." Moody reached into his pocket and pulled out several more bracelets. "Give these to your friends. Spread the word. We're going to rid this country of head trauma if I have anything to do with it."

"That's really admirable," Eddie said.

With no visible prompting, Lisa freed a can from the six-pack and handed it to Moody, who took three quick sips without removing the unlit cigarette from his mouth. He put the can down and seemed to forget about it.

"I'm excited to have you involved with us," he said. "You've gotten a lot of people's attention in the past few weeks. What we're working on, the big goal here, is a live delivery special when Susan goes into labor. That means we've got to get the story arcs up to speed. Right now there's about a one-month lag between what we're shooting and what we're airing. So when they start shooting you in January, that stuff will probably air the beginning of February. By the time we're into the middle of February, it will be more like two weeks or even a week in between. We've got a crew of editors and producers working pretty much twenty-four/seven digesting all this information we're throwing at them and turning it around into hour-longs. As far as details-wise, your field producer—Lisa?"

"Dell is going to be in the field with them."

"Your field producer, Martin Dell, can fill you in details-wise. Glad to have you on board."

"Can I ask you a question?" Eddie said.

"Sure thing," Moody answered in a flat voice that reflected the pained expression on his face.

"You're the one responsible for determining the general direction of these story lines?"

"Arcs," Moody said.

"I beg your pardon?"

"Story *arcs*. Lines are flat and straight. That's not very compelling. We're trying to create story *arcs*. I consider story to be an area of core competence."

"So you're responsible for arcing this particular story? That's your call?"

"It's your call, really," Moody said. Lisa pulled another can from the pack and handed it to Moody. He took the same three quick sips and placed it beside the first. "We're pretty organic about all this business. It depends an awful lot on what footage we collect. We can't just go making things up. It all has to happen first."

"I guess what I'm asking is, I want to be there when Susan, when my wife delivers our babies. My daughters, I mean. I want to be there for their birth."

To Eddie's relief, the smile returned to Moody's face.

"I can imagine why you would," he said. "I was at the birth of one of my kids and it was all sorts of special. That was—"

"Clarissa," Lisa said.

"My daughter Clarissa. It's a beautiful thing. I wasn't there when the other two were born, which was unfortunate. But it wasn't up to me. Their mothers didn't want me there. That's life. You see where I'm going with this?"

"No, I don't."

"Lisa?"

"It's up to Susan," Lisa said. "It depends on whether she wants you there."

"Well put," Moody told her. "I have a problem sometimes with indirectness. I'm aware of it, and I'm working on it. Point is, what Lisa said, so far as answering your question goes."

"You can't make any promises, is basically what you're saying?"

"Here's the thing," Moody told him. "This is the honest truth. A lot of these kinds of momentous occasions can get—"

"Overhyped," Lisa said.

"Overhyped," said Moody. "Did you know that I've been to three Super Bowls?"

An awkward silence followed, until Eddie understood that he was actually meant to answer the question.

"No, I didn't know that," he said.

"It probably sounds like a pretty good deal to you. But you know what I've learned?"

"What?"

"Sometimes it's better to see these things on TV."

PART FOUR

SEVENTEEN

THE FIRST TIME EDDIE appeared on *Law & Order* he arrived to the set and found more than a hundred people, make-up and wardrobe and catering and dozens of others whose jobs he couldn't begin to guess, running around with headsets on or earpieces in, half of them looking perfectly assured and the other half completely panicked. Every task was unionized, so a gaffer could be fired for picking up a camera or a cameraman for touching a boom. Eddie spent the day standing in place, waiting for lights to be set up, hoping above all that he wouldn't mess up when his brief turn at the witness stand arrived, which would cost everyone time and money and ensure that he'd never be hired again.

The director spoke briefly to the actress playing the Legal Aid defense attorney about to question Eddie, but not to Eddie himself, who didn't have enough lines to merit anyone's attention. There was no mention after the scene was over of how he'd done. He only learned that his performance was passable when he was hired back the next year. Nor had anyone ever told him he'd done something wrong during that second appearance, though he was never called in for a third. There had been other television appearances, perhaps a dozen in all. The crew that arrived in the imperial suite in the first week of the new year reminded him more of his student film days than of those experiences. He'd expected the enormous space to be packed on the day shooting started, but only six people came.

For two weeks he'd been living in the four-room suite by himself while Melissa visited her mother in California for the holidays. The visit seemed to conflict with her earlier description of their relationship, but Eddie assumed that Melissa's new fame had drawn her mother's attention. Eddie should have visited his own parents in Florida during this time, but he couldn't bear to face them. He couldn't trust them to keep any secrets, and he didn't want to spend Christmas lying to them. His unwillingness to lie about a young girl he was seeing was not a good sign, since this was about to become his whole life. From then on the crew would always be there, so Eddie would have to stay forever in character. He would have to inhabit the story completely. It was just acting, he told himself. But this flew in the face of his belief that acting was something other than lying. Besides, even acting had not ended well for him.

It was something of a relief, then, to see the size of the crew. Contrasting this production with the scripted shows he'd done gave Eddie the feeling that he was the professional among amateurs, that he was in control. The field producer, Martin Dell, helped put Eddie at ease. He was about Eddie's age, and he had none of Moody's eccentricities. He offered a firm handshake and what seemed like a genuine smile.

"Very nice to finally meet you," he said. "I'm looking forward to working together."

Dell moved about the room with relaxed attentiveness, as if already playing scenes out in his head. He waved over his associate producer, Kara, a tall woman with short red hair and a serious expression who introduced the rest of the group.

"For the most part," she said, "you're going to be followed by just one camera, managed by Hal here." Kara gestured at a large, unsmiling cameraman, who looked like a stoic from some postmodern parable. He had a beard he wore shaved tight along his jawline, as if to suggest the presence of a neck below, but it only added to the impression that his head had been dumped hastily onto the mound of his shoulders. "Hal's assistant, Kit, might also be helping out." Kit stopped briefly to wave a hand before he went back to carrying heavy equipment into another room. Kara pointed to a South Asian girl who was helping Kit carry equipment. "That's Roma. She's a production assistant."

"The thing to remember," Dell said, once Kara had introduced everyone, "is that it's called 'reality television' for a reason. We're trying to capture the truth. Occasionally we might ask you to repeat something just for clarity's sake. We might ask you to reenter a room for blocking purposes, that kind of thing. And we might ask you to be more explicit about some thoughts you have. But ultimately we're asking you to be yourself. I understand you've got some acting experience?"

"I used to act," Eddie admitted.

"We're not actually looking for you to act here. We just want you to live your real life."

Eddie wasn't sure whether any of them knew how far they already were from his real life. They clearly meant to treat his relationship with Melissa as real, even when the cameras weren't running.

"I get it."

"That's great," Dell said. "Don't overthink things. It will all be natural and easy."

"When does Melissa get back?"

"She's already back. She's getting prepped in the other room. Once we get you miked up, then we'll bring her in. Our sound guy, Yuri, will get on that."

Yuri spoke rather limited English for a man whose job was to make sure their words were comprehensible, but he moved with comforting efficiency. He unbuttoned Eddie's shirt and taped a small mike to his chest. While Yuri worked, Dell continued his patter.

"It's been a little while since you've seen Melissa, right?"

"About two weeks."

"In a few minutes she's going to walk in this room. Naturally you're going to be happy to see her. I want you to be true to that emotion. Nothing too dramatic, just try to convey the actual feeling you have. Then you guys are going to have a normal conversation. It's all right to talk about the show—you're nervous, you're excited—but not too much. Don't dwell on it. Just be excited to see her. And if you talk about anyone else, use proper names, not pronouns, so people know who you're talking about. Does that all make sense?"

Eddie wanted to assure him that he'd received plenty of direction before, but he remembered that he wasn't supposed to be acting.

"It all makes sense."

"We're going to get the camera rolling. You hang tight. In a little bit Melissa will be here."

He expected her to come bursting through the door as soon as filming started. He didn't think they would waste footage on him alone. But this was another change from his old television days—everything was digital; they didn't worry about wasted footage. The camera stayed on him for several minutes while he sat expectantly. He thought they might be trying to draw out the proper expression of anticipation. He tried to produce that expression, though he'd just been warned away from any conscious performance. They wanted genuine surprise. He tried to convey his readiness to be surprised. Instead, he turned tense. His shoulders rolled up toward his ears, and his thighs started to twitch. He thought of his worst acting experiences, in the months after Martha left. He wanted badly for the cameras to go away. Finally, he gave up and sat down with his head in his hands. That's when Melissa appeared.

"I'm back," she called out as she walked through the door. She carried two suitcases she hadn't taken with her when she left.

Eddie stood up and rushed over to her, surprised to find himself genuinely happy to see her.

"I missed you," he said. Perhaps the fact that there was some truth to the statement made him say it a bit too loudly, in a forced tone.

Melissa kissed him on the lips.

"I missed you, too."

"Fuck," said Dell, as he walked in from the other room. "Sorry, guys. You both are doing great. We've just got a sound problem on our end. Yuri, can you figure out what's going on with Melissa's microphone?"

Yuri approached Melissa without a word and pulled her shirt up over her bra. He took the mike from between her breasts and looked at it quizzically. He left her shirt perched up near her neck while he retreated to another room. Eddie wanted to say something to acknowledge the absurdity of the situation, but Dell grabbed his arm and pulled him aside.

"You're perfect," Dell told Eddie. "Except that, like I said before, sometimes acting experience can get in the way a little bit. We're not looking for you to act here. We're just looking for you to be you. Just try to be a little more natural."

Trying to be natural never worked, Eddie knew. Trying was the opposite of being natural.

"I'll do my best."

He looked back at Melissa, who suppressed a smile while Yuri stood with his face in her cleavage, reattaching her mike.

"Sound is good now," Yuri said.

"I hate to do this to you," Dell said, "but I need Melissa to step back outside with those bags and give everything another go."

This time she didn't wait long before returning to the room, dropping her bags, and calling out, "I'm back."

Eddie made an effort to act more like himself, whatever that might mean. He walked more slowly to the door, and he spoke more quietly when he said, "I missed you."

He was glad they'd been able to practice their awkward kiss, because when their lips met now it seemed natural enough, at least to Eddie. He couldn't say how it would look on camera.

"I missed you, too," Melissa said.

"How was your trip?"

"It was all right."

Her unhappy look seemed designed more for the camera than for him.

"What's the matter?" Eddie asked.

She turned away from him.

"You know how my mother is."

"I don't. I've never met her."

"She doesn't think that we should be together. She says it's not good for me to be with a man who left his pregnant wife."

"I didn't leave her," Eddie said, in genuine frustration. "She threw me out."

"Don't get angry with me. I'm just telling you what she said."

Eddie tried to calm himself. He imagined what he would say if the situation were real.

"The problem is that she's never met me. She just knows what she reads in the paper. I look like a jerk in the press, but if she met me in person, she'd feel differently."

Eddie was speaking for the audience now, trying to plead his case.

"Forget I said anything," Melissa told him. "We can talk about it some other time."

Eddie was relieved to have the subject dropped, but Dell stepped into the room.

"I think you should stick with this topic," he said in his most encouraging voice. "We're getting right to the core of something here, and it would be a shame if you gave up on it. I know this is hard, but just continue this line for a few more minutes."

He retreated from the room, leaving Eddie and Melissa facing each other. Eddie was somewhat pleased to see Melissa as uncomfortable as he was. She spoke in a soft voice he'd never heard from her before.

"I guess it's because my own dad left while my mom was still pregnant with me, and we never heard from him again. That's why she tends to side with Susan when she thinks about all of this."

When Eddie answered, he hoped that he sounded as sincere as she had.

"I'm going to be there for those girls. No matter what else happens, I'm going to be there to take care of them. I'm not going to be like your father was."

His voice had cracked toward the end of his speech, and he wasn't sure how that would sound. He hadn't intended the effect, but it seemed after the fact like a nice touch.

"That was all great," Dell said. "I'm glad we stuck with things. That felt really honest."

While Melissa unpacked, Dell led Eddie into another room for an interview. It had been explained in the contract that he would be interviewed up to three times a day and that the company could use the footage any way they saw fit. Beyond this he didn't know what to expect from these sessions.

"I just want you to stay relaxed," Dell told him. "A lot of people on these kinds of shows tell me the interview is their favorite part. It's a chance to really get your feelings across, to give the action some meaning."

There was a stool in the middle of the room and a camera on a tripod about fifteen feet away. Eddie sat down and turned toward the camera, though it was hidden now by all the light shining in his face. Eddie had been in plenty of spotlights before. He'd looked out from stages where all you could see were lights above and darkness below and you had to take on faith that there was an audience somewhere in between looking at you.

"Look over here at me," Dell said soothingly. He was seated just to the left of all the lights. "If you look right at the camera it really creeps people out. Since I'm the one you'll be talking to, it should feel natural to just pay attention to me."

As Eddie turned from the lights, his eyes began to adjust, but he still felt the heat coming off them. He was already sweating, and he imagined it would only get worse. Dell reached into his pocket and handed Eddie a cloth handkerchief. It seemed like the kind of magnanimous gesture a captor offers before the torture begins.

"This will take a bit of getting used to," Dell explained as Eddie wiped his face. "First off, as you probably know, I'm going to be cut out of all of this, so I don't want you to speak to me by name. And you need to repeat any question that I ask you before answering it. That part you'll pick up pretty quickly. The other thing is that I want you to speak in the present tense. We call these interviews 'ITMs'—in-the-moments. The idea is that we'll run a scene, and then this will serve as a kind of internal monologue. So I don't want you to tell me how you feel now about what happened with Melissa out there. I don't even want you to tell me now in the past tense how you felt at the time. I want you to describe the feelings like you're having them, like you're still in the moment. Does that make sense?"

Eddie realized then that all of Susan's voice-overs—her description of getting an ultrasound or her introduction of some artist at the gallery—were in this present tense. It seemed so natural when he watched it, but it was strange to be faced with doing it. He'd known that they would have access to everything about his external life, but now they wanted his thoughts, too.

"It makes sense," Eddie said.

"So let's start at the beginning," Dell told him. "How does it feel to have Melissa back?"

Eddie considered the question.

"It feels good. I'm happy about it."

"Don't forget to repeat the question."

Eddie wiped his forehead with Dell's handkerchief. He'd expected to get used to the lights, but they seemed to be getting hotter as the interview progressed.

"How do I feel to have Melissa back? I'm happy about it."

"Does it bother you to hear what her mother said?"

"Of course it bothers me."

"Repeat the question."

"Did it bother me to hear what she said? Yes, it bothered me."

"Remember, present tense. In the moment. And names instead of pronouns, so we always know who you're talking about even if we cut a few sentences."

"Does it bother me to hear what Melissa's mom said about me?" Eddie tried to put himself in the moment. "Of course it bothers me. The woman has never met me, and she's passing judgment. Not that I care what she thinks, particularly. But I guess what she's saying—that I'm a jerk who walked out on his pregnant wife—is something that a lot of people who have never met me think at this point."

"And you don't think it's fair?"

"No, I don't think it's fair. I would still be with my wife if I could. That was her decision. Not that she didn't have her reasons, of course."

"You're talking about the tape."

Eddie hadn't expected to be asked about the tape. It seemed that great effort had been made to separate their story from its origin, but perhaps that was no longer a goal now that he was going to be on the show.

"Yes, I mean the tape. But I had good reasons. I didn't just do it for kicks."

"What were those reasons?"

"I'd rather not say."

"Come on, Eddie. We're getting at something here."

Eddie thought about what he could say that wouldn't get him in more trouble.

"I was broke. We needed money for our family."

"You couldn't think of a better way to make some money?"

"It seemed easy. And harmless."

"You didn't think it would harm Martha?"

"Not particularly. But to be honest I didn't really care if she got hurt. That's not my problem. For years we lived to-gether, we were doing something together, and then I found out she'd never believed in me. She was just hanging around until something better came along. So when the time came I wasn't too concerned about whether she got hurt."

Eddie was amazed at what these lights and Dell's friendly persistence could do. He'd given them more in a few minutes than he'd intended to give them for the entire show. He needed to protect himself.

"What about Susan?" Dell asked. "You didn't worry that she would get hurt?"

"Do I really have to answer these questions?"

"Think of it as an opportunity. You were just saying how the press makes you look like a jerk. Now you can set the record straight, and I'll put it on TV."

"I shouldn't have lied to Susan. Not just about the tape. I honestly regret that."

As he spoke, Eddie realized how Susan must have felt. Just as he had felt when Martha left. She'd thought they were in something together, and she'd discovered he didn't believe in it. But he did believe in it. He did want things to work. Was this only because he'd seen the new Susan?

"I wanted to start a family. That's why I did it. I wasn't trying to get revenge on Martha or to make myself famous. I wasn't trying to recapture my old life. That life is over."

Dell seemed satisfied with this.

"Let's get back to Melissa. Are you worried that she'll agree with her mother, that she'll leave you?"

"Am I worried that Melissa will agree with her mother?" Eddie said, glad now for this convention, which gave him time to sort out an answer. It was at once easier and more difficult to answer a question that wasn't about his real life. "Melissa doesn't listen to what other people say. She knows the real me."

"Are you in love with Melissa?"

"Am I in love with Melissa?" There had to be a right an-swer to this, but he wasn't sure what it was. "We get along really well, and we have a lot of fun together, but we haven't known each other all that long."

"Are you still in love with your wife?"

Eddie remembered what Dell had said, about treating these questions as opportunities. What did he want to say to Susan? It had to be something true. Somehow she would recognize this one truth amid all the lies.

"Of course I'm in love with her." Eddie wiped the sweat from his forehead again. "She saved my life. That sounds melodramatic, but it's true. We met at a time when a lot of things had been going wrong, and she was the first good thing to happen in a long time. She came at just the right moment. I resisted that idea for a while. I don't really know why. I was lucky to meet her when I did. It's taken all of this to show me that. I'm sorry," Eddie said, catching himself. "I realize I've been using a lot of pronouns here. Do you want me to start over?"

"That's all right," Dell said. "I think that's all we need. You did great."

EIGHTEEN

EDDIE GOT UNDER THE covers with Melissa after changing for bed that night, but when she turned the lights off, he slipped out to sleep on the couch. In the morning he woke to find Hal kneeling on the floor, pointing his camera at him. Most of the crew were already in place. Eddie didn't know where they'd spent the night or how long they'd been back in the room, watching him. Kara, the associate producer, smiled for the first time since Eddie had met her.

"How did you sleep?" she asked.

Eddie was surprised that she would speak to him so openly while they were "in scene," as Dell had put it. He still didn't understand all the conventions of this game.

"I slept all right."

"Glad to hear it," Kara told him. "You've got a full day."

She didn't mention the obvious fact that he'd started the night in a different place than where she found him now, but Eddie suspected he'd be asked about it during his interviews.

He could say that he'd been having trouble sleeping, but it might be more dramatic to suggest a deeper problem. He'd been upset about what Melissa's mother had said. He'd gotten used to sleeping alone again.

Sitting up, Eddie discovered that a morning erection had slipped through the fly of his boxer shorts. When he tucked it away, Kara laughed.

"Don't worry," she said. "We've seen it all."

Was even this meant to sound reassuring? Eddie got up and walked to the bathroom. It was the one place in the suite where he could be alone. In the warmth of the shower he wondered what the day ahead would bring. Something dramatic, he guessed. Something that would make for good television. They had told him several times now he was just supposed to live his life, but he didn't know how to do that, since he hadn't really been living his life for months before the cameras came.

So much of Susan's show consisted of her doing things— necessary things, like going to work or to the doctor. Eddie had nothing necessary to do. He'd sometimes made his senior drama students read Aristotle's *Poetics,* and he thought now of a line from the book to the effect that characters exist for the sake of the action, not the other way around. If he'd been having trouble playing his character, perhaps it was because his character needed some action to perform. It would all get easier if he kept busy.

When Eddie got back to the bedroom, Melissa was gone. Some of the crew had left with her.

"She's taking a shower in one of the other bathrooms," Roma said after letting Eddie look around in confusion for a moment.

"How many bathrooms are there?" he asked. "It's a hotel room."

"It's an *imperial* hotel room."

Eddie wanted to put on Entertainment Daily while he waited for Melissa to shower, but he was embarrassed to watch in front of the crew. He thought he should be doing something better with his time. It was a strange worry to have. These people made television for a living. Before Eddie had decided on a course of action, Melissa returned in a plush Cue Hotel bathrobe.

"I have a surprise for you," she said.

"What is it?"

"We're going ice-skating!"

She'd always tried to appear adult and knowing in his presence, but now she was playing up her childishness.

"Why would we do that?"

Dell stepped in from the other room.

"We want you to express some surprise here, Eddie."

"I am surprised," Eddie said. "I'm quite surprised."

"Surprised in a my-girlfriend-planned-something-nice-for-me way. Not a what-the-fuck-are-you-talking-about way."

"I'll try it again."

After Eddie had expressed sufficient excitement about the outing, Melissa dropped her robe and dressed to go out. She moved with complete naturalness, not shy before the camera but not aggressive or exhibitionist. Eddie doubted that anyone watching her strategically blurred figure would guess that she'd never shown herself to Eddie this way before, though they might get a sense of the fact from Eddie's response. She turned to face him as she pulled on her underwear, even speaking to him, as if inviting him to look her over.

"I promise we'll have fun."

The SoHo Cue had granted the show complete access, and guests were being asked to do the same as they checked in. The clientele were the sort to be unfazed by such things, or else the sort to aspire to such unfazedness, so things proceeded smoothly throughout the hotel. Only when the camera crew left the lobby did the spectacle begin. Anyone who appeared on camera—even just an elbow or a leg—had to sign one of the waivers that Kara handed out like takeout menus. She didn't offer money for cooperation, but almost no one refused her. Most of the time it wasn't even necessary to flag these people down, since they naturally stopped to look as Eddie and Melissa passed.

The crew was small enough to get nearly lost amid the photographers and other onlookers who had taken to waiting for Eddie and Melissa outside the hotel. The minimal setup now struck Eddie as perhaps part of the point. In the past he'd occasionally wondered how these shows achieved the illusion of nonchalance, especially given what he knew about the effect a camera's presence could have on someone who wasn't properly trained to be in front of one. But the nonchalance was real, in a way. Not that anyone would ever forget that the cameras were there, but it was easy to forget that the footage being collected would be broadcast to the world. Now that there were onlookers, Dell and the others did less to intervene. Eddie and Melissa weren't ever asked to repeat a gesture or clarify a statement. They just went about their business. It might almost have been a home movie.

A car took them to Rockefeller Center, where they stood for a minute beneath the enormous Christmas tree while tourists took pictures. A visit to that tree had been an annual tradition in Eddie's family when he was growing up. Standing under it now, he thought about his parents. He regretted not going down to see them before the show started, and he regretted even more that he couldn't tell them what was really going on. At least he might say something about his childhood holidays during his afternoon interview. If he expressed it properly, he felt sure it would make the show. It would make him more sympathetic to the rest of the audience, and his parents could hear him say nice things about them, if they watched.

He couldn't be sure that they would. The last time they'd spoken, his mother had expressed such distaste for the whole thing. Of course, he'd expected her to be upset that he was running around with a younger girl while his wife was pregnant, and he'd done his best to assure her that it was a misunderstanding. But she seemed most upset by something he couldn't possibly deny, which was that he was on a reality show. She said it was beneath a boy who'd been raised as he was. Beneath a St. Albert's boy, she obviously meant, though she didn't put it that way. If she had, he would have told her that it was the striver in her talking. The parents of his rich friends would be happy to watch their sons on TV. Such things were beneath no one anymore.

Skates were waiting for them at the rink, but Eddie and Melissa went through the show of giving shoe sizes and paying for rentals while Hal circled with the camera. Melissa stepped awkwardly onto the ice, grabbed Eddie's arm, and brought him down with her.

"What happened?" she said, laughing.

"I think I broke my elbow."

She was already standing back up, still laughing. She skated away, and it was obvious that the fall had been a performance. Melissa was an excellent skater. It was probably why this activity had been chosen. She looked beautiful as she moved, and Eddie thought of her body as he'd seen it just an hour earlier. For whom was she performing? Men watching on TV would envy Eddie for having her. He was near the point of envy himself. After a moment Melissa circled back and helped him off the ice.

Eddie hadn't been ice-skating since he was a child, and he was exhausted after about an hour of it. He wanted to sit on a bench for a while, but there were more activities planned: lunch at the Carnegie Deli, a carriage ride through the park. He could already see how their fun-filled life was going to be contrasted to Susan's difficult pregnancy. There was nothing he could do about that, and making a point of not enjoying himself would only reveal him as unpleasant. Anyway, he *was* enjoying himself, although it wasn't the kind of day he would ever plan on his own behalf. It was supposed to conform to some universal idea of a romantic winter day in New York, and as such it was a day an actual New Yorker could only find ridiculous. If Susan had ever suggested they go for lunch at the Carnegie Deli, he would have told her it was a tourist trap. But this very fact made it novel to him. He'd spent his entire life in this city, and he'd never done these things that other people associated so closely with it. The fact that he wasn't quite himself made it all right to enjoy such things now.

They had tickets that night for the Broadway opening of *Unabomber: The Musical,* but first they went back to the hotel to change. When Melissa went to the interview room, Eddie lay down in bed, hoping for a short nap, but his cell phone rang. Alex was calling. Eddie wanted to silence it, but the timing—the call arriving at the first moment he was free to answer—seemed meaningful.

"I hear you're being difficult," Alex said.

"What are you talking about?" Eddie was genuinely surprised. "I do everything they ask me to do."

"But they've got to ask you first. That takes time and money. You don't sleep where they want you to sleep. You don't say what they want you to say, even when you know perfectly well what that is."

"I'm trying to cooperate. There's nothing in my contract about where I'm supposed to sleep. There's nothing about what I'm supposed to say."

"There's nothing in your contract that says you get to watch your daughters being born, either. They're running that shit live. You think they're going to let someone they can't trust go anywhere near one of those cameras when the time comes? Someone who won't say what they want him to say? Someone who won't sleep where they want him to sleep?"

"Who told you I was being a problem?" Eddie asked. "No one said anything to me. If they'd asked me, I would have done my best."

"You don't need to worry about that. Just keep in mind that the information is flowing. And they want you to step things up."

"All right," Eddie said. "I can do that."

AFTER THE SHOW, THEY ate at a French restaurant in midtown, the kind of expensive place that Justin sometimes mentioned going to, in a tone that suggested he'd rather have had a burger. The maître d' brought Eddie and Melissa to a booth in the back corner, where the effect of intimacy was somewhat undermined by the cameras already waiting for them.

"You're a good skater," Eddie said after they'd ordered cocktails.

"My stepfather used to take me when I was little. He was a semipro hockey player."

Eddie had no particular reason to doubt this, but he did.

Over dinner, they split a bottle of wine, and they were both fairly drunk by the time they got home. Eddie hadn't said anything to Melissa about sleeping in bed with her that night. It was awkward to mention, and he'd worried that someone might overhear. The nondisclosure agreement couldn't possibly mean that just one wrong word in public would ruin him, but he wanted to please the producers, and each time he dropped the mask he found it harder to recover. He could speak to the crew so long as he was speaking as the Eddie they were filming. When he gave any indication that this Eddie wasn't real, he struggled to get back into the part. He'd always found it a self-serious pretension when temperamental actors refused to break character—asking to be called "General Washington" in their trailers, eating craft service with wooden teeth. But now he found it necessary. Perhaps he should have learned the trick sooner, though such behavior wasn't really indulged when the role in question was "Young Guy #1" in a toilet paper commercial.

Melissa gave him a long good-night kiss and draped an arm across his chest before turning the lights off. They both lay for a moment without moving before Eddie extracted himself from this embrace. The king-sized mattress was large enough to allow for plenty of distance between them, and Eddie moved to one edge, giving Melissa the rest of the bed.

He woke in the middle of the night to find that she'd rolled over and pressed herself against him. Her hand rested gently on his outer thigh, and it was moving slightly. He whispered her name, but he got only a light snore in response. For months he'd been starved for the kind of attention Melissa was unknowingly providing. He felt himself stirring, and he tried to pull away from her touch, but there was nowhere to go without falling out of bed. She might have been awake, teasing him while continuing on with her fake snore. He said her name again, and she rolled over to her side of the bed.

NINETEEN

"THINGS SEEM TO BE going well between you and Melissa,"
Dell told Eddie a few days later.

"They are."

"Can you put that in a complete sentence, so we can use it?"

"Things are going really well with Melissa right now."

It was true. Some kind of threshold had been crossed on
the first night he'd stayed in bed with her. There was nothing
sexual about it. He'd just woken up the next morning committed to the role. Everything was easier after that. Instead
of making dozens of tiny decisions each hour, he'd made one
big decision, after which the rest became instinctual. He did
everything for the cameras, even when the cameras weren't on.
He hadn't wavered since then.

He'd worried at first about losing himself in the part, but
the more committed he became to showing the camera what it
wanted, the more persistently he felt the presence of an unseen
self. It was nothing so tangible as a voice, but if it had been

it would have said something like, *The person they're look-ing at doesn't exist, but I am in here, and I am real.* It must have been that he'd had an inner self all along, but he'd never experienced it in this way. It had only developed in resistance to something. Susan would call the thing he was talking about his soul, Eddie thought. Whatever it was, he felt oddly protec-tive of it. So long as he kept it inside, they couldn't do anything to it. They could film every move he made, but they couldn't film his mind. They could film him while he slept, but they couldn't film his dreams.

Not that they didn't try. Dell's interviews were designed precisely to capture what went on inside, which might have been why Eddie still had trouble with them. Only once had he been completely honest in that room, in his first interview. Since then he'd dedicated himself to withholding. This frus-trated Dell and the others, who tried various tactics to get what they wanted out of him. They became more adversarial. The sessions got longer. Melissa emerged from the interview room after twenty minutes with a smile on her face; Eddie got grilled for an hour. By now he was convinced that they turned up the temperature and brightened the lights as the hour wore on.

"Does that worry you?" Dell asked.

"Does it worry me that things are going well with Me-lissa?"

"No offense, but you haven't got the best track record. Martha, Susan—they seem to have gone on to better things. Are you scared of losing Melissa?"

Only a few days before, he would have protested this char-acterization.

"You want to know if I'm scared of losing Melissa? No, I'm not. Melissa knows the real me, and she'll stand by me."

"So you don't think that Susan knows the real you?"

The main effect of these interviews was to make him eager to get out into the world. That was the easy part. Most days weren't as busy as the first had been, but they had a similar structure to them. Eddie and Melissa slept in each morning, and the crew was already in place when they got up. Sometimes they were told what was planned that day, so they could discuss the activity over breakfast. Otherwise, they speculated instead. After their morning activity, they returned to the Cue. Liquor was provided at every turn—mimosas at breakfast, wine at lunch. The crew's goal was to get them at least a little drunk for their afternoon interviews. After the interviews, which would have been exhausting in any case, they slept it off and prepared for the evening. They ate out every night. Naturally there was more to drink at dinner. They came home and went to bed, often falling asleep before they'd extracted themselves from their performed embrace.

All the while another order was being imposed, one that Eddie knew about but couldn't apprehend. All of this was happening in the service of the show. It only had meaning once it was shaped and aired, and he couldn't know what that meaning was until they appeared in an episode. The crew collected far more material than they could possibly use—enough material to make almost anything they wanted.

They'd been shooting for almost three weeks when Dell told them they would be featured that night. He didn't say anything more, except that he wanted to film them watching themselves.

"This is so awesome," Melissa said as the opening credits ran. She seemed not quite to have believed that this was coming, as though she'd been auditioning for a part she'd only now received. The episode began as many did, with Susan seated at the front desk of the gallery, talking with her coworkers. This time, Tomaka was reading the *Daily News*.

"Listen to Peerbaum's column," she said. " 'Handsome Eddie Hartley has been making the rounds with his teenage girlfriend. Most recently, the pair were spotted canoodling in a back booth at Paradise Regained, the new hot spot in the Meatpacking District.' "

"Can you imagine being that girl's mom?" Susan asked.

It was such a perfect segue that Eddie couldn't believe it had been spontaneous. The next shot showed Melissa on television for the first time. A title at the bottom of the screen introduced her in midconversation with her mother.

"You don't understand," Melissa said. "He's really sweet. He's just been misunderstood."

"No man who leaves his pregnant wife is 'really sweet.' "

Melissa's mother seemed familiar to Eddie, though she didn't look all that much like her daughter. He'd probably seen a photograph of her somewhere without remembering it. "I don't think he's good for you."

The argument continued while they drove to the airport. Melissa went through security, and the screen showed a plane taking off before fading to commercial.

"You're getting a lot of airtime," Eddie told her, trying to sound happy about it.

When the show came back, Melissa was in a cab to the Cue. Shots of her ride home were interspersed with shots from the interview room.

"Of course I think about these things my mom says," Melissa told Dell. "About how Eddie is no good. But people don't understand him like I do."

Eddie sat in the hotel room with his head in his hands, waiting for Melissa to arrive. Watching the scene, Eddie's excitement at seeing himself back on television was tempered by surprise at how old he looked. When he pictured himself in his mind, he was twenty-one or twenty-two, as he'd been during the bulk of his television work. Occasionally those images could still be found on TV, and nothing had come along to replace them. He didn't just look old but also nervous and ill at ease, though this suited the tone of anxious anticipation.

In some ways, the fact that he was watching from the same room he saw on-screen was stranger than the fact that he was watching himself. Eddie almost expected the show to unfold in real time, as though Melissa were out in the hall with her suitcases at the same time that she was sitting next to him.

"I'm back," Melissa said as she walked through the door. Eddie watched himself hurry to meet her.

"Welcome home," he said. "I missed you."

They kissed, and Melissa said, "I missed you, too."

"What's the matter?" Eddie asked as Melissa turned away.

"You know how my mother is," she said. "She doesn't think that we should be together. She doesn't think it's good for me."

The screen cut to Eddie in the interview room, looking as uncomfortable as he'd felt at the time. "Does it bother me to hear what Melissa's mom said about me?" he asked. The fact that he was asking himself the question made him sound defensive, and the sweat running down his face made him look guilty. "The woman has never met me, and she's passing judgment. Not that I care what she thinks, particularly."

They cut back to Melissa.

"I guess it's because my own dad left while my mom was still pregnant with me, and we never heard from him again. I think about what Susan is going through."

Back in the interview room, Eddie said, "To be honest I didn't really care if she got hurt. That's not my problem."

After a brief shot of Melissa unpacking with tears in her eyes, the show went to commercial.

"I was talking about Martha and the tape," Eddie called

out, knowing that Dell was listening to them from the other room. "I never said I didn't care if Susan got hurt."

The show was more than half over, and it had been dedicated almost entirely to them. Eddie thought they would have to go back to Susan after these commercials, but they returned to Melissa telling Eddie that she was taking him ice-skating. They didn't use the look of excited surprise Eddie had attempted to generate after Dell's direction. Instead they went with his spontaneous response.

"Why would we do that?"

Then they showed Melissa back in the interview room.

"I know Eddie's upset about my visit home. It's been a real strain on our relationship. I thought it would be nice to give him a surprise. Take his mind off of things."

Melissa skated expertly across the screen with a smile on her face, racing toward Eddie on the ice.

"I think I broke my elbow," he complained.

Everything was being presented to make him look as unpleasant as possible, until a turn came. Melissa helped Eddie off the ice, and they skated around together. Eddie smiled a genuine smile. The cameras followed them off the ice.

"She saved my life," Eddie said back at the hotel. He wiped the sweat from his forehead. "That sounds melodramatic, but it's true. We met at a time when a lot of things had been going wrong, and she was the first good thing to happen in a long time. She came at just the right moment. . . . I was lucky to meet her when I did. It's taken all of this to show me that."

The credits rolled as Eddie and Melissa rode a carriage through the southern entrance of the park. When the show was done, Eddie said nothing about that closing line. They'd taken the only true thing he'd said in weeks and twisted it to mean something else entirely, but that bothered him less than he thought it should. It had been a mistake to think that any declaration to Susan would make it through to her by these means. Anyway, expressions of love weren't going to get him back to her. He would get back when it was clear that his return would make good television. This episode could only help in that regard. In the meantime, he needed to guard that inner self more carefully. They could only touch what he let them have.

THE CALLS BEGAN BEFORE the credits were over. Some didn't surprise him. He'd been hoping to hear from his parents, and despite their tone he was glad that they'd watched the show. They asked what on earth was going on with this little kid, when he was going to straighten things out with Susan, how their unborn granddaughters were coming along. Eddie tried to answer all these questions in a fashion that would reassure them while also providing usable footage for the show. The conversation took place on speakerphone, with the crew listening. After his parents hung up, Kara called them back to get permission to air their voices.

The next call came from an unrecognized number. After a moment's consideration, Dell told Eddie to pick up. Eddie said hello, and a voice he didn't recognize replied.

"Who is this?" Eddie asked.

"C'mon, Handsome Eddie," the voice answered with some embarrassment. "You know who this is. It's John Wilkins."

"Wilky," Eddie said. "Sorry about that. How have you been?"

"I've been great. Ever since our reunion I've been thinking that we ought to get together more often. Like old times."

"That would be nice."

"My wife and I were just saying how we'd love to have you and Melissa over for dinner."

"I'll have to check our schedule. Things are pretty busy right now."

"Just let me know a night that works for you, and we'll sort things out on our end. I don't know if you remember, but my wife does interior design. In all modesty, I've got to say, our apartment looks great. I think it would really work on camera."

When Eddie got off the phone, Dell came out from the other room.

"Who was that?"

"A guy I went to school with. We weren't even friends, really."

"What does he do? What's he like?"

"He's a lawyer," Eddie said. "He's got a couple of kids, I think."

"Don't bother calling him back," Dell said.

Other calls came—from St. Albert's classmates, from cousins, from actors he'd worked with on student films and tiny plays, from seemingly anyone he'd ever met who still had his cell phone number and wanted to be on TV.

Shortly after the next episode aired, Eddie opened a copy of *CelebNation* to find an article with the headline "Handsome Eddie's First Kiss." There was a full-page photo of a woman with short blond hair sitting on a couch with two young boys in her lap. It was the dimples—not on her face, but on the kids—that gave her away.

She'd acted with him in *The Crucible,* his first play at St. Albert's. Eddie was Giles Corey—not a starring role, but big for an eighth grader. While his friends formed layup lines on the court in the St. Albert's basement, Eddie and a sophomore from Melwood named Karen sat Indian-style backstage, reading lines with knees touching. Karen was pretty in a pudgy, dimply way, and she sat with her uniform skirt hiked up to show gym shorts beneath. She smelled of something chalky and flo-ral. Eddie didn't know whether all girls smelled this way, since he hadn't been that close to one for any length of time. The other boys in his class knew girls in the natural course of things. Over the summer they sailed and took tennis lessons with girls in Bridgehampton, and they came back to school with stories obviously embellished but rooted in some kind of fact. Once a week Blakeman and some half dozen others went to danc-ing school, where they learned with these same girls to foxtrot and to waltz. (Eddie had thought this was a joke the first time he'd heard about it, but it was true.) These experiences in hand, they walked unembarrassed on free afternoons the few blocks uptown to Spence or down to Melwood and waited outside for school to let out. Meanwhile, Eddie took the train home with his mom.

Back in Queens the boys knew girls for the simple reason that they went to school with them. Despite the odd anachro-nism of its separate, single-sex entrances, the parochial school that Eddie would have attended in the absence of his St. Al-bert's scholarship mingled the genders completely, and the few neighborhood boys he was friendly with were sexually pre-cocious in ways that would have shocked the swagger out of his ultimately sheltered classmates. When Tommy Lanetti told Eddie about cutting school to finger Jennifer Minovic in the back of the Sunnyside Center movie theater during a lunch-time screening of *Turner & Hooch*, Eddie could tell by his style of recounting that every word was true.

Around Karen, Eddie was quiet and shy, and she responded teasingly. After the third or fourth rehearsal, she invited him to walk her home. In the lobby of her building on Fifth, she intro-duced Eddie to the doorman and the elevator operator, calling each by his first name. It thrilled Eddie to refer to grown men in this way. Upstairs the apartment was empty. Karen fetched cans of Coke from the kitchen, and they sat drinking them on the living room couch.

"You're kind of hot," Karen said. "You know that, right?"

Eddie wasn't sure whether she expected an answer, but he told her, "I guess."

Karen laughed.

"You're going to be starring in these plays by the time you're my age."

She said this as though they were of an entirely different generation. Her attitude implied a hard-won knowledge she wished to convey to him but knew could only be had by subjecting one's soul to the smithy that was ninth grade. When she'd finished her Coke, she set the can down and calmly kissed him. They went on for half an hour, until Eddie told her he had to be home for dinner.

So it had been for the remaining five weeks of rehearsal. They always messed around right out in the living room, suggesting to Eddie that there was no risk of an adult coming home. Perhaps Karen's parents wouldn't have been bothered by discovering him on their couch, his hand beneath their daughter's uniform skirt. The whole thing was so strange to Eddie that he couldn't know.

The arrangement only lasted as long as the play. When Karen's father brought a bouquet of flowers backstage at the last performance, she didn't introduce him to Eddie. When he casually brought up the possibility of seeing each other over Christmas break, Karen explained that her family was going to Jamaica. Eddie wasn't sure she would have appreciated an eighth grader waiting unannounced outside her school, so he made no effort to track her down in the spring. What had already happened was enough. He had confidence for the first time in his life, and that confidence was bound intimately to the belief that he could act. And Karen was right: by sopho-more year, he was the star of the show.

All of this had retreated to a dark corner of his memory until he picked up the magazine that day. But he recognized Karen on the page, and it came flooding back. Perhaps she was really the one to blame for setting him on the disastrous path toward acting. Though it didn't seem so disastrous any-more. This article more than anything else made Eddie real-ize something he'd been too busy to understand sooner: he was a regular on a television show. He'd gotten what he'd always wanted.

Karen worked in finance now. She was divorced and rais-ing her sons on her own. She described rehearsing *The Cru-cible* with Eddie. "He was younger than me," she said. "But he was kind of a wild one. He talked me into taking him home after rehearsal. I have to say I wasn't too surprised when I saw that tape. I could have told you back then he had it in him."

TWENTY

"WHAT ARE WE DOING this morning?" Eddie asked over breakfast a few weeks later.

Melissa worked a bit of egg from a corner of her square hotel plate.

"I've got class," she answered. "You're on your own."

Since the beginning of the semester in late January, she'd attended school just often enough to call herself a student without possibly learning anything. There'd been a spike in applications to the university since Melissa had joined the show, and so long as she mentioned the place once in a while she could have passed her courses without showing up at all. But Dell wanted her there occasionally for the sake of the story arc. On those days, Eddie usually walked her to campus and waited in a nearby coffee shop. Sitting among the students, he looked old and out of place, which was part of the point.

"What class?" he asked.

"It's called Physician, Heal Thyself. It's a seminar on the career of Martha Martin."

"You're kidding me."

Melissa laughed.

"Yes, I'm fucking kidding you. It's on postwar Italian cinema. *Neorealismo.*"

She rounded the last vowel out with an excited flourish.

"Do you want me to go with you?"

"I think I can find it myself."

As far as Eddie could tell, there was nothing planned for him in Melissa's absence. The prospect of a truly unscheduled day—his first in more than a month—appealed to him. There would still be an audience wherever he want, but nothing interesting enough to air was likely to happen, so he could relax a little bit.

"I think I'll go for a walk," he said as they finished breakfast, speaking as much to the crew as to Melissa. If they had some other plan for him, they would have to let him know. But they didn't.

"See you after class," Melissa said. "We can do something nice tonight."

Once the extent of Eddie and Melissa's popularity became clear, Moody had sent a second cameraman to the Cue. Now Hal was assigned exclusively to Eddie. He followed quietly, but Eddie always knew he was there. The two of them left the room together and took the elevator downstairs. The crowd outside the Cue had grown in recent weeks, but Eddie felt something new as he exited the revolving door, some difference in the tone of their anticipation. They pressed in with more urgency than usual.

"What do you have to say to him?"

Eddie was asked all sorts of ridiculous things when he stepped into public. His job was to smile and keep walking.

But it took discipline he didn't yet have to ignore a direct question posed in this way.

"Say to who?"

"Patrick," several voices called out at once.

The man who'd asked the initial question shoved a copy of the *Daily News* into Eddie's chest. "Paddy's Pain," the headline read. " 'Creep Teach Stole My Girl.' "

"What do you have to say to him?"

Patrick was shown crying on the front page. The photo seemed to have been taken recently. He'd grown some fitful facial hair since going off to college, and his face looked fuller. He was holding up a photo within the photo—he and Melissa slow dancing together, perhaps at one of their proms.

"They'd already split up," Eddie said. "I didn't take her from him."

This seemed to strike the crowd more as an admission than a defense. Eddie stood dumb while they took pictures of him holding the paper. He wasn't sure whether Patrick knew what was actually going on, but it seemed likely that he did. Eddie hadn't even thought about Patrick, so he didn't know how his character was supposed to relate to him. He couldn't play the scene. He folded the paper under his arm and walked back inside as the photographers pushed in. He felt on the point of crying himself, but he worried how the tears would look. Would they humanize him or dramatize his guilt? Would they seem calculated? If he held them back, he'd be blamed for his coldness instead. This was his problem—if he was anything less than completely committed, he became lost. If he stopped to make a decision, it was always the wrong one. If he connected the self inside with the show he was putting on, both would suffer. He needed to act on instinct, and instinct told him to retreat.

Back in the elevator, Eddie's surprise turned to anger. He

didn't believe for a moment that Patrick was hurt. He just wanted a piece of the story. Melissa had probably recruited him. At the very least, she'd known it was coming, and she'd sent Eddie out to face it alone.

"Have you seen this?" he asked as he charged back into the room. He threw the paper down on the desk where Melissa sat with her laptop open, pretending to prepare for class.

She looked up with tears in her eyes. They trailed down her face, ruining the makeup that she hadn't been wearing when Eddie left the room. The tears looked real enough, and they kept coming now. Eddie himself had never mastered crying on command.

"I've seen it."

He was playing the scene all wrong. His anger would look defensive, even cruel. He realized they'd set him up for this, which only made him angrier.

"What are we going to do?" he asked, trying to control the tone of his voice.

"I don't know." Melissa seemed to be genuinely considering the question. "I never meant for anyone to get hurt."

Eddie reached out for her, and she began to cry again.

"The important thing is that we still have each other," he whispered, loud enough for his mike to pick up.

"But that's just it." She turned her face to meet his squarely. "I think I'm still in love with him."

She couldn't do this now.

"What the fuck are you talking about?"

"Don't yell at me."

"We had a deal."

"Is that how you think of us? Like some kind of deal? An arrangement of convenience? This has all changed you. You're not the same person I fell in love with. When I saw Patrick's face on that newspaper, I remembered how simple things were back then. How innocent we were. I started having feelings for him again."

Whatever effort he made now to get things under control had to happen on camera. Otherwise it wouldn't be real.

"This isn't a matter of convenience for me," he explained. "When I say we had a deal, I just mean that we promised to stick together through the good times and the bad times. This is tough for both of us, and I don't want to see Patrick hurt any more than you do. But we can get through it."

Eddie's voice weakened as he spoke. When he'd finished, he saw a look on Melissa's face that he hadn't seen before: he'd impressed her.

"You're right," she said. "I'll stick it out for now."

"TELL ME ABOUT WHAT happened out there," Dell asked Eddie in the interview room after Melissa had left.

"You know what happened," Eddie said. "I got ambushed. Everyone here knew what was coming except for me."

Dell didn't deny the fact.

"Why don't we just stick with Patrick for the moment?"

"Fuck Patrick," Eddie said. "This had nothing to do with him. You guys set me up. Moody probably put Patrick in touch with the papers personally."

"That might be true. To be perfectly honest, I don't know how it happened. That's not part of my job. But how it happened isn't really the point. I'd like you to talk—in the moment—about seeing that paper. How do you feel as you look at that photo of Patrick?"

Eddie tried to return to character.

"I feel bad about it," he said. "Patrick didn't do anything wrong. I'm sorry he got hurt. He's the best student I've ever had, and I wish him only the best."

"And what did you feel when Melissa told you she still had feelings for him?"

Eddie took a slow drink of water. For the first time it struck him that this development might be a good thing. He didn't want to stay with Melissa; he wanted to get back to Susan. If Melissa had somewhere else to go, it made it easier for them to separate.

"I guess I should have known," Eddie said. "I mean, everything happened so quickly between us. I still have feelings for my wife. I can hardly blame her for having feelings for Patrick."

"It sounds like you would almost be relieved if Melissa went back to him."

"I'm not saying that. I'm just saying that I never expected this to be easy."

By the time the interview was over, Eddie had his bearings back. He might even have made himself sympathetic, or given Moody the material to make him sympathetic if Moody wished to do it. Of course, there was at least as much material to make him into a villain. Eddie wouldn't know for another two weeks which option they chose, but this didn't bother him. All that really mattered was that he was interesting. If the audience came to think it would be a tragic mistake for Susan to take him back, that only helped his chances.

In the meantime, Eddie could see why Melissa had brought Patrick into the story. She wouldn't allow herself to be left behind. She'd come to depend on the camera, and she wasn't going to return to unwatched obscurity when Eddie went back to Susan. Introducing Patrick meant that she had a story of her own once Eddie was gone. And he had no objection to that, provided she stayed as long as he needed her. But her native understanding of the world they'd entered no longer struck him as such a great thing. She wasn't his guide; she was his competitor.

TWENTY-ONE

THE NEXT EPISODE BEGAN with Susan at her prenatal yoga class, but it soon shifted to Eddie and Melissa, who were the focus of the rest of the hour. Eddie could see why no one had warned him what was waiting for him outside the hotel. He did so much better this way. The disbelief on his face looked real, because it was real. He clearly saw this development as a nuisance, which made him seem uncaring. When they cut back to the suite, he perfectly played the selfish man, disturbed by the intrusion of the boy he'd hurt, projecting his guilt by yelling at Melissa for something she couldn't control. Even Eddie felt moved watcing Melissa say that she'd never meant for anyone to get hurt.

"He was my old boyfriend," Melissa explained, catching up the rare viewer who wasn't following along online. "Eddie was his high school drama teacher, and that was how we first met. When people started asking about Patrick, Eddie just lost it. I wish he wouldn't take it out on me."

They cut to Eddie in the interview room.

"Fuck Patrick," he said. The first word was censored, but no one would mistake it. "This had nothing to do with him."

Beside him, Melissa gave an audible gasp.

"You really went for it," she said.

He should have known they would use that remark. They worked through hours of interviews to capture something like that. The moments when he let his private self out were precisely the ones they would turn against him. But he still suspected that looking like a jerk would help his cause.

His angry face left the screen, replaced by a grainy, shaky video. At first, it was difficult to make much out, but the baroque cross in the center of the shot established the setting for Eddie, and he quickly found Patrick at the lectern beneath it. A moment after Eddie oriented himself, a title at the bottom of the screen did the work for the rest of the audience: "St. Albert's School Graduation." The audio was hardly comprehensible, but titles had been added so viewers could read Patrick's speech, or at least the few sentences about Eddie. The speech had been cut so that the closing remarks, about how much Patrick owed to St. Albert's, seemed to refer to Eddie as well.

"How did they get that?" Eddie asked.

"I honestly don't know," Melissa said. "I was sitting with his family, and no one was recording it."

The video made a nice endpoint for their side of the story, so Eddie expected the episode to return to Susan after the commercial. Instead Melissa walked down Broadway alone. She had on the same clothes she'd been wearing during their argument about Patrick, which probably meant this footage had been taken while she was on her way to class. It seemed an oddly anticlimactic moment to finish the show. But Melissa continued past the building where her classes were held and walked west through Washington Square. She approached the Washington Diner on Sixth Avenue, and the camera pointed through the window to show Patrick waiting in a booth inside. The window framed a shot of Melissa walking past the counter as Patrick stood to meet her.

While the credits rolled over this ambiguous ending, Melissa shifted expectantly beside Eddie. He realized that the next scene in their drama was meant to play out now. This was one of the strangest things about televised life: you were called upon to respond to the producers' construction, and those responses then became part of the construction itself. In this case Eddie found it easy to meet expectations, since he really did feel betrayed.

"You told me you were going to class."

"I can explain." Melissa stood up from the bed and crossed the room dramatically. "He just wanted to meet, to talk about everything."

"You could have told me. Did you think I wouldn't let you see him?"

"I thought it would be simpler this way."

"Simpler for me to find out by watching it on television? I mean, Jesus, Melissa. There were cameras following you. Did you think I wouldn't find out?"

It gave Eddie satisfaction to know that she was stuck. She couldn't admit that she'd wanted him to learn what she'd done this way precisely so that they could play out this scene.

"I guess I didn't think about it. I planned to tell you before it ever made it to the air."

"Have you been seeing him a lot?"

"It was just that once."

"Did anything happen?"

Melissa looked for a moment like she might respond with indignation, but instead she spoke softly.

"We just had lunch together. You have to trust me."

As Eddie wondered what his character ought to make of all this, he discovered with some surprise that he genuinely cared whether she was telling the truth. He didn't want to believe she'd been talking with Patrick all this time. He imagined her calling Patrick after she got home from Blakeman's party that night, telling him how drunk his old teacher had been, texting him the photo she was about to Teese out to the world. Eddie couldn't say why this possibility bothered him, but it did. It made him feel like a fool, and that feeling made him angry.

"I'm supposed to trust you?" he asked. "Why on earth should I do that?"

"All we did was talk," Melissa said. "I promise you."

He was tempted to push her further, but for once he had the high ground. He was finally in the right. There had to be a better way to use this fact.

"I believe you," he said. "Let's forget it ever happened."

Melissa didn't seem happy with this answer, and Eddie could tell that she wanted another chance to provoke the scene he'd avoided.

SHE WAS ALREADY DRESSED to leave when Eddie got up the next morning, but she'd waited for him to wake up and catch her sneaking out.

"Where are you going so early?" he asked before he could consider his options.

"I'm headed for the library to get some work done before class."

She obviously wanted him to object, to prove his jealousy and possessiveness. He felt obliged to offer some resistance.

"Can't you study here?"

"It's too distracting with your skulking around. It's weird

how you don't do anything all day. You're a grown man and you don't have any job."

Eddie could see the whole crew preparing now for a full-blown altercation, but he still meant to play his moral advantage. She was the one sneaking around on him.

"Can I see you when you get out?"

This response deflated her.

"Meet me on the south end of the park at noon," she said. "I'll be coming out of class then."

As soon as she left, Eddie turned on Entertainment Daily to watch reactions to the previous night's episode. He was ready to hear people vilifying his treatment of Patrick. He would finally be the center of the story. Instead, Marian Blair announced that Justine Bliss was dead.

"The beloved singer's long, courageous struggle ended a few minutes after midnight," she told the camera. "The nation mourns the loss of a child."

A montage of Justine played over her last single, "Gettin' My V Worked Up." Eddie had heard the reports in the previous few days—that she'd contracted pneumonia, that her condition was back to critical, that her family had been called to her bedside. He'd assumed these were efforts to revive interest in her story. But this news seemed definitive. He doubted that even Moody was at the point of faking deaths. Eddie felt unable to generate appropriate feelings of sadness and anger. All he could do was wonder how such feelings might be approximated for the camera.

To avoid overacting in response to his absence of genuine emotion, Eddie turned off the TV. He collected the morning papers from the hallway and brought them into the room. The *Daily News* showed a candlelight vigil that had taken place outside the hospital when word first broke after midnight. "A Star Burns Out," the headline read. "Nation

Mourns End of Our Bliss." Eddie brought the paper back to bed and opened it to Peerbaum's column, expecting an elegy for Justine. Instead he found a photo of himself with his arm wrapped protectively around Melissa. "Enough is enough," the column began.

I'm writing this just a few moments after hearing what the whole world will have heard by the time these words are printed, that our angelic voice has been silenced. Like everyone else, I am sad. But I'm also angry, because this child didn't have to die. We all let it happen. And I want to hold on to the anger, to remember how it feels, so that we might take action to make sure we don't ever have to feel this way again.

I will always remember where I was when I got the news. I was finishing the column I thought you would all be reading this morning, a column about the rivalry between Eddie Hartley and Patrick Hendricks. That all seems silly and unimportant now, but I wonder if that isn't part of the lesson. Last night, during the era that will forever be Before the End of Bliss, I watched Patrick Hendricks stand in a house of God and praise Eddie Hartley, and I watched Eddie dismiss Patrick with a word I can't print in this paper.

What does this have to do with Justine? Let me fill in the blanks. Doesn't the fact that Eddie Hartley was even allowed to teach a boy like Patrick in the first place tell us everything we need to know about ourselves? Isn't it time we started taking lessons from people like Patrick instead?

Eddie skimmed to the bottom of the page, more or less taking in the substance of the arguments. He was famous for selling a sex tape, for abandoning his pregnant wife, taking up with an underage girl. These were the things the culture celebrated. Apparently they were also the things that had killed Justine. Eddie hadn't literally pushed the girl down the stairs, of course, but he might as well have.

"In the wake of this tragedy," the column concluded, "America is faced with the same choice facing Melissa: Patrick or Eddie? I hope we all choose wisely."

Peerbaum had probably already finished his column about Eddie when the news came in. He was on a deadline, and so he'd repurposed what he had, seasoning it with moral outrage to cover the fact that it was no longer fresh. It might not have been fair, but that was beside the point. Peerbaum had helped to create Eddie; he obviously felt entitled to destroy him. But that wasn't quite right. It wouldn't destroy him at all. Peerbaum was building him up even bigger. Even on the day after Justine died, they were talking about him. People were interested.

The rest of the paper supported Eddie's interpretation of Peerbaum's column as a last-minute adjustment. Surprisingly little mention was made of Justine apart from the lead story. The news had come in when it was too late to scrap the issue. The page next to Peerbaum's described the desperate effort of Melissa's mother to separate her daughter from Eddie, to get her back with Patrick, who had always been a "calming influence" in her life. The article called Melissa's mother a "classic beauty" and a "retired actress." Eddie looked at the photo in a bottom corner of the page, and he remembered the sense he'd had when he saw her on the show, that she was familiar from somewhere. Oddly, the grainy newsprint of the head shot increased the feeling. He imagined staring straight into her eyes, her eyes staring back. A smudge on the page gave her face a dirty complexion, which settled the question. This woman had thrown the eggs at him.

At first he suspected Melissa's intervention. It would have been easy enough to recruit her mother to help nudge their story along, push them onto the front page. But the incident coincided so neatly with Susan's admission that she wanted Eddie back. The timing had been too good. Moody had done it. But why enlist Melissa's mother? Eddie was still being too naive. This woman was an actor—an extra—hired for two different minor roles.

The satisfaction of discovery quickly collapsed when Eddie realized how many more questions the discovery raised. Who else was in Moody's company of players? Not Melissa—they'd met long before Moody's arrival in his life. Or so it had seemed. But how could he really know when Moody had arrived? Susan had spoken to Alex one day, and that evening she was throwing Eddie's things out the window in the most dramatic fashion possible. If Moody's involvement could reach back that far, it could go back much further. Moody found Morgan in Hollywood and sent him back to Blakeman's apartment. Moody hired Martha Martin to be in that play with Eddie. Moody reached down from the sky to twist Eddie's ankle on the basketball court during eighth grade tryouts. In all his life, there'd been no chance happenings. Everything had been willed by some invisible source obscure to Eddie, all for the purpose of a story being told. Everything had conspired to bring him to this point.

Eddie set down the paper and laughed. As he looked again at the image of Justine, it only made him laugh harder. It was a cruel laughter, and it might easily be used against him, but he couldn't stop himself. Even her death seemed part of the vast web. How did he know Justine was real? He'd never seen her in person, only on TV or in magazines. Supposing she was real, it didn't seem beyond Moody's powers in that moment to bring death upon her and resurrect her when the story was done.

He knew this was all crazy. He had to pull himself together before he met Melissa. But this feeling—that he was walking through a world that had been meticulously constructed only so that he could walk through it—increased when he went outside. People recognized him, looking him over with anger or disgust. Others just went about their day. But even they seemed to be following directions. Eddie was walking through a soundstage. A church bell down the block sounded the hour as he arrived at the building on the south side of Washington Square that held Melissa's class. Students began to stream out, but Melissa wasn't among them. After a few minutes, a girl in a navy sailor's coat and black jeans separated herself from a small group to approach him.

"You're Eddie Hartley, right?"

Eddie nodded, but he gave her no other prompt. She would have to take charge of the scene.

"Are you here to see Melissa? She wasn't in class today. She's never in class, you know. She says it's because you don't want her to go, because you didn't graduate and you're afraid she'll leave you if she does. I think it's terrible what you do to her."

A day before, he would have told this girl that she didn't know what she was talking about, that he'd always encouraged Melissa. If she'd persisted, he would have told her to mind her fucking business. And he would have been on tape screaming at a well-meaning college kid because Melissa stood him up.

"You're sure she wasn't in class?" he asked instead, in a concerned voice. "She seemed so excited for it this morning."

"I'm sure." But the girl seemed doubtful now.

"Thank you so much for telling me."

She stood restlessly, as though waiting for Eddie to dismiss her from the scene.

"If you see her," he said, "tell her that I'm worried about her."

Eddie turned away and took out his phone. He had to leave Melissa a message expressing concern. He did wonder, out of simple curiosity, where she'd gone. She was with Patrick, of course. Were they eating lunch at that diner? Were they at some impromptu memorial for Justine? He would find out soon enough. There was no point disappearing on him if she couldn't make a scene out of it. She would tell him where she'd been, or else tell him some transparent lie. Either way, he would lose his temper and look bad. And that wouldn't be the end of it. She'd come back to Eddie for a time. She had to, because leaving him immediately would spoil the drama. She'd drag out her decision so long as it remained interesting, until the whole world was clamoring for her to make a choice. By the time it was over, Melissa and Patrick could have their own show. He left a voicemail asking where she was. He tried to make his tone express only worry.

On the way back to the hotel, he began to develop a plan. To pull it off, he would need to improvise. He passed a luggage store on Broadway and walked in. The salesman inside recognized Eddie and offered him half price on everything. He was the first person in days to respond with real excitement to the cameras. It was as though Eddie had stepped off the set. Eddie picked two large suitcases, which he asked to have delivered to the Cue. Now he would need something to put in them. He hadn't accumulated many possessions while living at the hotel, but he wanted the effect of carrying over-stuffed bags out of the room. He went into another store and bought a pile of clothes, not bothering to try them on.

Back in the room, he packed everything except a few stray items, which he left on the bed beside the open bags. As he waited for Melissa, he played the next step out in his head. He imagined her possible reactions, and he considered the best way to respond to each one. He felt some of the old excitement he used to get before going onstage, back when he still thought he had some talent, when he expected to convince the audience.

The part he missed least about acting was waiting around. As an extra or a bit player, you sat for hours on set until the moment you were needed. You were expected to be ready whenever you were called into action. You quickly did your part and sat again. Friendships were built, and occasionally romances began, but mostly these long stretches practiced you in the ways of tedium. Stars might use the time for elaborate practical jokes or to sleep in their trailers, but neither of these options was open to someone as easily replaceable as Eddie had been.

Now he was the star, and his room at the hotel was nicer than any trailer, but the waiting itself felt the same in its mixture of anticipation and boredom. The only other person in the room was Hal, who almost never made conversation while holding the camera. That wasn't so bad, perhaps, because it meant he wouldn't ask Eddie about the suitcases. Three hours passed, and then a fourth. Eddie worried that Melissa wouldn't come back after all. She might wait until morning, or return in the middle of the night, appearing to take great care not to wake him while making sure to do the opposite. He couldn't wait until then. He was on the edge of giving up when he heard a key card in the door. He picked up the last of his things and worked them slowly into the bags, so that Melissa caught him zipping one of the suitcases as she came in.

"What are you doing?" she asked.

"Where have you been all day?" Eddie tried to make his voice express concern. "You didn't go to class."

"I was with my mother," she said. "I'm a nineteen-year-old girl. I like to see my mom sometimes."

Eddie thought she might be drunk, and this seemed to work in his favor.

"Was Patrick there?"

Melissa tried to look surprised by the question.

"How did you know?"

"I just guessed," he said softly.

He could tell she'd expected anger from him. She'd been looking forward to the blowout to come. Now she had to recalibrate.

"It's been a weird day," she said. "For some reason I needed to see him again."

"I understand."

He left the bag half closed and crossed the room to her.

"You're not mad?" she said.

"I was mad at first. But I've been doing a lot of thinking. I know Justine's death hit us all pretty hard. When a tragedy happens, you learn things about yourself. You wanted to be with the person who matters most to you. And I'm not that person."

"Don't take it that way, Eddie."

"This day has put things into perspective for me, too," he continued. "We both knew this couldn't last. I'm too old for you. You don't really want to be with me."

"That's not true," Melissa said. "What are you doing?"

She inflected the question as if she meant it to pierce through the veil of their narrative and reach Eddie directly. She wanted him to know he was making a mistake.

"I'm trying to be honest," Eddie said. "With myself as much as with you. We should have tried that a long time ago."

"You've got it all wrong," she said. "I went to see Patrick to tell him we weren't getting back together. I'm a little mixed up right now, but I told you I'd stick it out, and that's what I plan to do."

"You don't need to say that. You don't owe me anything. Just follow your heart."

"My heart wants to be with you."

"I'm sorry," Eddie said. "Ever since I heard the news about Justine, my wife and kids are all I can think about. It was wrong for us to do this. I realize that now. We just lost ourselves for a while. I can't undo all the hurt I've caused, but I'm going to try to make things right. You belong with someone your own age, and I belong with my wife."

Eddie felt the tears running down his cheeks. He tasted the hint of salt on his lips, and he had to hold back a smile. He was crying on command. He turned from Melissa and finished zipping his bag.

"Is this really it?" she asked.

"I love you," Eddie said. "I want you to know that. You've got a long, wonderful life ahead of you. I hope you'll think of me sometimes and smile."

He worried he was overdoing it. But it wasn't really possible to overdo these things. He put an arm around Melissa and he kissed her forehead in way that he hoped would appear fatherly.

"Tell Patrick I'm sorry," he said. Then he picked up his bags and walked out of the room.

TWENTY-TWO

EDDIE FELT A PIERCING sense of solitude as he left the hotel. He didn't regret what he'd done. He wasn't even sad, exactly—just inexplicably lonely. Had he become so attached to Melissa that the idea of losing her could have such an immediate effect? The audience waiting outside looked disappointed by his appearance, as though they recognized this change in him right away. He headed up the block untouched until he got to the corner, where he turned to make sure Hal had made it safely through the crowd. But Hal wasn't there. Eddie wasn't being filmed.

Hal never fell behind. If he wasn't there already, he wasn't coming. Eddie continued walking, his sense of isolation more acute now that its source had revealed itself. He hadn't meant to be banishing himself from the show. He'd only meant to take control of the story. Moody's decision to cut him loose didn't make sense. Eddie was a bit uncooperative, but he was also the most interesting thing about the show. He imagined asking Moody about the decision, and just as he had the idea he stopped at a streetlight to find Moody next to him. For a moment he thought he was imagining it.

"What's going on?" Moody asked lazily, as though they were old friends who'd just bumped into each other.

Eddie tried to take the same tone.

"I'm leaving Melissa."

"So I gathered. I was hoping there might be something I could do to help you reconcile. Every relationship has its rough patches."

"It's too late. We're done."

The unlit cigarette bobbed in the corner of Moody's mouth as he sighed contemplatively.

"Can I give you a ride?"

"Do you have someplace in mind?"

"I assumed that you did. You packed those big bags. I imagine you're taking them somewhere. I'm just offering you a lift."

He waved to a black town car creeping along beside them, which pulled over at his signal.

"I think I'd like to walk," Eddie said.

"There's nothing sinister going on here," Moody insisted. "I've done a lot for you, and I'd just like ten minutes of your time."

Eddie might have kept walking if he had anywhere to go. The trunk popped open and Moody took the bags. Eddie took a seat in the back of the car while Moody walked around to the other door. A tinted glass divider separated them from the driver, and the windows—also tinted—were closed. It was like leaving one world for another.

"Where can I take you?" Moody asked as the car pulled through the light. He smiled at the searching look on Eddie's face. "You didn't think it out beyond leaving the hotel?"

"I guess not."

"It's not too late to turn around. We're making great television."

"If I go back to Susan it would make great television, too."

"You can't do that right now, I'm afraid."

"Why not? We both know Melissa is going to wind up with Patrick. Why do you need to drag things out when everyone knows how it's going to end?"

"Dragging things out is the whole point, Eddie. That's all life is: dragging things out when everyone knows how it's going to end."

"Don't you think it's good for the story arc—for me to get back to Susan before the kids are born? People are feeling pretty sad about what happened to Justine. It would be nice to have a wholesome development."

"You're a villain right now, the object of everyone's anger and sadness about Justine's death, the emblem of everything that's wrong with us. I can't send you back to Susan. What's wholesome about that? You need to be punished, so everyone feels like they've learned something. Maybe there's some justice in the world and we aren't as broken as we thought we were in our most cynical moments."

"And how is that supposed to happen?"

"I was hoping I wouldn't have to tell you. You do so much better when you don't know. To begin with, you go back to Melissa and forbid her from seeing Patrick or her mother. Over the next few episodes, you become more and more controlling and paranoid."

"Until she leaves me."

"That's right. None of this magnanimous older brother stuff."

"And why would I do that?"

"We were hoping you would do it without meaning to.

Let's face it, Eddie, your judgment isn't always superlative. But we're obviously past that now. I'd love to appeal to your better nature, tell you to do it because it's what's best for everyone, but I'm going to try the mercenary route instead. You're going to do it because I'm going to pay you half a million dollars to do it."

"I've got triplets," Eddie said. "You're going to have to do better than that."

"The half a million is for you," Moody told him. "That's the first part of the deal. The second part is that I'll take care of your wife and kids."

"But I won't be there?"

"It's possible that you'll work your way back. Right now Rex seems like a much more solid bet."

"I want to be there when those kids are born."

"Where's your sense of justice, Eddie? If you get the big reward, what does that say about the ways of the world?"

"I don't want to be a villain anymore. I want my life back."

"You can't have it," Moody said. "I bought it, and it belongs to me."

"It doesn't," Eddie said. "What you have is just a fiction. It's pictures, it isn't the real thing."

"If you believed that, you wouldn't be running away. The pictures *are* the real thing. This is the life you wanted. You don't get to have it both ways. I bought everything. After it's all played out, I can get some good work for you. I'm sure we can find you a fine story arc. You can be on TV as long as you want."

"But I have to give up my family first?"

"You already gave them up, Eddie. You signed everything over to me for a thousand dollars a week. This isn't a choice I'm offering you, some Faustian bargain. We struck that bargain months ago."

"I can tear the whole thing down," Eddie said. "I don't care about some nondisclosure agreement. You can sue me if you want, because I've got nothing."

For the first time that Eddie had ever seen, Moody lit the cigarette he kept forever in his mouth. It was the only sign that Eddie had made an impression.

"How much do you know about my background?" Moody asked after taking a long first drag.

"I read that you used to be some kind of priest, that you escaped from a monastery."

"That's slightly overdone," Moody said. "I was never ordained. And I didn't live at a monastery. I was staying at a retreat house in Minnesota, run by the Order of St. Clement. Spent the summer there after my first year at the seminary. I understand you went to Catholic school. Have you ever been in a place like that?"

"We did an overnight retreat each year up in Westchester. Mostly I remember being bored."

"Imagine that, but for a few months. There were about a dozen permanent residents. Maybe another dozen visitors like me, on retreats. Not all seminarians—some parish priests and some laymen just looking to recharge, I suppose. The entire time I was there, I felt intensely lonely. There wasn't anyone in particular I was missing. I wasn't especially close with my family. I didn't have many friends. I kept to myself anyway, so I thought this would be just the thing for me. But I was miserable. Then this film crew arrived. For years the order had been sending a priest around to parishes throughout the state, asking for money and recruiting people to come on retreats, but that was too expensive. They wanted to make a video to send around instead. When the crew got there, something lifted for me."

He paused as if he had offered Eddie a kind of riddle.

"So you had some contact with the outside world. A bit of normal conversation."

"It wasn't really that. The film crew didn't talk with us. They were big on that. They didn't want to alter what they were observing. What lifted me was the idea that there was an audience. All my life I'd wanted to do good. I'd been an altar boy. I'd studied theology in college and gone to the seminary, where I was first in my class. But none of it mattered once no one was watching. If I believed in God, I would have believed that he was watching, right? But it turned out I didn't. Somehow I got that far along without even asking myself the question."

Moody had kept the windows closed, and the back of the car was filling with smoke. He stopped to flick ash from his cigarette, and he lazily applied it to the floor mat with his foot.

"But the crew had their own problems. The things that were really going on in that place couldn't be captured on film, because they were meant for God, not for the audience. They happened inside people. I watched all this, and somehow I knew what the audience would want to see. I started to intervene in little ways. When I saw someone praying, I suggested that he look up a bit more, or put his hands in a reverential pose. All minor stuff. I expected some resistance from the priests, but they cooperated completely. The order had cut back their budget, and they were hoping this film would save the place. They would happily tilt their heads a few degrees in one direction if it would make a difference. And it did make a difference. I knew it would."

"So you found your talent," Eddie said.

"It's not a talent, exactly," Moody clarified, ignoring Eddie's sarcasm. "It was just good timing. These priests, they wanted the video to lead the audience to God. But I realized they had it all wrong. They needed the audience because there is no God. The more I considered it, the more I saw in the audience everything I'd been taught to see in him. Never visible, but always present. Many and one at the same time. We exist for the audience—on a basic level, it created us. The audience gives us free will, but it expects us to use that freedom in a way that pleases it. If we don't, we are banished to hell. Do you know what hell is?"

Eddie laughed. "Getting taken off the air."

"This isn't a joke," Moody said. It was the first time Eddie had seen him angry, but he quickly regained his usual calm. "The next week, the documentary crew packed up, and I asked to come with them. I told them I could help in the editing process. I knew what the place was really like, and I knew how to capture it on-screen. They'd seen that the tinkering I'd been doing had given them better footage, so they offered me an unpaid internship. Two years later I was running the production company."

"So you went from the priesthood to *Date Rape Drive-In* and *Puppy Mill Tycoon*."

"It turns out the audience wanted *Puppy Mill Tycoon*," Moody said simply. "They wanted *Date Rape Drive-In*."

"That sounds like a story you tell so you don't have to feel bad about lying to people and making work that isn't any good."

Moody dropped his cigarette to the floor of the car and stomped it out before lighting another.

"I don't know what you mean when you say that word, good. I'm not being facetious. I really don't. Probably you really don't know either. In the world I used to live in, good is whatever God wants. That's it. There's no other measuring stick. There is no good before God. When we say that God is good, all we're saying is that God is God. In the world I live in now, it's the same thing. There's only one criterion. What does the audience want? Does the audience want you to be honest? Does the audience want you to be kind?"

Moody paused, and Eddie realized he was once again expecting a response.

"The audience wants us to be interesting," Eddie said.

"You're getting there," Moody said. "But it's simpler than that. The audience only has one way of expressing its interest—by watching. They might watch because they love you. They might watch because they hate you. They might watch because they're sick. Doesn't matter. Is that good or bad? The question doesn't make any sense. Good is whatever the audience watches."

"But if the audience is so important, don't you want to improve them? Couldn't you train them to want something better?"

"You still don't get it, Eddie. There is no 'something better.' The audience is all there is."

"It's a nice little parable," Eddie said. "But it has nothing to do with me."

"Here's what it has to do with you. You think I've got no standards. But I do have standards. And I don't care about the money. The money is just a manifestation. I care about the audience, and I won't defy them. I want you to know that you can't threaten me. You want to tell the world it's all bullshit? If you do that I'll lose a lot of money, and I'll never recover that five million from you. But I'd rather lose that money than do something the audience doesn't want. It's important that you believe me when I say this. Don't try to call my bluff, because I'm not bluffing."

"Neither am I," Eddie said. "If I ruin the show, Susan will have to come back to me. There won't be anywhere else to go."

"How do you think she'll feel about that? She could have come back to you at any time. She's not chained up. She's sticking with the show because she wants to be on the show."

"She'll change her mind."

"So let her change her mind. Give her a chance to decide for herself."

"And what do I do in the meantime?"

"I have a plan for you," Moody said. "The audience has a plan for you. It involves going back to Melissa and taking on the sins of the world. If you do that your wife and your children will be set forever. And you'll have a television career for as long as you want one. But we've got to get moving on this. I let you out of this car, and you walk back to the hotel. You don't even take the bags out of the trunk. That never happened. I drive away, and Hal is waiting for you outside the hotel."

Eddie could see it all playing out. He knew it would work exactly as Moody described. Everything always did. But for all his gnomic authority, Moody wasn't actually omnipotent. If he were, he wouldn't bother talking Eddie into anything. He'd just make it happen. And he didn't actually own Eddie. For all the pressure he might apply, Eddie could still say no. That was still under his control.

"I won't do it," he said with as much finality as he could manage.

Moody took this with surprising equanimity.

"Too bad," he said. "It would have been great TV."

Though Moody made no sign that Eddie could see, the car pulled over and the doors unlocked.

"Where do I go from here?" Eddie asked.

"You go wherever you want. I can't stop you. You'll still be getting your weekly check until the contract expires. The imperial suite at the Cue is waiting, but if you don't want to stay there, it's not my job to find you other accommodations. You're on your own."

Eddie had expected to find himself across town, but it seemed they had been driving in circles, because Moody dropped him near Washington Square, not far from where Eddie had waited for Melissa that morning. This time, Moody didn't offer to help with the bags. Eddie took them from the trunk and placed them on the sidewalk. Before the car pulled away, a window opened.

"One more thing," Moody said. "You've still got a chance to do a selfless act. Stay away when those babies are born. The hospital is going to be covered with security, so you won't get to her anyway, but you shouldn't even try. You need to understand that she doesn't want you there. If you force yourself into the situation, you'll be causing needless suffering for Susan and the kids."

The window closed and the car sped off, leaving Eddie alone with his luggage. He felt ridiculous carrying all these expensive clothes he'd bought for show. On the corner, two homeless men were begging for change. Eddie brought the two suitcases over and put one in front of each of them.

"Do you guys need some clothes?" he asked. "All brand-new. They still have tags, so you can sell them if you don't want them."

Unburdened, he walked into the park. A crowd of students had gathered beneath the victory arch, holding candles and photographs of Justine, singing a song of hers that Eddie vaguely recognized. He stood on the edge of the crowd and swayed along.

"Here you go, man," said a girl beside him. She passed him a candle and lit it from her own. She looked like the girl he'd spoken to that morning outside Melissa's class, but her hair was cut short. She gave no sign of recognition.

"Thanks," he told her, putting the thought out of his head. He lifted the candle, watched its flame dance to Justine's song, and wept.

TWENTY-THREE

THE METROPOLITAN HOTEL HAD not struck Eddie as particularly shabby when he spent his first night there after Susan threw him out, but that was before his months at the Cue. Now the place's condition spoke of his own declining prospects. The brown paint on the lobby walls was peeling through to a coat of blue beneath. The ceilings were water stained, and half the lights were out. The man at the front desk barely looked up from a televised tribute to Justine to hand over the key to Eddie's room, which stood at the top of a narrow staircase. It was barely large enough to fit its full-sized bed, and the television on the bedside table looked nearly two decades old.

How had he arrived at this place? Moody had been right. He'd signed everything away a long time ago. Leaving the Cue wouldn't bring Susan back. Nothing would bring her back if she didn't want to come back. And, honestly, who wouldn't choose Rex Gilbert over him, if offered the choice?

So what was he doing here? He'd exercised his freedom, but what kind of freedom was freedom to choose his own banishment?

At least he had money coming until Susan gave birth and his contract ended. After that, he'd need to figure something out, but that might not be so hard. After all, he was famous now. He'd even done a bit of decent acting. There had to be some way to make something out of that. Moody wasn't the only producer in the business. Eddie would have to wait until his contract ended to sign another deal, but he could start planning right away. He needed to talk to Alex in any case, to discuss the repercussions of what he'd done. But soon after settling in the room, he discovered he didn't have his phone. He'd packed it in one of the suitcases he'd given away. For the moment, everything was quiet. The sense of disconnection calmed Eddie. He felt a pulse within him, the inner self.

IT WAS AN ODD feeling to wake the next morning with nothing to do, but not an unpleasant one. He wondered what else would be different about the day. There weren't any crowds waiting when he went to the corner to buy the morning papers. No one gave him a second look. By itself this didn't mean much, Eddie thought. There were no cameras to signal his worthiness for attention. Turner Bledsoe could probably walk down the street in New York without being recognized.

Back in his room, he worked carefully through all the papers without seeing his name. All the gossip stories were about Justine, but they found plenty of ways to mention other stars. Martha and Turner would be attending the funeral, to be held that night at the Staples Center in L.A., and Martha said she was especially moved by Justine's death as a new mother herself. The service would be simulcast at Madison Square Garden as part of the Stomping Out Head Trauma Gala, whose celebrity attendees included Susan and Rex.

Eddie watched an hour of Entertainment Daily before changing to a news channel, where a commentator argued that Justine's death had altered everything. America finally needed to break its addiction to celebrity gossip. Even this man didn't think to connect Eddie to the problem. It amazed Eddie to see how quickly Moody had written him out of the story. But the real test would come when the next episode of *Desperately Expecting Susan* aired. The show was nearly in sync with real time now. The producers were turning footage into episodes in a matter of days. They couldn't cut Eddie out entirely—it would be too abrupt, bad television. They would have to make some mention of his departure. He hoped they would eventually use his good-bye to Melissa. It was the best performance he'd ever given, and he wanted to see it aired. It might give him some sense of finality, let him go back to the world as himself and figure out what came next. But all this speculation came to nothing, because that night's episode was preempted by funeral warm-up coverage.

Guests filed into the Staples Center, stopped along the way by a red-carpet correspondent who asked where they were when they first heard the news about Justine and who had designed their mourning wear. Interior shots showed the arena darkened, apart from a spotlight on the casket at center court. While the seats at the Staples Center filled up, 2True cut to the head trauma gala. Susan sat courtside at the Garden, with Rex's arm wrapped protectively over her shoulder.

"The story of the night so far," the New York correspondent reported, "is Rex and Susan. After months of will-they-or-won't-they, the famous 'just friends' have declared their couplehood. 'In a great tragedy you realize you don't have time to waste,' the pair said through a publicist. 'You have to show your true feelings.' That's a bit of heartwarming news we could all use about now."

Eddie felt a surprising lack of bitterness as he turned the TV off. Mostly the scene had given him an urge for human company. He wanted to see someone who really knew him, who had known him before any of these changes. He thought of Blakeman and Justin, but without his phone it wouldn't be easy to contact them. He could go to Blakeman's place, but there would inevitably be a crowd there that he didn't want to face. It was just as well. He couldn't explain things to Blakeman. He didn't want to answer questions about Melissa and Patrick or Susan and Rex. He wanted to speak with someone who wouldn't care about any of that. If possible, he wanted to speak with someone who didn't even know about it.

BY THE TIME HE woke the next morning, he knew who that person was. He waited for the school day to begin before walking to St. Albert's, so that he wouldn't see any of the teachers or the boys. He wore the same clothes he'd been wearing for two days—the only ones he had. It had been impulsive to give those bags away; he could have used their contents now.

Outside the school, Stephen McLaughlin sat on the sidewalk, holding his sign.

"Handsome E," he said. "I haven't seen you in a while."

"I got fired," Eddie told him.

"Doesn't surprise me. I've been trying to tell you for years these people have no loyalty."

"I should have listened."

Stephen smiled in recognition.

"How's your mother doing?"

"She's good." Eddie lowered himself down beside Stephen. "She lives in Florida."

"You get down to see her much?"

"Not as much as I should."

"She's a nice woman. She always looked after me when my dad was being tough."

"I should get down there more."

"And how about your wife?"

Eddie thought Stephen might know something after all, but his face showed only casual interest.

"She's pregnant," Eddie said. "Due any day now."

"Congratulations. Boy or girl?"

"Girls. Three of them."

"That's wild," Stephen said.

They sat together for the rest of the morning and into the afternoon. They didn't talk about much. But that suited Eddie—sitting quietly next to someone who'd always known him. Nearly every day for three years Stephen had sat in this place, saying almost nothing. His life took place inside his head. What happened on the sidewalk wasn't nearly as real to him as whatever was going through his mind. This had always seemed a little sad to Eddie, but not anymore. Eddie felt a bit as he had while sitting next to Susan at church. He'd stopped going once she threw him out, and now he realized that he missed it. He also realized that Susan had never gone to church on the show. The new Susan—the champion of Richard Oh's melted figurines—would have seemed out of place kneeling in a church.

ON HIS THIRD DAY with Stephen, Eddie bought them each a sandwich, and they ate lunch together. Each day he arrived late enough in the morning and left early enough in the afternoon that he never saw anyone from St. Albert's who might recognize him. He wondered what they would make of him in his dirty jeans and old sweater. He had a long way to go before he matched Stephen's torn clothes and six-inch beard, but he thought he could get there eventually.

When the weekend came, Eddie bought the same sandwich and ate it on the sidewalk alone. After he'd finished, he wandered the neighborhood for most of the afternoon. As evening fell, he arrived outside the bar where he'd gone on the day he got fired. It was crowded now, but the same old man sat at the bar. Eddie took the empty stool beside him.

"Good to see you again," Eddie said.

The man looked over with neither recognition nor surprise, as though used to being known to people he didn't remember meeting. He lifted his glass in a silent greeting. Eddie ordered a beer, along with a burger that he ate while watching *Puppy Mill Tycoon* on the muted television. He'd finished his food and ordered another drink when a woman walked up beside him and pointed to the screen.

"Isn't that just around the corner?"

Eddie looked up to see his old apartment building.

"That's where Susan Hartley lives," the woman continued. "Why are they cutting to it live? Do you think she's having the babies?"

As the woman said this, Susan emerged from the building, supported by Rex. Her face was covered in sweat, and she was breathing heavily. The camera turned to show a black Escalade waiting with an open door. Everything in Eddie wanted to get up and run to her, but he knew she'd be gone before he got there. The best way to know she was all right was to stay there and watch.

"Can you take this off mute?" he asked the bartender.

"What's she saying?" the woman called out.

Susan's face filled the screen now, and her mouth was wide

with terror, but she didn't seem to Eddie to be saying anything in particular. The whole bar's attention now turned to the TV.

"Can you put some volume on?"

"She's saying 'Eddie.' That's her husband's name. She's calling out his name."

"No she's not. She's just screaming. She's got three kids trying to get out of her. I'll bet that hurts."

"It looked like 'Eddie' to me."

"Turn up the volume."

Still no one moved. Susan called out again in silence, and Eddie threw down enough cash to cover his tab.

If he was wrong, he would ruin everything by coming for her. Moody would pull the plug and they'd be forced to raise the kids with nothing. That was assuming Susan took him back. Destroying her last chance might prove worse in her eyes than everything he'd already done. But Eddie's children were being born, and he wasn't going to watch it on TV.

He ran downtown, in the direction of Walters Presbyterian, the hospital where Susan's doctor worked. He was still a few blocks away when the sidewalks grew crowded with spectators. They couldn't have all arrived in the past half hour, Eddie thought. They'd been camped out, waiting for this moment. As he pushed his way through, they pushed back.

"Wait your turn, like everyone else," said a girl about Melissa's age. Then she recognized him and called out, "It's Handsome Eddie!"

Eddie continued pushing ahead.

"What are you doing here?" the girl asked.

"I'm here to see my wife give birth."

The people who'd been resisting him now surged to push him toward the hospital. A line of security guards stood at the threshold, but the crowd overwhelmed them, carrying Eddie into the revolving door. The lobby was filled with people, including more guards, but they didn't seem to notice him, and the ones from outside hadn't made it through the door. Eddie ran to the reception desk.

"My name is Edward Hartley," he told the woman there. "My wife has gone into labor."

She made a show of looking the name up, though she must have known exactly who he was.

"I'm sorry," she said. "I've had strict orders from the patient's family not to let unauthorized visitors up."

"What family?" Eddie asked. "I am her family."

The receptionist signaled to someone behind him, and Eddie turned to find a row of guards approaching. He couldn't see any way through them. If somehow he did manage to get by, there would be more coming. He didn't even know where Susan was. He had no chance of getting to her. He was preparing to surrender himself when an arm wrapped around him protectively. Martin Dell stepped between Eddie and the guards.

"You're not supposed to be here," Dell said.

"I want to see my wife."

"Moody told me to make sure that doesn't happen."

"Are things all right with Susan?"

"I'm not a doctor," Dell said. Reluctantly he added, "She was asking for you."

Eddie sensed an opening in Dell's tone.

"Do you remember what I told you about Susan in our first interview?" he asked. "It might have been the only honest thing I've said in the past two months. I need her, and she needs me. Right now this isn't about the show. It's about real people. My wife wants me to be up there."

Dell shook his head, as though angry with himself.

"The only way I can help you without losing my job is if it looks like you snuck your way in."

"How do we get around Moody?"

"Moody's on a flight from L.A. He's been tying things up with Justine's family. We were planning to induce tomorrow. The timing was a surprise, and everything is pretty chaotic."

"So what should I do?"

Dell looked briefly around the lobby. He waved at the guards, who let them through to a small pocket of open space near the elevators.

"Go back to the door and run up to the desk again. After the receptionist turns you away, sprint toward the elevators. I'm going to try to grab you, and you push me away. When you get to the elevator bank, you see the guards and run for the stairs. We'll get an aerial, from upstairs down the stairwell, and you're running up. We'll send some guards up after you, about half a floor behind. She's on the sixth floor. You barge in the door and say, 'Where is my wife, is she okay?' How does that sound?"

"Do you think it's going to work?"

"It's the best shot we have. Moody's on the ground in half an hour. This is all live, so if you're in the picture by then, he can't pull you out of it."

Eddie retreated to the doorway to wait for his signal. He was grabbed again, this time by Yuri, who taped a mike under his shirt. Dell brought the cameras and lighting into place. Eddie wasn't sure if they would cut to him live or save the footage to show Moody later. Either way, he had to make it work. Dell waved his arm and Eddie ran to the desk.

"My name is Edward Hartley," he said. "My wife is in labor."

"I'm sorry, Mr. Hartley," the receptionist said. "We have strict orders not to let you up."

Before she'd finished, Eddie had turned and headed for the

elevators. When Dell stepped in his way, Eddie tossed him aside with more force than he'd intended. The line of guards waited at the elevator bank, but Eddie slipped by them into the stairwell. He took the first two flights as quickly as he could, listening for the sound of pursuers. Approaching the third landing, he realized how long six flights would be, and he slowed to catch his breath. He would have stopped entirely, but there was a camera above him. The person he was playing wouldn't stop to catch his breath. Eddie's chest was pounding and his throat began to constrict, but he pushed on. Between the fourth and fifth floors, he heard something pop in his leg, and a shooting pain went through his body.

Hal waited on the sixth floor with a camera on his shoulder. He waved Eddie through the door and into the waiting area, where another camera captured his arrival.

"Where is Susan?" he called out. "Is she all right?"

Annie and Tomaka and Rex sat together, none of them talking. They looked up at him but didn't answer. Eddie crossed the room to them.

"Where is she?" he asked again. "Is everything all right?"

"The doctor just left," Annie said. "You barely missed him."

"I was downstairs," Eddie said dumbly, still trying to catch his breath. "I was waiting there."

"We know," Annie said.

"What's happened?"

"There's been some kind of complication."

"What do you mean?"

"I don't really know. The doctor didn't say much. Only that things weren't going smoothly. He wanted to talk with family, and I told him you were on your way. But he couldn't wait any longer."

"Is she in danger?"

"It's tough to tell. You know how doctors are. He said he'd be back soon."

Eddie looked into her face, trying to determine how much of this was real. If Tomaka or Rex had been talking, he might not have taken it seriously, but he didn't think Annie would lie to him. He was still out of breath, and his leg was burning.

"I'll be right back," he said. "If the doctor comes, don't let him leave. Tell him I'll just be one minute."

He limped to the bathroom, found an empty stall, and vomited. First he emptied his stomach of his burger and his drinks. After that he kept gagging, bringing up only bile. When he'd finished he stayed crouched over the toilet, looking at the mess in the bowl and crying. He turned to find the stall door open and Hal pointing a camera at him. He stumbled past Hal to the sink, where he washed his mouth and wiped his face before walking outside. Annie had moved to open a space between her and Rex. Eddie sat down. It seemed strange to introduce himself to the man who was supposed to be sleeping with his wife, so he only nodded in greeting. Rex nodded back. Up close he was astonishingly handsome, not quite real, and Eddie felt the strange urge to reach over and touch his face.

The doctor arrived a few minutes later with a manila folder and a look of tired concern.

"Mr. Hartley?" he asked.

"That's me," Eddie said. "Can I get in to see my wife?"

"I'm Dr. Rupert." The man looked at Eddie, and then at one of the cameras. "Perhaps you could walk with me for a moment."

Eddie wondered whether he was just trying to make things more dramatic or actually expected some privacy. They walked down the hall while Hal followed a few steps behind.

"They told me there's been some complication."

"I'm afraid your wife has ruptured her uterus. There's been some hemorrhaging."

"Is this for real?"

"Very much so. The truth is that it may be quite serious."

"The babies?"

"The babies should be all right in any case. That's the good news. Obviously they're a bit premature, but we expected that with multiples. Our real worry at this point is the mother."

"What does that mean, our worry?"

"She's lost quite a bit of blood, and she's still bleeding. The first thing they're trying to do now is get that bleeding stopped. But it's a serious situation."

"Could she die from this?"

The doctor answered the question with a moment of silence.

"The first step is to get the bleeding stopped," he said finally. "Then we've got to get her a transfusion. We're trying to find some matching blood on the premises. I'm not sure how much we're going to need."

"I'm a match," Eddie said. "I can give blood."

"We'll need to get you straight to the tenth floor. I'll call up. They'll be expecting you."

Eddie started to walk away, but the doctor grabbed his arm.

"We're going to do our best here," he said, seeming to look both at Eddie and beyond him. "No matter what happens, you're going to have three healthy daughters."

As the elevator doors closed, Eddie took a deep breath. Susan would want him to pray for her, he thought. There had to be some special prayer for difficult childbirths, but he didn't know that prayer, so he said the Hail Mary. He said it to himself, without closing his eyes or bowing his head or moving his lips, so that anyone watching would think he was just standing there, doing nothing. He finished just as the doors opened on the tenth floor, where a nurse was waiting.

"Mr. Hartley," she said. "We've got a room set up for you. I just need to ask a few questions first."

"All right."

She went through a series of impressive and frightening diseases—HIV, hepatitis, blood cancers—asking whether Eddie suffered from any of them.

"No," he said.

"Have you ever been an intravenous drug user?"

"No."

"Have you had multiple sexual partners within the past year?"

Eddie looked over at the camera before answering, "I have not."

"Have you eaten something in the last few hours?"

He told her he'd eaten a full dinner, and he didn't mention that he'd just thrown it up.

"Follow me."

Eddie had never donated blood. It seemed at first like giving a sample at the doctor's office, but they filled two bags instead of a syringe. It frightened him to think that Susan might need that much blood. He couldn't believe he'd had so much to give up. Watching it leave his body, Eddie felt sick. His throat was still itchy with vomit, which he struggled to swallow down. Hal stood in the corner, moving his camera between Eddie's face and the blood leaving his arm. When the second bag was full, the nurse brought Eddie a cookie and a Dixie cup full of orange juice, like something from lower school snack time at St. Albert's.

"This will get your glucose back up a bit," she said. "Take your time, sit until you feel comfortable."

But Eddie couldn't eat, and he didn't want to sit. He had to get back to the sixth floor, to find out how Susan was doing. As soon as the nurse left, he tossed the cookie in the trash and stood up. He rushed out of the room, still dragging his bad leg. He was halfway down the hall when he collapsed.

TWENTY-FOUR

WHEN HE WOKE IN the dark room he first felt the warm pinch of an IV in the crook of his right arm. Next came the burning throughout his face. One of his eyes had swollen shut. Dried blood clogged his nostrils, straining his breath. He reached to clear it out and found a splint taped over his nose. When he pushed at it, a shock of pain jumped to the back of his eyeballs and reverberated through his head. He let out what he thought would be a yell but sounded only as a low moan. A shadow in the corner seemed to move in response.

"What happened?" Eddie asked in its direction.

"You fainted." He recognized the voice but thought he must still be dreaming. "You fell facedown and broke your nose. Chipped a tooth as well. The whole thing looked a lot worse than it actually is, I'm told. Blood everywhere."

"How long have I been asleep?"

"You were in and out through the night," Moody said.

"It's morning?"

"Past noon."

"How is Susan?"

"She's great. So are the girls. Everyone is just fine."

Relief deadened all the pain for a moment. This was followed by the bitterness of the possibility that he would be kept from them.

"Shouldn't you be up there overseeing things?" he asked Moody.

"I've been waiting for you to wake up. I wanted to have a few quick words."

"You mean you wanted to stop me from seeing them?"

"Quite the opposite, Eddie. We're all one big happy family."

"So you won't be suing me?"

"Suing you? For what?"

"For busting past security? For telling that nurse I never slept with Melissa?"

"That's all behind us. Why would I try to sue the most popular man in America?"

"I thought I was the villain?"

"When was the last time you went online?"

Eddie tried to remember. There had been no computer in the hotel room, and his phone had disappeared.

"It must have been while I was still at the Cue."

"Then you've missed a lot. Your penance is done, Eddie. People are moved. You gave it all up at the height of your fame. You said good-bye to Melissa. Gave away your possessions to the needy and spent your days sitting outside with some kind of street corner guru. You've attained wisdom. People think you're some kind of saint. You've put a lot of us to shame. If Eddie Hartley can change, there's hope for all. The video of you crying at Justine's memorial has more than a million views."

"You drove me to that memorial."

"Of course I did. But you did a lot of the work yourself. With the luggage, and whatever was going on with that bum outside the school. You've always been better when you didn't know."

"You've had cameras on me all week?"

"That's what I've been paying you for, Eddie. It's in the contract."

"Then why did you try to stop me from seeing Susan?"

"Try to stop you? I walked you right to her, Eddie. I was producing the whole thing live."

"Dell said you were in L.A."

"Did you think I would be on the other side of the country just when my biggest star is ready to pop?"

"You were with Justine's family."

"Justine is the past, Eddie. We're worried about what comes next."

"So that was another lie."

"You're still thinking about things in the wrong terms, Eddie. It was great television, is what it was."

"Was Susan really in any danger?"

Moody sighed. In the darkness, Eddie imagined the cigarette bobbing in his grinning mouth.

"For our purposes, she was."

"I thought she might die."

"That's exactly my point. You were very relatable."

"I was terrified."

"All that should matter to you now is that Susan is safe and your kids are healthy."

For a moment, it was all that mattered.

"So now what?" Eddie asked.

"We've got a show to do. I got the overnights, and they were the best ratings we've ever pulled. You beat out Justine's funeral. Your collapse was an iconic television moment, Eddie. You know what was so great about it?"

"What?"

"It was real, Eddie. That's what everyone responded to. This is what people needed after Justine—a happy ending, some redemption. We're going to turn the culture around. Peerbaum's working on the column now. He's even got a quote from me. I don't usually like to insert myself that way. Authorial intrusion can be a real downer. But in this case it seemed appropriate."

"What did you tell him?"

"Just that I did a little soul-searching myself. I'd let some of my field team go too far. The idea that a television producer would practically tackle a man, trying to stop him from getting to his wife when she was in danger—I was as sickened by it as anyone else. Dell represents all that's wrong with the reality business, and we've gotten rid of him."

"But it wasn't his fault."

"It's got to be someone's fault, Eddie. We can't all reach the Promised Land together. That's how the thing works. Marty understands. He made it to the mountaintop, which is more than a lot of people get. And he's being well compensated. Let's get back to the matter at hand. We're going to usher in a new era of authenticity. You've even inspired Rex. Next week he's coming out, and *CelebNation* has the exclusive."

"Rex Gilbert is gay?"

"You're honestly asking me that? You must be the last one in show business to know."

"I'm not really in show business."

"You sure as hell are now."

"So I get to go home with Susan? We're getting back together for good?"

"That's right. But to keep everyone honest, there's going to be some changes. It's going to be live-streamed. Twenty-four/ seven access, so everyone knows it's on the level. We're going to earn people's trust. We just need you to sign the forms."

"When do I get to see my girls?"

"As soon as we finish with the paperwork."

"I can't exactly move yet."

"We've got a few minutes."

"Am I allowed to talk with Susan about it first?"

"I'm afraid not. Understand, you're under no pressure to sign. No coercion is going on here. You want to take some time to convalesce, figure things out, that's your business. But you can't get on camera before we've taken care of the contract, and you can't see Susan without getting on camera."

After he'd signed everything and Moody had left him alone, Eddie fought his way into the bathroom to clean up. It would be his last time off camera for a while, so he hoped to make himself look presentable, but there wasn't much he could do. His swollen right eye was purple on its lid, fading into a sickening yellow around the lower rim of his right cheek. This would get better eventually, but the damage to his nose seemed more likely to persist. It couldn't really be seen beneath the splint, but when he explored it with his fingers he found a bump halfway down the bridge, after which the whole thing sloped slightly askance.

He wasn't so handsome anymore. At least for now he was a little bit monstrous, in fact. There was something to be said for the overall effect. He'd been brought low so that he could be raised up, but he still had the scars from his fall. He didn't feel any better suited to playing a saint than a villain, but at least he had a part again. He hobbled out of his room. Whatever had popped in his leg the day before had tightened. He couldn't bend his knee, so he stepped into the camera's eye in a parody of a military march.

Emerging from the elevator on the sixth floor, on his way to see Susan after all this time, he tried to imagine what she'd been through in the past few days. Had her life ever been in danger? He didn't want to believe she'd let him be deceived about such a thing, though she hardly owed him honesty. Perhaps she hadn't known Moody's plan. Or she'd thought that Eddie knew it, too. He'd have to ask once the cameras were off, whenever that time came.

"Your face," Susan said in greeting as he limped into the room.

"I fell," Eddie responded, trying to smile.

"They told me. It gives you some texture. I like it."

"How are you feeling?"

She looked tired, and she was damp with sweat.

"I'm still in a lot of pain," she said. "But they've given me something for that. Sorry if I seem a bit out of it."

"That's all right. It's just great to see you again."

"They told me you saved my life. I wouldn't have made it without that transfusion."

"We had a real scare," Eddie said.

"We did," Susan said. "But everything is okay."

"Where are the girls?"

"The nurses have them. They should be back soon."

Eddie pulled a chair beside the bed and took Susan's hand.

"I'm sorry for everything."

"It all worked out," Susan said.

Before Eddie could respond to this, the door opened and three nurses arrived, each carrying one of the babies.

"Hello, Dad," the first nurse said. "Do you want to meet your daughters?"

"Yes, I do."

"Let me show you how to hold her."

She approached with one arm holding the baby, who was swaddled so tightly in a blue hospital blanket that she might have been a package about to be dropped in the mail. Eddie reached out his arm and the nurse placed the bundle on him. The baby was smaller than his arm from the elbow to the wrist, and Eddie felt terrified of her. How fragile, this thing that had been placed into his care. But she seemed to fit so naturally.

"Say hello to your oldest daughter," the nurse said. "This is Martha Hartley."

"It seemed appropriate," Susan said. "Martha's the one who made this all possible."

Eddie looked into the child's tiny, milky eyes. She twisted her mouth in what might have been a yawn or a burp. He'd never seen anything so beautiful in his life.

"She looks like you," he told Susan.

The other girls were set down, one on Eddie's other arm and one on his lap.

"Meet Justine and Regina."

"Regina?" Eddie asked.

"I decided that one should be named after Rex," Susan explained. "He was really there for me when things were bad. I hope that doesn't seem weird."

Eddie didn't care what they were called. They were his, and they were all connected in a place where names had no meaning.

"Why don't we get a picture of the happy family?" the nurse asked, though everything was already being captured by camera. She took Susan's phone and stood in front of Eddie and the girls.

"Smile," she said.

As soon as the picture was taken, the girls began to cry in their rolling bassinets, first one and then all three together.

"They're hungry," Susan said.

"What do we do?"

"The nurses showed me, but I need your help."

Eddie propped Susan up with pillows and brought the girls over, one at a time. Susan opened her hospital gown and took two of them while Eddie fed the third a bottle.

"Come over here," Susan said.

He sat beside her on the bed, and the entire family was together.

There was so much he meant to say, but he couldn't while the cameras were on. It wasn't that any of it conflicted with Moody's story, just that he didn't want it to be broadcast to the world. He wanted it to belong to them. Susan turned up from feeding and looked at him. What passed between them then lasted only an instant. It wasn't something that could be captured or reproduced, but Eddie was almost certain it was real.

THEY LEFT THE HOSPITAL two days later. The sidewalk was filled as though for a parade. As he pushed Susan's wheelchair through the oversized revolving door, Eddie read the signs being waved at them. "Congratulations Eddie and Susan." "The Hartleys Give Me Hope." When they came into sight, a cheer spread up the block. Guards created a path to the black Escalade waiting on the corner. Eddie helped Susan up and clicked the three baby carriers into place. A camera mounted on the back of the driver's seat tracked Eddie's motion while he struggled to climb in after them. The shake of the starting car sent the girls into a syncopated round of screams.

"I guess we just let them cry it out," Susan said.

Eddie watched through the front windshield as the driver pulled into traffic. When the light changed, they continued west.

"Where are you going?" Eddie asked. "Our apartment is in the other direction."

"I'm taking you to your new place," the driver answered. "Plenty of room for the family."

They turned uptown on Park Avenue. In the nineties, they turned onto a side street and pulled up in front of a four-story brownstone that made Eddie think of the places where his richer St. Albert's classmates had lived. The driver got out first and opened the curbside door. He helped them both to the street and carefully handed down the babies. Hal was waiting on the sidewalk with his camera. He followed them to the front door but stayed behind as they crossed the threshold. Eddie didn't see any cameras in the front hall, which meant that they might be anywhere. A tall woman with neatly cut black hair greeted them.

"Mr. and Mrs. Hartley," she said in a perfect British accent. "My name is Priscilla, and I'll be managing your house." She hadn't had that accent, Eddie remembered, when she'd stood beside him at the bar and told him that Susan was calling his name. "Why don't I show you to the nursery first, then I can give you a full tour of the place?"

A banner above the nursery door read "The Von Verdant Gallery welcomes home Martha, Justine, and Regina." Below it was a painting of a pink stork carrying three bundles, signed by Graham Turnbough. Susan grabbed Eddie as they walked inside.

"It's got everything," she said. "Can you believe it?"

Eddie looked over the three cribs, the three changing tables, the pile of diapers.

"These diapers are a gift from our friends at Pampers," Priscilla said. "And Fisher-Price has outfitted the nursery with phthalate-free toys appropriate for ages zero to three months."

"That sounds good," Eddie said as they each set one of the babies in a crib.

"The nurses and the nanny get here tomorrow," Priscilla continued. "But we're on our own tonight."

"How big a staff have we got?" Eddie asked.

"The numbers aren't important. It's just to make sure the children have what they need."

They went through the rest of the house, beginning with the home gym in the basement and ending with the pool inside the rooftop bubble. Eddie imagined his girls growing up thinking this was just what life was like. On their way back downstairs, they stopped on the third floor.

"I've got another surprise for you," Priscilla said.

She opened a door to reveal a room filled with stretched canvases on easels and a table covered in brushes and paints.

"My own studio," Susan said. She turned to Eddie. "Did you have anything to do with this?"

Eddie shrugged.

"I've always wanted to paint," Susan said to Priscilla, who seemed to exist in part as a stand-in for the audience. "All these years working at the gallery, I really wanted to be an artist myself."

They both now looked expectantly at Eddie.

"She's very talented," he said, improvising. "All she needed was a little push, and I think this might be it."

At the end of the tour, Priscilla left them sitting together on the living room couch. Eddie wanted to say something, but one of the babies started crying, and the others quickly joined in. They walked to the nursery together.

"I guess this is our life," Susan said. "We're going to have to grab private moments where we can."

Just after ten o'clock, all three girls fell asleep at the same time. Eddie and Susan used the chance to get ready for bed. In their room, Eddie discovered that his closet was filled with the clothes he'd given away on the street.

By the time he'd brushed his teeth and undressed, Susan was already under the covers.

"Get in," she told Eddie. "Who knows how long we've got until we're up again."

Eddie lay down beside her. He had so much to say, but the camera was still on.

"I really did miss you," he said.

"Why don't we turn out the light," Susan answered.

"I love you," Eddie told her, once the room was dark.

From the production suite next door, Moody engaged the night vision on the bedroom camera. In the darkness, Handsome Eddie Hartley reached for his wife so naturally it was impossible to say whether he even knew we were watching.